THE LADIES' LANTERN

A DELAFIELD & MALLOY INVESTIGATION

BOOK 5

TRISH MACENULTY

PRISM LIGHT PRESS

SOMEDAY beneath some hard
Capricious star—
Spreading its light a little
Over far,
We'll know you for the woman
That you are.
— Djuna Barnes, "The Book of Repulsive Women"

"We are living now. We shall not be living long. No one can tell us we shall live again. This is our little while. This is our chance....Perhaps I can call you; you who have dreamed and dreaming know, and knowing care. Move! Move from the things that hold you. If you move, others will move. Come! Now. Before the sun goes down."

— Susan Glaspell, "The People."

Contents

Prologue
May 1916 — Dublin

Ellen's stomach lurched when she saw the blood-spattered wall. The smell of gunpowder lingered in the air.

"And what of their bodies?" she asked. "Did they not even get a decent funeral?"

"No need to create more martyrs," the man in his drab captain's uniform said, puffing out his chest. "General Maxwell has promised there'll be no more treason whispered here for a hundred years."

She jerked her head toward him, clenching her fists, willing her legs to stand firm. He was a stout man with a pock-marked face and a pouting, self-satisfied expression.

"You English call it treason when people fight for the right to rule themselves?" Her voice shook with rage.

He shrugged. "The Irish can't rule themselves. The leaders are nothing but a collection of half-mad poets."

She turned her eyes away and stared up at the looming prison. Her brother was in there somewhere among the other thousands of men and women. He would be scared, but he would not show it. Her eyes traveled back down to the wall with its dark stains.

"You have a choice to make, Miss Malloy," the man said in a jovial voice, as if he found the situation somehow amusing.

"Do I?" she asked and cast her eyes once more at the thick gray wall of the prison.

Chapter 1
Louisa

"On account of what the government considers improper activities in military and naval matters, this government has requested the immediate recall of Captain Boy-Ed and Captain Von Papen as they are no longer acceptable, or personae gratae, to this government."
— U.S. State Department, December, 1915

The morning held its breath as a black motorcar chugged to a stop at the curb in front of the pier. The driver got out and opened the back door. As the crowd surged forward, police spread their arms to keep on-lookers back, and two German men in long black coats and top hats climbed out of the back seat. The temperature had dipped below 20 degrees overnight and had only crept up a few degrees since sunrise. Bundled in coats and scarves, Louisa, Ellen, and Carlotta watched Captains von Papen and Boy-Ed stride toward the pier where the steamship *Noordam* waited.

"It would be unfortunate if their ship caught fire in the middle of the ocean," Louisa said, thinking of all the men who had drowned in the unforgiving sea because of German sabotage.

"I have no doubt those two hooligans will continue to cause mayhem wherever they go," Ellen said.

Louisa and Ellen shared a look. They had risked their lives to expose the German plot to sabotage American ships. Together they had managed to steal a brief-case containing the accounts kept by the Germans and get the information to a newspaper. It was enough to seal the fates of von Papen and his sidekick, Boy-Ed. But America had still not entered the war.

"I hope they burn in hell," she muttered.

Carlotta brought her gloved hand to the scar across her lip. Her nose was crooked from the beating she had taken from von Papen when he discovered she was helping Louisa. Her lovely face would never look the same.

Louisa put an arm around her and pulled her close. As horrible as the beating had been, at least she no longer made her living in a brothel. Carlotta stepped back, and a moment later an egg sailed over the jeering crowd, splattering von Papen's back. He wheeled around and glared.

"Carlotta," Louisa whispered. "You shouldn't have done that."

"That's right," Ellen added. "Eggs cost good money."

"It was a rotten one anyway," Carlotta said.

Louisa and Ellen chuckled, and Carlotta crossed her arms in satisfaction.

The *Noordam* was a huge black vessel with a yellow and green funnel. As a Holland-based ship, it would be safe from German torpedoes, unlike the *Lusitania* that had been sunk in the Irish sea, ending the lives of more than 1,200 passengers and crew members, including the love of Ellen's life, Hester French. The crowd watched the two men stride up the gangplank to the ship. The ship's horn blasted as the gangplank was lifted and stowed.

Louisa gazed over at the motorcar which had brought the two men and saw a broad-shouldered man in an expensive coat, leaning against the car. She thought she recognized him. Standing next to him was a huge man, whom she assumed to be a bodyguard from his watchful manner. She didn't remember the first man's name, but she had often seen him in von Papen's company. He must have felt her looking at him, for he turned a cold gaze her way. She looked away quickly. Franz von Papen may be expelled the country, but he was leaving behind his spies and henchmen.

"Let's watch it leave," Carlotta said as the crowd dissipated.

So they waited, shivering in the breeze that sheared off the surface of the water. The smokestack belched as a tugboat pulled the ship across the rippling river.

The ship's horn sounded once again.

"It's gratifying, isn't it? Seeing them leave our shore?" Louisa asked.

"It won't bring Hester back," Ellen said, her hand drifting over her belly.

In about two months' time, the baby would be here. What sort of mother would Ellen be, Louisa wondered. Would she be able to pour her heart into the child in spite of its unfortunate origins? She couldn't begin to imagine what her friend must be feeling.

It had taken Louisa months to learn the truth about the child that Ellen carried. After surviving the sinking of the *Lusitania*, Ellen had gone to Germany, ostensibly to help her Irish countrymen acquire arms from the

Germans to foment rebellion in Ireland. Once there she pretended to offer her services as a spy for the Germans. She later told Louisa she was so numb from the grief of losing Hester that she didn't care what happened to her. Then a German intelligence officer had forced himself on her, and Ellen, who had no sexual interest in men, was going to have a baby.

At the curb in front of the pier, Louisa hailed a cab, and the three of them huddled together in the backseat.

"Suzie will have something warm for us when we get back," Louisa said.

"I still can't believe she's getting married," Ellen said. "But Mr. Sweet seems like a nice gent."

"He's a good sort," Carlotta confirmed. "If he hadn't stepped in when von Papen was beating me, that lobcock mighta killed me."

Mr. Sweet, the butler at a German opera singer's brothel, had brought Carlotta to Louisa's house after Von Papen had beaten her for telling his secrets.

"Well, you're with us now and no one will do that to you again," Louisa said, ignoring the profanity. "And with Suzie getting married and leaving us, we'll all have to learn how to be more self-sufficient."

"Speak for yourself and your pampered mam," Ellen said. "Suzie was never *my* servant."

"Tell me, how do you plan to publish your magazine and take care of a baby when the time comes?" Louisa asked. "If you want to do both, you'll need help."

"I've told you both a hundred times, I'll take care of the baby," Carlotta interjected. "It's not like I can do much else."

"And your help is welcome, girleen," Ellen said, patting Carlotta's hand.

"Well, don't count on me," Louisa said, looking out the window. Snow fell against the glass in big fat flakes. "I know nothing about babies, and since I'll most likely never be a mother myself, I have no need to learn." She couldn't admit even to herself how much she wished that were not the case.

They rode silently along the snow-lined streets. Christmas decorations hung from lamp posts. A group of children stood in front of a shop window, mesmerized by a display of reindeer and toys spilling out of a sleigh. A peddler stood on the street holding up a pole with perches of small birds. He must have clipped their wings to keep them from flying away.

"You ladies do know," Carlotta said, her voice grim. "that getting rid of them won't change a damned thing. It's like rats. You kill two and 20 more will replace them."

Chapter 2
Ellen

Virgil Thorn kicked snow off his feet and grinned as he entered the hallway, carrying a stack of magazines.

"Fresh from the printer. The January issue!" he said.

"Just under the wire," Ellen said, taking the stack from him so he could remove his overcoat and fedora.

She could hardly wait to peruse the pages of the very first copies of *The Ladies' Lantern*. Wouldn't Hester have been proud of her!

Thorn followed her into the parlor that had been transformed into a magazine office by placing two desks on either side of the arched entrance to the dining room. The former editor of *The Ledger*, as dapper as ever in a three-piece suit, a gold watch chain hanging from his pocket, was a wiry, energetic man, and though they had once been antagonists, Ellen had forgiven him for being British and hired him to edit her magazine.

Ellen stared at the cover with its picture of a woman holding a lantern high. The first edition of *The Ladies' Lantern* was finally in her hands. She didn't say it out loud, but she was more excited about this achievement than she was about having a baby, a baby that had been forced on her by a German brute. If a torpedo hadn't sunk the *Lusitania* and sent her into a spiral of grief, she would not be in this situation, what with her swollen ankles and having to constantly relieve her beleaguered bladder.

"You did it," Louisa said, looking over Ellen's shoulder. Louisa's rose water *eau de toilette* wafted in the air. Fortunately, it wasn't a lavender scent, for that was what Hester had worn, and Ellen couldn't keep from weeping whenever she smelled it.

"Not by myself," Ellen said. "Half the articles are written by you. And if Mr. Calloway hadn't sold off his newspaper, I wouldn't have the illustrious Mr. Thorn here as an editor."

"Now all we need are readers," Thorn said. "Lots and lots of readers – if we want to sell advertisements, that is."

"Many women will be delighted to read a women's magazine that's about more than just 'bonnets, babies, and butter cookies,'" Louisa said. She looked around the room as if she were searching for something.

"I'm not so sure," Ellen said, admitting to a nagging worry. "Margaret Sanger's magazine didn't last but an issue or two. Your gloves are on the sofa, by the way."

"Because it was only about one topic, birth control," Louisa said, picking up her kid leather gloves. "Your magazine covers a whole range of causes."

"*Our* magazine," Ellen said.

Ellen wished Louisa had the same passion for *The Ladies' Lantern* that she did. She worried that Louisa thought magazine writing a poor replacement for her weekly syndicated column with readers around the country.

"No time to rest on your laurels, ladies," Thorn said. "We need to get started on the next issue. Thank heavens we're a quarterly and not a monthly."

"I'm heading over to the Heterodoxy Club for lunch. Maybe I can get an interview with Inez Milholland about the changing home," Louisa said, pulling on her gloves.

"Who's that?" Thorn asked.

Ellen looked up at him sharply. "She's the lady who rode the white horse in the suffrage march in 1913. I saw her myself. Magnificent." Of course, she would never forget that march. It was where she'd met Hester French. Ellen had thought Hester nothing but a silly rich woman pretending to care about the plight of the lower classes, but then as she'd gotten to know Hester, witnessed her kindness, and heard her peals of laughter, she'd fallen hopelessly in love. All the locked doors in her heart had opened wide.

Louisa's mother, Anna, entered the room.

"Oh, they're here!" she said, leaning her cane against the desk, and picking up one of the magazines. When Ellen had first met Anna, the woman could barely walk but she had changed over the past few months and miraculously become quite mobile, using a cane instead of relying on an invalid chair.

Anna had offered to help with the circulation for the magazine, which oddly enough, considering the old woman had never worked a day in her 60-odd years, she did well. She used the telephone and her superior tone and blue-blood voice to twist arms and sell subscriptions. Having a hand in the magazine had given Anna a purpose, which only confirmed to Ellen that the life of the idle rich was not one worth living. Now that she was rich herself, thanks to Hester's fortune, she would have to take care not to become one of those that she despised. Hester, though wealthy, had filled her time fighting for social causes. And it was Ellen's intention to honor her with a magazine dedicated to such causes.

"By the way," Thorn said. "Did you know that the Germans gave Franz von Papen the Iron Cross as soon as he arrived back home?"

"Of course, they did. He's a hero to them. Think of all the havoc he wreaked while he was here," Louisa said. "He arranged for the sabotage of American ships, he forged passports so German men would return home and fight, and he tried to get us in a war with Mexico."

"Did Suzie make coffee this morning?" Anna asked.

"She did," Carlotta said, carrying a silver tray as she entered from the dining room. "I'll fix you a cup, ma'am."

Carlotta set the tray down on the coffee table.

"What's an Iron Cross?" she asked as she poured a cup for Anna, who had somehow never lost the illusion she was someone who should be waited upon hand and foot. Carlotta usually obliged.

"It's a military honor," Thorn said.

Carlotta touched the scar on her lip.

"Sure. He's a real hero when it comes to beating women," she muttered.

Every time Ellen thought of von Papen's filthy hands on this girl, she seethed.

"You helped bring him down, girleen," Ellen said. "We all did, come to think of it."

Carlotta had been von Papen's favorite girl at Martha Held's brothel until she spilled his secrets to Louisa. Then she paid the price.

"I never did hear the whole story," Thorn said. "Weren't you some sort of double agent, Miss Malloy?"

"That's a story for another day," Ellen said. She *had* served as a double agent for the British, working in the offices of the Hamburg-American Shipping Line and for her trouble had wound up almost dead in a box in the hold of a ship. She didn't care to relive those events.

Louisa put down her cup of coffee and stood.

"I'm off to the Village, where the radical women bide their time in cafes and tea shops, gathering their strength to take over the world." She leaned over to kiss her mother on the forehead. "Ellen, you'd better put your feet up. Your ankles are as big as an elephant's."

Ellen looked down at her feet. She'd taken to wearing woolen slippers instead of shoes because of the constant swelling. It was as if the baby had taken over her body and might never return it.

As soon as Louisa was out the door, Suzie came downstairs, wearing her wool coat, knit hat, and scarf.

"I have an appointment to get fitted for my wedding dress," she said.

"Oh no, you're not going without me," Anna said. She rose from her chair by the window and grabbed her cane. "Carlotta, fetch my coat and scarf, please."

Ever since Suzie had announced her engagement, she was no longer the housekeeper and cook. Instead she was Anna's "dear friend." Ellen suppressed a smile.

"All right, Anna. You may come along," Suzie said.

After Suzie and Anna left, Ellen lowered herself to the sofa. She wondered how on Earth they would get along without Suzie to run the house. Carlotta was willing to help out but she was no Suzie. She was practically a girl, and her recent job experience at the brothel did not entail managing a house.

"Are you feeling all right, Ellen?" Carlotta asked. "Can I get you something?"

"I would appreciate a cuppa," Ellen said. She wasn't one to ask for help but she'd been awake all night with charley horses in her calves. This having a baby business was no picnic. She felt like a fortress under siege.

With the house to themselves, Ellen and Virgil discussed the April issue of the magazine while Carlotta went upstairs to clean the bedrooms.

"We need a copy editor," Thorn said. "It would also help to have someone to sell advertising full time. I think we should also hire an entertainment writer to focus on the motion picture industry."

"How is the motion picture industry a woman's issue?" Ellen asked.

"Women are becoming rich from it," he said. "Anything that offers a path to independence and self-sufficiency for women should be of interest to your readers. They aren't only actresses, by the way. Many of the scenario writers are women. There are even lady directors."

"I suppose there's a case to be made," Ellen admitted.

A knock on the door startled them.

"Are you expecting someone?" Thorn asked.

Ellen shook her head and struggled to get up to answer the door.

"Now, now." Thorn waved his hand at her. "I'll get it. My title is not only editor-in-chief but also butler-in-chief."

Ellen gratefully sank back down. Thorn left, and a minute later, a man with a thick Irish accent asked, "Is Miss Ellen Malloy in?"

Christ on the Cross. She knew that voice. She struggled to rise from the divan as a young man with blue-green eyes and sandy hair came in. His mouth dropped open when he saw her there as big as a house.

"Ellen?" he asked. "What...?"

She had no idea why her younger brother was standing in the hallway of Louisa's brownstone or what to tell him about her enormous belly.

"Martin," she said. "What are you doing in New York?"

"I took a job as a courier," he said. "I thought I'd surprise you. But I'm the one getting the surprise, aren't I?"

"It's a long story," Ellen said. "Come in."

"Is this *Anglo-Saxon* fella your husband?" Martin asked, indicating Thorn.

"Certainly not," Thorn answered.

"Come to the kitchen, Martin," Ellen said. "I'll explain everything. You might do some explaining as well."

They sat across from each other at the old wooden table in the kitchen at the back of the house. She gazed at her brother. He wore a thick sweater of Irish wool, and his hands bore the callouses of a boy who grew up hauling nets full of fish. He had the strong, jutting jaw that all the men in her family had, but the cheeky grin was all his own.

"How did this happen to you?" Martin asked looking at her belly.

"Do you really not know, Martin?" she asked.

"Oh, I know all right. What I want to know is who?" His gaze rose toward the ceiling as he did some mental calculations. "Must have happened while you were in Germany helping the Brotherhood get arms. Did Plunkett do this? Or Roger Casement?"

She had befriended both men while she was in Germany after the sinking of the *Lusitania*, but it stopped at friendship.

"Don't be daft," Ellen said. "Plunkett is much too pious and devoted to his fiancée, and Roger Casement fancies the fellas. Anyway, it doesn't matter who it was. He was a terrible man, and his name is better left unsaid."

Martin shook his head.

"A German?"

Ellen nodded.

"Did he force ya?" he asked, his eyes narrowing.

"Does it matter? 'Tis done." She rolled her head in a circle to loosen the tension in her neck.

"You didn't even tell us."

"And why should I?" she asked.

All of a sudden, he smiled, showing his crooked teeth. "A wee Malloy coming into the world."

"A wee Murphy actually. Mr. Murphy, Hester's brother-in-law, has a dead cousin back in County Cork that's standing in for my husband. I'm a widow. A rich one." She held up a hand with a wedding band on it. "Of course, I'm keeping my own name. But the baby's last name will be Murphy."

"Rich? How'd that happen?"

"My friend Hester that died last year when the *Lucy* sank left me her fortune," Ellen said.

"A fortune, eh?"

"I sent some money to Mam. I thought you knew."

She thought back to the mass funeral the Irish had given for the *Lusitania*'s dead on a breezy day in May. She'd buried a part of herself on that breezy day in May.

Martin whistled. "I knew you were grieved to lose your friend but I didn't know just how close the two of you were." He gave her a sympathetic look. He knew she'd never been interested in men romantically.

Ellen lowered her eyes, her grief washing over her anew.

"Let's turn the attention to yourself, boy-o," she said. "Why aren't you home in Ireland? Who hired you to be a courier? As if I don't know. Was it John DeVoy, publisher of *The Gaelic American*?"

"I'm after delivering messages from the Brotherhood to *Clan na Gael*. Messages too important to be delivered by cable," he said. "And yes, Mr. DeVoy is one of my backers."

Clan na Gael was the American arm of the Irish Republican Brotherhood. Their main objective was to free Ireland from the English, a plan of which she approved, but they also supported a foolish alliance with the Germans, including with that scoundrel Franz von Papen.

"Von Papen is a brute, you know," she said. "He's been declared *persona non grata* here in the United States for his misdeeds."

"He'll be even more useful to us in Germany," Martin said with a shrug. "There's an uprising a-coming, Sister, and we need weapons. With German rifles — or I should say Russian rifles captured by the Germans — we can drive out the English invaders. The hell with waiting for home rule."

"Martin, I was there. In Germany. I knew Captain Boehm, the head of the Abwehr, their intelligence unit. They have no intention of helping Ireland. Trust them, and you'll all wind up dead," she said.

"Captain Boehm? Is he the culprit?"

Ellen shook her head. "Boehm was more of a father figure, if you must know. The culprit was a Major with the intelligence service. A cold-blooded brute."

She would not say his name, but she would never forget the cruel eyes of *Oberstleutnant* Walter Nicolai and how he'd manhandled her body as it were a thing meant only for his satisfaction.

"Well, I'd rather be dead than a vassal in the feckin' British Empire," Martin said with a flash of anger.

They sat in silence, trapped in their own thoughts. Outside, the wind jostled the bare limbs of the linden tree in the back yard. The baby kicked, and Ellen rubbed a hand across her belly. She gazed at her brother and remembered when he had been but a toddler, sucking his thumb by the turf fire. Even as a child he'd been a rebellious hellion, sneaking out of the house to chase the chickens.

"So, you're bringing messages from the Brotherhood. What are you taking back home?" she asked.

He rubbed his fingers together. Money, of course. Money for a rebellion.

"'Tis a bad business, brother," she scoffed. "You'll get yourself killed and break her heart, you will," she said. Their old mother in the Claddagh, who had already lost one son in Gallipoli.

"Not as bad as when she finds out she's got a grandchild and no one told her." He leaned back, crossed his arms and gazed at Ellen with knowing eyes. He had her there.

Chapter 3
Louisa

Louisa would not cry. As a society writer, she'd been to hundreds of weddings. Why should she cry at this one? Just because the bride happened to be Suzie, whom Louisa had loved since she was a baby? The same Suzie who had been born into slavery and worked for Louisa's family from age eleven to the day Louisa's father was murdered and the money gone. She had been the only servant to stay with Louisa and her mother to take care of them, managing the household so they didn't wind up in the poorhouse. Suzie, now in her sixties, wearing satin and pearls, after all these years was getting married. Louisa sobbed.

Louisa's mother, on the other hand, was dry-eyed. Instead of weeping, she smiled blissfully.

"Doesn't she look lovely?" she sighed.

The couple said their vows in St. Philips Episcopal Church in Harlem, a new church with a Negro congregation, in front of family and friends in the nave. Included among the guests was Martha Held, owner of the German brothel where Franz von Papen and Karl Boy-Ed had been regular customers, along with several of her girls. Mr. Sweet was the butler and bouncer for the establishment, and, Suzie had sold lingerie to the girls as a way to infiltrate the establishment, which is how she had met the delightful Mr. Sweet. Today the girls were dressed in an attempt at respectability.

Suzie's niece, Pansy, was her sole attendant. After a kiss to seal their vows, Suzie in her long dress and Mr. Sweet in his black silk top hat marched down the aisle to the triumphant "Wedding March" by Mendelssohn.

Afterwards, guests enjoyed a reception in the church hall with a three-tiered cake, punch, and canapés. Ellen, flush with her new wealth, had insisted on paying for all the food and for the chamber orchestra even if she were too pregnant to attend herself. While the orchestra played "If You Were the Only Girl in the World," Louisa watched Suzie dancing in Mr. Sweet's arms. One was never too old to fall in love, it seemed. She felt a pang of pity for herself.

Would she ever know anything akin to Suzie's happiness?

After some wedding cake, Louisa and Anna said their good-byes to the happy couple, and walked back to their brownstone a few blocks away from the church. The weather had turned bitter as wormwood, and for some reason there wasn't a taxi anywhere, as if they were all hibernating like bears. So mother and daughter walked home in the freezing cold, their breath turning into vapor before them. It seemed strange that Suzie would not be waiting for them with warm stew and freshly baked bread. She would be cooking for Mr. Sweet from now on. And who would cook for them?

"I wish Ellen could have come," Louisa said.

"Pshaw," Anna replied. "She should be in confinement. She certainly shouldn't be working on that magazine. The womb and the brain compete for energy, you know. She'll be lucky if that child is not somehow deficient. I did absolutely nothing for six weeks before you were born. It's medically proven that a woman in the family way should not be exposed to anything that is not beautiful."

"Mother, not everyone believes that. Besides, I'm quite sure Ellen would go mad without the magazine to distract her. Not to mention that since Mr. Calloway sold *The Ledger*, I need the work."

"Work? You were a society writer for *The Ledger*. She's turned you into some sort of muckraker," Anna said.

"I was doing muckraking at *The Ledger,*" Louisa said.

"Not under your own name!" Anna said.

It was true. Any investigative pieces Louisa wrote for the newspaper had been published under a pseudonym, but those pieces had been the most exciting. She'd been kidnapped, threatened with a gun, exposed sex traffickers, and uncovered a spy ring. The articles she was writing for Ellen's magazine seemed quite dull in comparison. Now she was interviewing suffragists, union women, and birth control advocates — all important issues certainly but without either the glamor of her society beat or the danger of her investigations. At least, the electric bill was getting paid, and there was plenty of food in the cupboard.

They rushed up the steps, entered the house, and hurried into the parlor to warm themselves by the fire.

"How was the wedding?" Ellen asked from the desk where she examined a mock up for the next cover of *The Ladies' Lantern.*

Carlotta sat on the couch, knitting a misshapen bootie. She'd only just learned how to knit.

"Beautiful! Suzie looked stunning," Louisa said. "I brought cake for the two of you. Or I suppose I should say the three of you." She glanced toward Ellen's rotund belly.

Louisa looked for a place to put down the cake among the magazine pages scattered over the coffee table.

"Ellen, dear, don't you think it's time you looked for a new space for the magazine office?" Louisa asked.

Louisa's home had always been her refuge from work. Now there was no refuge.

"Oh, don't send them elsewhere," Anna objected. "I like having people around."

"I haven't had the time to look for another space between growing a baby and trying to get the first issue out," Ellen said. "But I am not deaf to your entreaty, Louisa. I'll find something."

"Please do it soon. I'm about to lose my mind. I mean, for heaven's sake, I have to see Virgil Thorn in my house every morning before I've even had a cup of coffee..."

"Well, if you got up earlier," Ellen said, "you could have your coffee before he showed up."

Louisa glowered at her. Ellen had grown impudent after inheriting Hester French's money. Actually, Ellen had always been impudent. It was one of the things that Louisa liked most about her. But her mother was right. Louisa had been a society writer. This idea of a progressive magazine for women was Ellen's dream. Not Louisa's. Louisa didn't even know what her dream was anymore.

"Do you think a story on whether women should change their names after marriage or wear wedding rings is serious enough for our readers?" Ellen asked. "So few women actually buck these old traditions. Even Margaret Sanger uses her husband's name."

"As long as society treats women as chattel to be owned by men, then yes, those are serious topics," Louisa said. "Though I do think Suzie Sweet has a nice ring to it."

"And if you'd married Forrest Calloway, would you've taken his name?"

"I suppose I wouldn't have minded being Mrs. Calloway. But we'll never know, shall we?" She hoped her voice didn't betray her regret at the way things had turned out. If she had accepted Forrest Calloway's marriage proposal, she would now be living in a grand house overlooking Gramercy Park. In spite of her early pledge to not marry, she had initially accepted his proposal. She did love him, after all, but after the sinking of the *Lusitania* and with Ellen missing, she could not think of marriage. So, she'd rejected his offer, had a fling with an engaged British spy, and now shared her cramped brownstone with her mother, Ellen, Carlotta, a magazine office, and soon, a baby.

"Ellen, why do none of your story ideas involve going to parties? I miss oysters and champagne."

"Would you prefer to be paid in champagne?" Ellen asked.

The irony was not lost on Louisa that Ellen had once been *her* assistant at *The Ledger*. Now their roles were reversed.

"I'd settle for writing about the opera once in a while." Louisa rubbed the bridge of her nose. "I did get that interview with Inez Milholland. She says all these new household gadgets like dishwashers and such have freed women from drudgery so we can do more important work."

Ellen stood and crossed the room, thinking.

"You could interview Emma Goldman. She's just been knicked for advocating for birth control," Ellen said. "She's at the Tombs."

It took a moment for Louisa to catch her breath. An article by the editor of Goldman's anarchist magazine, *Mother Earth,* had incited an insane woman to try to kill Louisa two years earlier. Fortunately, the woman was dead now, but anarchists were still a dangerous bunch in Louisa's opinion.

"I think I'll go upstairs for a nap," Louisa said, "while you come up with a better idea."

"Louisa," Ellen said, reaching down to the sofa so she could lower her unwieldy body. "Perhaps, you might fetch the midwife instead."

Louisa stepped toward Ellen, who had gone white as a sheet of paper.

"Oh, Ellen. Is it time?" she asked.

Ellen grimaced and uttered a groan.

The midwife didn't have a telephone. So Louisa grabbed her coat and ran out the door.

Chapter 4
Ellen

"Try to think of something nice," said the midwife, a stout woman with a Russian accent.

Nice? Ellen groaned. As the pains increased in intensity, her mind catapulted back to the day she had plunged into the icy waters of the Irish Sea after a torpedo hit the *Lusitania*. She remembered dragging herself onto a life raft, searching the surface of the water for Hester. Then, after she and others were rescued, she had walked amongst the hastily built coffins, looking at each bloated body, each swollen face, and not seeing Hester anywhere. The only thing she'd found was Hester's pink hat.

These were her thoughts now as her body turned into a machine full of cogs, gears, and chains all activated in the task of cranking out a human being.

The hours dragged on until finally the grandfather clock downstairs chimed 12 times to ring in a new day. With each hammer strike inside the clock, the contractions rushed one on top of the other like colliding boulders tumbling in an avalanche.

As bad as it was, though, Ellen welcomed the pain. It was the first real sensation she had experienced in all these months since Hester's death. As the calm voice of the midwife encouraged her, her flesh split in two. She clenched her teeth and clutched the sheets, screamed, and then in an enormous wave of agony what felt like a sack of fat and bones spilled out from between her legs. Ellen stared at the ceiling, gasping. It felt as if she had been turned inside out.

The sudden wail of life startled her.

"Here's your Valentine's Day gift, a baby girl." The midwife wrapped the baby in a tight cocoon and put it next to Ellen, who held the small, mewling creature against her skin, its head covered with something that looked like cottage cheese.

What was she supposed to feel? She'd been under the impression that a wave of maternal love would flood through her. Instead, she simply felt curious. It was so small and vulnerable. How had the human race survived, she wondered? *Something, some instinct, keeps us from leaving them by the roadside.*

The midwife clamped the umbilical cord and then cleaned up the afterbirth.

"You're as healthy as a horse," the midwife declared. "And you've got a fine baby."

Ellen had hoped the arrival of the baby would ease her sense of loss after Hester's death, but nothing would do that. And yet ... the baby was hers. She must protect it and provide for it. Then she admonished herself, the baby isn't an "it." The baby is a "she." All little girls deserve love and protection. Even her own Mam, who was no paragon of motherhood, had not allowed their father to take out his anger on the children when they were young.

"Put her to your breast. She's had a long ordeal just as you have."

Ellen did as she was told. The little mouth clamped on her nipple and sucked with a ferocity that surprised her. She wasn't but a few minutes in the world and already she was demanding her due.

"What will you name her?" the midwife asked.

"Hester," Ellen whispered. "Hester Murphy." Ellen would think her of as "little Hester," so as to differentiate her from her true love, Hester French.

After the midwife had cleaned her up and left, Carlotta and Louisa stood in the doorway.

"How are you feeling?" Louisa asked.

"Like death on a biscuit," Ellen replied.

Carlotta came closer and peered at the baby.

"You done good, Ellen," Carlotta said.

The baby had nursed her fill and fallen asleep, her tiny wet mouth open, eyelids fluttering as she dreamt. What does a baby dream about, Ellen wondered.

"I'm knackered," she said, exhaustion placing its heavy hand on her own eyes.

Carlotta reached down and put the baby in the wicker bassinet beside the bed. Ellen dropped into a deep sleep and dreamt that she lay in a long wooden box, shaped like a coffin—the same kind of box that she had been trapped in by a German spy, drenched in darkness for hours. In the dream, the darkness was a living thing, resting on her chest, drinking her life force.

A wave of relief swept over her when she was awakened by the door to her room opening. Louisa entered, bearing a tray with a bowl. The baby was back in the bed with her. Carlotta must have put her there. Ellen wondered she hadn't rolled over and suffocated the little thing.

"I made you some cream of celery soup," Louisa said. "Suzie gave me her Fannie Farmer cookbook before she left. She said anyone who can read can learn how to cook."

Louisa placed the tray on the side table and then stared down at the baby that was just beginning to fuss, kicking her legs out as if she were raring to get up and run out the door. At that moment, the ginger cat leapt on the bed and stared at the baby in surprise. Carlotta ran in and scooped up the cat.

"It's bad luck to have a cat around a baby," she said. "We have to get rid of it."

"You'll not be getting rid of my cat," Louisa said sharply.

"I'm only saying…"

"I hear what you are saying, and I am telling you, Gin-gin stays. It's still my house."

"No one will take the cat away," Ellen assured her. "Let me try some of this soup you made."

She spooned a mouthful of soup and grimaced. "Louisa, did you even taste it?"

"No."

"You're supposed to taste the food before serving it. This hasn't a drop of salt or pepper."

"Oh." Louisa frowned in disappointment.

"Perhaps, you might bring a salt shaker up."

"I will." Louisa turned and hurried out of the room.

Maybe they should hire a cook, Ellen thought. Then she dismissed the idea. Having Hester's fortune thrust upon her had become such a burden. Every time she thought of the money, she thought of the reason she had it: Hester was dead. She despised herself every time she encountered a problem that money could solve. *Let a poor person take care of it.* That was the rich man's solution to every problem.

The baby whimpered and Ellen brought her to her breast. The child had the appetite of a whale.

"That's what ye are," Ellen whispered. "A tiny whale."

She thought of the next issue of the magazine with all its unfilled pages. Had she been mad to think she could blithely continue working when the baby came? A shadow seemed to come into the room then and settle over her, heavy as pile of stones.

Chapter 5
Louisa

"Well, mother and baby seem to be doing fine this morning," Louisa said, entering the dining room where her mother was reading the newspaper. This wasn't exactly true. Ellen, in fact, looked haggard, but Louisa was sure that was just from the travails of birth.

She poured herself a cup of tea (as no one had yet figured out how to make coffee) from the silver service on the sideboard. "Are we out of cream?"

"Of course, we are. With Suzie gone and Ellen having babies at all hours of the night, we've become a house of savages," Anna said.

"One baby, Mother. Singular. Have you seen her yet?"

"I have." Anna sniffed. She sat at the table, reading *The Evening World*. "She's got all her fingers and toes. I counted just to be sure."

Louisa glanced at the headlines on the front page of the paper that Anna was holding and noticed Billy Stephens' byline. He had helped her shift from writing society stories at *The Ledger* to writing about the murder of a police woman — the story that had changed her trajectory from mere society columnist to investigative reporter.

"Mother, may I have the front page?" she asked.

With a show of annoyance, Anna extracted the front page and handed it to her.

Louisa perused the article. "Two watchmen in the Woolworth Building spied a light on in one of the offices on the ninth floor. Upon unlocking the door with their pass key, they discovered Bernard Benson, Attorney at Law, with a bullet hole in his temple."

Good opening, she thought. Billy knew how to recreate a scene in a few sentences. Reading further, she saw that while no money had been found at the scene, there was a drawer full of pawn tickets. The reader was left to surmise that the man had killed himself over debts. She sympathized with the dead man, remembering her own financial struggles before her column was syndicated, financial struggles she had feared she would face again after *The Ledger* shut down and she lost her syndicated column. But fate had intervened with Ellen's inheritance and her passion for publishing a magazine.

Would I have killed myself before going to the poor-house, Louisa wondered. No, she would never have left her mother to fend for herself.

She turned back to the story. Mr. Benson left behind a wife, Judith, née Steinberg. Louisa paused. She remembered a Judith Steinberg from Barnard. A vivacious brunette who cared little for studying and dropped out after her first year to get married. Poor Judith, she thought.

After finishing the article, Louisa glanced at the other headlines. Another ship sunk by a torpedo, Rockefeller inspecting workers' conditions in the Colorado mines, and a Zeppelin raid on London. The war in Europe was exacting a dreadful cost. The only hope of ending it anytime soon was for America to declare war on Germany. Yet who could wish for American men to die on foreign soil?

"What a pity," her mother said, out of the blue.

"A pity?"

"That he killed himself. If he'd been murdered, then his widow would at least get some insurance money."

"Are you referring to this story about the man in the Woolworth Building?"

"I am. How do you think we were able to buy this townhome?" Anna asked. "Your father had squandered our fortune, but at least he had a life insurance policy.

Of course, I had no idea about the state of our financial affairs when he died."

Louisa remembered her own sadness and confusion after her father's death. When she had stood at his graveside, a shadow fell across the world. Everything darkened.

"I went to Barnard with Judith," she said, more to herself than to her mother. "I should visit her and offer my condolences."

"I'm sure she needs some sympathy. And not just for the loss of her husband. She's probably lost everything," Anna said.

Louisa's mother was surely thinking of her own precipitous fall from the heights of society after her husband's death. Louisa took a deep breath. Her father's murder had haunted her for years. How could a man so kind and gentle have gotten himself into such a fix? She knew the answer now. He was a man who loved other men, and that had meant his demise. Knowing the truth could never erase the pain of his loss.

Her mother turned to the society page.

"Oh, look, Mrs. Cornelius Vanderbilt hosted a ball last night at her Fifth Avenue palace. If you were still a society writer, surely you would have been invited. I remember when Grace was just an upstart. Cornelius was effectively disinherited when he married her against his family's wishes. Nevertheless, she's clawed her way to the top." Anna dropped the paper to eye Louisa. "Don't you miss it, Louisa? The glitz and the glamour? The intrigue?"

"I do not miss it," Louisa said, which was not entirely true.

"Well, I do," Anna said, turning her attention back to the paper. "At least when you were writing about society, I could keep tabs on my old cronies."

"Mother, do you honestly care about all that? Aren't you enjoying your work, signing up subscribers for Ellen's magazine?"

"I suppose so," her mother admitted.

Louisa finished her tea and went into the parlor to plan her day. Snow fell in quiet clumps outside so she would wait to visit Judith. She stared up at the family portrait above the mantel. It had been painted by a famous artist back when her parents were young and she was but a girl of eight. In the painting, they exuded the wealth and privilege of their class — her father seated in a throne-like chair, her regal mother standing at his side, with an impish Louisa on his other side, leaning in toward him. He'd been the one to love her, the one to admire her drawings and read the stories she wrote. In turn, he'd told her stories from his own wondrous imagination. She still missed him, his soft gray eyes and the way his voice had crooned her to sleep at night. She'd been the luckiest little girl in the world.

She thought about the baby upstairs — a little girl with no father at all and a former prostitute for a nurse-maid. One thing was certain: Ellen would never marry a man. She would have to be both mother and father to the child. Louisa had always thought one of the benefits of Ellen's relationship with a woman would be the avoidance of an unwanted pregnancy. Could she love her unwanted child, she wondered. The haunted look in Ellen's eyes was foreboding.

Anna came into the parlor and settled into her chair by the window where she liked to watch the world go by.

"Mother," Louisa asked, "did you love me when I was a baby?"

"What kind of question is that?" Anna said and waved her hand at the air as if to push away the question. "All mothers love their children."

"We both know that isn't true," Louisa said. She couldn't remember her mother ever once expressing love for her.

"You will never understand maternal feelings."

The remark stung more than it should have, and Louisa was about to say something she might regret, but she was stopped by the clink of the metal flap over the mail slot. She clamped her mouth shut and went to see what had arrived. She opened a square, cream-colored envelope and found the invitation she had been dreading.

> *The Honor of Your Presence is requested*
> *for the wedding celebration of*
> *Sadie Treadwell and Forrest Calloway.*
> *on Saturday, the thirteenth of May,*
> *one thousand nine hundred and sixteen*
> *at ten in the morning*
> *The Pierre*
> *Breakfast reception to follow*

"Did you get a valentine?" Anna asked when she came back into the parlor.

"Just the opposite. A wedding invitation," Louisa said. She swallowed and forced a smile to her lips. "In May. I'll have to get a new dress."

"The current fashions are hideous. It's this damnable war. Ankle bones everywhere," Anna groused. "It looks as if the designers simply ran out of fabric."

Louisa put the wedding invitation into a drawer.

"I suppose I should be on my way," she said. "I told Ellen I'd get her a story today."

"In this horrible weather?"

Louisa didn't care about the bad weather anymore. She needed to get out. She didn't want her mother or anyone to know how deeply she regretted breaking off her engagement with Forrest.

"I don't imagine a little snow will hinder the women who meet at the Heterodoxy Club." She snatched her coat from the hook by the door and hurried outside.

The sting of the cold air almost felt good.

You didn't want to marry, she told herself. *You wanted Forrest to be happy. Don't you dare cry.*

A disobedient sob wormed its way out of her chest. Fortunately, no one was around except for an old man begging on the corner. She looked at him, his stained trousers and brogans held together with string. He smiled up at her and she felt a wave of — not pity, but admiration. He hadn't given up on life. She took a quarter from her purse and handed it to him.

"Bless you." He stared at the coin in his palm.

"No, bless you," she answered.

She dabbed at her eyes with a handkerchief and hurried off to catch the El. She'd had her moment of self-pity. Now, she must get on with her work.

The Heterodoxy Club had been formed by a group of women in 1912 in reaction to the proliferation of clubs for men where women were forbidden. The meetings offered something more, however, than just a counterpoint to the men's clubs. The Heterodites, as they called themselves, were a diverse mix of socialites and reformers, Bohemian artists and professional women, suffragists and socialists. So many opinions among them all. Louisa had attended a few of the meetings to get a sense of their leanings and also to interview the speakers. Now it was time to ask for their help in garnering articles for *The Ladies' Lantern*. She would not write all the articles for this issue. She simply couldn't.

The Heterodites met every other week for lunch. On this day they were meeting at Polly's on MacDougal Street. A tall waiter wearing an apron that hung to his ankles showed her into a private room where about 15 women were seated at small, round tables, drinking coffee and gabbing loudly.

Mabel Dodge, with her hair cut in a short wavy bob and mink around her collar, smiled and invited her to sit. This was a singular honor as Mabel, known as Bohemia's "lion hunter," was an attractive woman whose social graces magnetized others and who brought in famous people of every stripe to mingle in her salons. Wealthy and intelligent, Mabel Dodge had the rare ability to make everyone around her feel at ease.

"Louisa, have you gone from society writer to radical?" Mabel asked with a grin. She drummed her fingers on the table, and Louisa tried not to be blinded by the emerald stone on her hand.

"I suppose I have," Louisa answered and handed her a copy of *The Ladies' Lantern*. "I'm looking for writers for a new women's magazine."

"Interesting," Mabel commented with a cursory glance at the magazine.

After the routine club business, Mabel rose and announced that the formerly syndicated society writer Louisa Delafield had a request to deliver to the group.

"Good afternoon," Louisa said, standing before the gathering of women. "I'm here on behalf of Ellen Malloy, publisher of *The Ladies' Lantern*, a magazine for socially conscious women."

"Oh, God. Not another *avant-garde* rag." The complaint came from Mary Vorse, a large-featured woman of at least 40 years, who had made a name for herself writing about the Triangle Shirtwaist Factory fire. "We already have *The Masses, Bruno's Weekly, The Dial, The Little Review*, et cetera."

If I must win over anyone, I must win over Mary, Louisa thought.

"Those are all fine publications, but *The Ladies' Lantern* is directed specifically toward women," Louisa explained. "While most of the magazines for women are single topic publications, such as birth control or suffrage, we cover a wide range of topics from labor and reproductive issues to changing mores."

"Bully for you. Are you asking for financial support? We've already given to Margaret's magazine and Charlotte's magazine and Emma's magazine. Why should we give to yours?" another member asked, waving a dismissive hand at her.

Louisa took a deep breath before continuing her pitch.

"For one thing, we aren't asking for money," Louisa said. "Some of you may remember the reformer Hester French, who died in the sinking of the *Lusitania*. She left her fortune to Ellen, and so Ellen is funding the magazine herself. We simply hope you might provide a few articles on whatever cause you choose to write about."

Louisa handed out copies of the first issue of the magazine, and gave the women time to peruse it.

"Who is this Jenny Smith?" Mabel asked.

"Me," Louisa admitted.

"And Roberta Jones?" Mary chimed in.

"Me."

"Did you write all the articles? You must have been busy."

"Not all of them. But we didn't have much time to find other writers."

"You really could use some cartoons," one of the women said.

"Yes, a lighter touch."

"I agree," Louisa said. "Do you know a cartoonist?"

"Perhaps some philosophy? Or an article about psychology," another suggested.

"Wonderful ideas. That's why I am asking for your help and your input," Louisa said.

"But you see, we're busy. We're writing plays and novels and poems along with articles for our own magazines," one of the poets said.

"We'll be happy to publish your poems and stories. And in case you were wondering, Ellen will *pay* you," Louisa said.

"Well, now," Mary said with a shrug. "What will it hurt to throw an article or two her way?"

The others laughed in agreement.

"Sign me up," said the stunning Ida Rauh, whom Louisa knew from her society writing days. Ida was so much more than a beautiful heiress. She had graduated from law school and was a labor union activist as well as an actress and a poet. She'd have plenty to say. Louisa wanted to jump for joy, but she refrained.

"How about an article on women's sexual desires?" Mabel suggested. "Something we are alleged not to have. Although Sigmund suggests otherwise."

The woman chuckled with knowing glances.

"And what about an article about menstruation?" someone else suggested. "Why do men believe that it renders women unable to function, unable to hold a job?"

"Menstruation? How about masturbation. Now, there's a taboo!"

Louisa couldn't believe her success. She only hoped it wasn't temporary. They might contribute articles for this issue, but Ellen needed to sustain the magazine, and for that she needed a stable of strong writers, writers whose names weren't Louisa Delafield.

Louisa extracted promises for nearly half a dozen articles. Ellen would be thrilled. Or at least Louisa hoped she would be.

"You really should talk to Djuna Barnes," one of the women told her as she was leaving. "She's absolutely the most brilliant woman I've ever known."

Louisa only knew Djuna Barnes from her "stunt girl" reporting — articles where she enacted events such as being rescued by firemen, and so forth. She had also done a piece on what it was like to experience forced feeding in an effort to explain what was happening to the suffragists in jail. Her acerbic wit glimmered in every line she wrote — even when it was about something horrible. Louisa had never met the woman, but her curiosity was piqued. She'd have to be on the lookout for Djuna Barnes.

Chapter 6
Ellen

Ellen held the baby's foot in her hand as the ravenous creature fed at her breast. This was not the blissful experience she'd been told it would be. She should be working on her magazine, not lying around like a cow. If only she wasn't so tired.

Louisa came in the room and hesitated at the sight of Ellen's bare milk-filled breast, but Ellen was too tired for modesty. Louisa averted her eyes and said, "Ellen, there's a man at the door who says he's your brother."

"That would be Martin," Ellen said. "Tell him to come on up."

"All right," Louisa said. "Do you want to ... cover up?"

Ellen pulled a quilted baby blanket that Suzie had made for her over the nursing baby's head.

"That better?"

Louisa smiled, but her eyes betrayed her discomfort with the proximity to things of a bodily nature. She left, and a few minutes later Martin stood in the room, holding a huge bouquet of pink flowers.

"Where'd you get flowers in the dead of winter?" Ellen asked.

"There's such a thing as florists, Sis," he said. "They import flowers from all over the world."

"Must be expensive," she said.

He set the flowers down on the dresser and sat on the edge of the bed.

"I make good money in my current employment," he said. "I might not have the fortune of an heiress, but I'm doing well enough. Let me see that baby."

Hester had fallen asleep while still sucking. Ellen gently pulled the baby away from her breast and handed her to Martin. When he took her in his arms, the baby opened her eyes.

"It's a blessing she gets to meet you before you come to your end," Ellen said. It would do no good to chastise him, but she couldn't help but fear for his safety. It was bad enough to be involved in the activities of Sinn Fein, or the Brotherhood, back home, but to travel to America on their behalf would surely bring him to the notice of the British secret service.

He ignored her dig.

"She's got her uncle's good looks, she does." He looked into the baby's eyes and said in a sing-song voice, "I promise I'll be around to take you to the altar on your wedding day. Yes, I will."

"Martin, while you're making promises, promise me you'll be careful," she said. "You canna trust the Germans. You know that, don't you?"

"I am careful. What is the wee one's name?" he asked.

"Hester Murphy," she said. "My Hester's sister, Katherine, is married to John Murphy. He's the one who found a conveniently dead relative to be my husband."

"So you said. Are you all right, Elleenie? You're looking rough." Martin gave her a quizzical look, as he rocked the baby in his arms.

"I'll be fine. I just gave birth." She didn't tell him about the shadow, about the almost unbearable pain that had wrapped a fist around her heart. She would fight it off. She had to.

He hummed to the baby as he paced around the room.

"I'm sticking around for a couple of weeks, you know," he said. "The Irish Race Convention is coming up. If you're up and around by then, you should come with me."

"Oh, I'll be up and around by then. I've got a magazine to put out," she said. "But I won't have time for any of that *Clan na Gael* foolishness."

"Foolishness? Ellen, this convention will determine whose side the Irish Americans are on — those who support an uprising or the Nancy boys who believe in the false hope of the Home Rule Act, which they conveniently suspended because of the war." He sat down on the bed.

"I know which side you're on, hothead. You and that John Devoy and his newspaper."

"And which are you on?" He placed the baby back into her arms.

"I'm on Ireland's side, but not those who would collude with those murderous Germans. That's where you lose me."

Little Hester fussed, so Ellen let the baby suck on her pointer finger to calm her.

"I understand your anger and your grief. That business with the *Lusitania* was terrible indeed." His voice grew soft and urgent. "But, Sister, this is Irish freedom we're talking about now, the right to our sovereignty. Come to the convention with me, will you?"

She gazed into his eyes. She'd always marveled at how sometimes they were sky blue and other times green as grass. She thought of their childhood adventures. Alone neither would have survived the bullying of their older brother, Michael, but together they had out-smarted him time and again. Perhaps it *would* be better if she kept an eye on him.

"All right, I'll come," she said. She couldn't say she had no interest in the movement for independence. It's just that it had been going on for centuries, and all they ever accomplished was the spilling of Irish blood. "Now, let me get some rest."

Martin leaned over, kissed her on the brow and then gently ran the palm of his hand over the baby's head.

"She's got hair just like yours truly," he said.

Ellen looked at the fine gold hair on the baby's head. Was that from Martin or from the Aryan father?

"By the by, did you say you know John Murphy?" he asked. "Owns some kind of factory, doesn't he?"

"Yes, he took it over from Hester and Katherine's father."

Martin ran his hand over his own hair and smiled.

"And he's a friend of yours, is he?"

"I wouldn't say friend, but I know him all right."

Martin whistled as he walked out of the door. What was he plotting now?

While the baby dozed, Ellen grew anxious. She had seen what had happened to girls in a world full of wolves. How could she keep the wee girl safe? Just herself and not a maternal bone in her body? She wasn't up to it. She fretted until she wore herself out.

She roused an hour or so later when the bedroom door creaked open, and Carlotta came in with a tray.

"Suzie brought over stew and homemade cornbread," Carlotta said. "That woman sure knows how to cook."

"Praise the saints. Why didn't she come up?"

"Didn't want to disturb you," Carlotta said.

Ellen took one bite of the stew and moaned.

"Christ on the cross, this is good," she muttered. "I fear Louisa will never learn how to cook, no matter how many cookbooks she consults."

"I brought up your newspaper, too. I know how you like to keep up with the news."

Ellen had subscribed to John Devoy's *The Gaelic American* for months now. It was important to keep abreast of the doings of the Irish radicals here in America. They were fomenting rebellion, and who knew where that might end? She did love the typeface of the masthead, and wondered if she might do something equally as arresting for *The Ladies' Lantern*. Who knew typeface could be so fascinating?

There on the front page was a notice about the upcoming Race Convention: "Preparations for the Great

Gathering at the Hotel Astor on March 4 and 5 Completed by the Committee. Names of Delegates Should Be Sent To Secretary Moore At Once. No Man Not In Favor of Complete Irish Freedom Need Apply For Admission."

Ellen shook her head. DeVoy and his cohorts had no room for compromise. It felt as if she were standing on the shore watching a shipwreck about to happen, and there was nothing she could do to save a single soul including her brother. She needed to get out of this bed, needed to talk to DeVoy and plead, cajole, or threaten — anything to get him not to endanger her brother.

The baby let out a sob.

"Oy, what is it now?" Ellen asked.

She looked down at the fussing baby. Suddenly a memory breached the wall she had erected around her mind and she felt Nicolai's hands holding her down as he grunted like a wild boar above her. She set the baby down on the bed and called for Carlotta to come get her. She had a terrible feeling she might harm the wee thing.

Chapter 7
Louisa

Louisa handed Virgil Thorn her typed interview with Inez Milholland. She poured some tea from the pot on the table and sat down on the couch while he read it over.

"I've asked the women at Heterodoxy for more articles, and several of them agreed," she said. She took a sip of the tea, feeling the warmth of the cup against her palm. "I can't write them all, you know. I'm not quite sure I'm cut out for writing about all these causes. There are so many, and I'm no expert."

"You are certainly better suited for covering soirées, balls, and tea dances," Virgil said and looked up at the painting of her family hanging above the mantel. "However…" He looked at her with one eyebrow raised, "your investigative powers are not insignificant."

"Thank you, but these stories for *The Ladies' Lantern* require neither a knowledge of society's mores or the ability to dig into scandals. And most of those women at the Heterodoxy Club are busy with their own publications. Every day another magazine starts up."

He spread his hands on the desk, leaned forward, and said, "The difference is we don't have to worry about funding. However, it wouldn't hurt to diversify our investors. You know, our old boss Calloway spends tens of thousands on these Broadway productions. Why don't you see if he has any interest in supporting the magazine?"

Louisa cringed at the thought.

"Forrest got out of publishing for a reason, and I won't grovel for money. Especially when Ellen has plenty." She set down her cup and saucer, stood and walked across the room to look out the window. "I got an invitation to his wedding."

"So did I," he said. "I'm sorry, Louisa. I know you and he were once..."

She turned and looked at him.

"I'm happy for him," she said with a smile plastered to her face. "I really am. I wish him nothing but success in all his ventures."

Thorn's eyes lit up.

"By the way, his latest investment has all Broadway abuzz. It's a musical, featuring Al Jolson. I'm rather interested in seeing it myself," he said.

"Interested? As in dying to see it?"

"Dying? Of course not. Maybe a bit," he said, looking up at her with a sly grin. "Why don't you go with me on Saturday night?"

Louisa looked out the window and pondered the invitation. Why shouldn't she go? After all, she loved musicals almost as much as Virgil did. Forrest Calloway might be there. But he might not. What difference did it make?

"I would love to go with you. It will be fun," she said. "I need to get out in public more often. The way I used to."

"Back when you covered the people who really matter," Anna sniffed.

"Oh, Mother. They only matter to themselves," Louisa said.

"We can go to the Paradise, afterwards. All the stars go after the shows." Virgil pretended to be casual about the prospect, but she guessed that he loved the idea of being surrounded by the wealthy and the famous.

"The entire time you were the editor at *The Ledger,* I had no idea who you really were," she said.

"At present, I'm still your editor," he said. "I picked up a book of poetry by one of those Bohemian women. We should run a review of it."

He handed Louisa a slim book, more of a booklet actually. She read the title aloud. "*The Book of Repulsive Women*. Intriguing title. And it's by Djuna Barnes. She's a journalist. I didn't know she was also a poet."

"An artist, too, apparently."

Louisa perused the book of poems and drawings. Such a strange sensuousness to the language. One verse in particular:

We'd see your body in the grass
With cool pale eyes.
We'd strain to touch those lang'rous
Length of thighs,
And hear your short sharp modern
Babylonic cries.

This woman was more and more intriguing, and it seemed more than a coincidence that someone had recently mentioned her name. Something tugged at Louisa's consciousness. She must meet Djuna Barnes. She didn't know why, but fate seemed to be nudging her with a sharp, pointed finger.

"I'll do better than a review," Louisa said. "I'll find the poet and interview her myself."

"Perfect," he said. "In the meantime, there's not much for me to do until we get some more stories. I'll be back by tomorrow."

He left, and Louisa wondered if agreeing to go to the musical was a good idea. What if Forrest *was* there? And what if his bride-to-be was with him? She would have to summon every ounce of dignity she could muster to face them.

Carlotta came back from the market with the ingredients Louisa had requested.

"What're you making?" Carlotta asked.

"Parsnip fritters," Louisa said, consulting her Fannie Farmer cookbook.

Louisa mashed the boiled parsnips and seasoned them. She shaped the mixture into small, round cakes, rolled them in butter and then sautéed the fritters. In a smaller pot she made a butter sauce.

Carlotta sat at the small wooden kitchen table and chopped up the parsley.

"Miss Louisa, were you a debu...?" She struggled to find the word.

"A debutante? Where did you hear about debutantes?"

"I read it in the paper. It said girls got to have parties and balls."

"No, I wasn't. Coming out parties are only for rich girls, and we'd lost our fortune when I was only 12."

"So, it's a coming out party?"

"Yes, the girls are introduced to society so they can find an eligible man to marry. A rich eligible man."

"Then I guess I had a coming out party when I was 15," Carlotta said. "Only we weren't looking for husbands."

Louisa stopped what she was doing and looked over at Carlotta, her dark hair pulled into a low bun, her long, graceful neck bent as she looked down at the knife in her hands, chopping parsley. Louisa knew exactly what sort of coming out party Carlotta must have had. The bids for her virginity would have been astronomical. She wanted to take the girl in her arms and weep for her, but she knew Carlotta would brook no pity. Instead, Louisa used the spatula to remove the fritters and place them on a platter.

Ellen poked her head into the kitchen. "Is it lunch yet? I'm famished."

"I can bring your lunch to you," Carlotta admonished.

"No need. I'm going stir-crazy," Ellen said. "I'll set the table."

Louisa took off her apron, went into the dining room and placed the plate of fritters on the table along with a platter of cold cuts. Anna sat placidly waiting to be served, her linen napkin on her lap. Carlotta brought out a pitcher of milk and poured a glass for Ellen.

"Drink," she said and nodded at Ellen's chest. "You need to replenish the stores."

"What's that smell?" Ellen asked just as Louisa sat down.

An acrid odor tingled Louisa's nostrils.

"Hell's bells, the sauce is burning," she said, rushing back into the kitchen.

Carlotta burst out laughing. "If Miss Louisa is cursing, then we're in trouble."

Louisa poured the burned sauce into the sink and went back into the dining room to eat with the others. She didn't mind taking over the cooking but she did mind feeling like an utter failure at it.

"I overheard Virgil discussing bringing on a copy editor," Louisa said. "That seems a bit much, doesn't it? Another person coming in every day."

She took a bite of the parsnip fritter. The taste was fine, but the texture was dry. They really did need the sauce, but they all ate what was on their plates out of politeness or hunger.

"I know what you're saying, Louisa, but for crying out loud I just had a baby. I promise I'll look for a space for the magazine soon."

Louisa bit her lip. She hadn't meant to nag Ellen about the crowded conditions. And Ellen didn't look much better than she had after the birth. It was as if a dark cloud hovered over her.

They had almost finished lunch when they heard the baby crying.

"I just fed her," Ellen said and burst into tears.

The outburst silenced all of them briefly.

"I'll look in on her," Anna said. "You go rest in the parlor."

"Thank you," Ellen said and rushed out of the room.

Louisa inhaled sharply.

"I don't think Ellen is doing well," she said quietly.

"She's got the baby blues. It's common," Anna said. "She'll get over it."

One of the household chores that Suzie had fostered in Louisa during her teenage years was dish washing. The family fortune and all the other servants were gone by then, and Suzie said she had enough to do what with cleaning, cooking, laundry and managing the dwindling finances. Now that Suzie was gone, Louisa had returned to her old chore. There was something soothing about the steam from the water, the warm suds, and the repetitive motion of wiping dishes.

The best thing about washing dishes was that it was a job at which she could not fail. And at this particular moment in life, she teetered on the brink of feeling like an utter and complete failure. It wasn't her fault that

Forrest had sold *The Ledger* and that therefore she lost her syndicated column. And yet, no other newspaper had scooped her up. Worst of all, she'd begun to wonder why Forrest hadn't waited for her. Why had he given up so easily. Why had he gone and fallen in love with Sadie Treadwell?

What was wrong with her, she wondered, that she was an old maid. She was still attractive. She may be older than most girls in the marriage market, but she was younger than Sadie, and Forrest wasn't young either. How could he have gotten over her so easily? She wondered if he knew or guessed about her affair with the British spy Reggie Grant.

Had that affair really had been a mistake? It was no longer the 19th century. Women had lovers. Some women had multiple lovers. Some women had men and women lovers. But she wasn't some women. She wanted sex accompanied by love. She wanted what she had once rejected. She wanted one man. And she could no longer have him.

Suddenly she thought of her college friend Judith who had just lost her husband to suicide. There were worse ways to lose a man than to another woman.

The last dish done, she turned off the water and dried her hands.

Chapter 8
Ellen

As soon as the baby was asleep in her bassinet, Ellen made her way down to the parlor where Thorn sat at the desk, working.

"Louisa wants me to find another place for our offices," Ellen said.

Thorn looked up in surprise.

"Should you be out of bed?"

"My gran had eight kids. She was up and about after every single one within a day, feeding chickens and boning fish. I've been doing nothing for days."

"Good heavens!" Anna commented from her perch by the window. "How many of those babies survived?"

"Half of 'em," Ellen said, "my mean old da included. What needs doing, Mr. Thorn?" She was desperate to work or she would surely lose her mind.

"I want your thoughts on these illustrations. Where is Louisa? She was supposed to interview that poet, something-or-other Barnes."

"She's taking a nap," Carlotta said, leaning over to sweep some dirt into a metal dustpan. "Said she has to go to the Village tonight for something called a salon? Might be out late."

Ellen examined the illustrations and pictures Thorn wanted to include in the next issue. She found it easy to get lost in her work and forget all about the fact that she was now a mother, to push away the shadow licking at her.

An hour later, Carlotta came in, holding a whimpering baby.

"Ellen, Hester is hungry. And I've got some washing to do including a barrel full of dirty diapers."

Ellen set down the pages and rose to take the baby.

"I'm mighty grateful for your help, Carlotta." The girl had taken on the diaper chore without a second thought.

Ellen sank onto the couch as little Hester's whimpering turned into a howl. Ellen fought the urge to drop the baby and run out the door.

"Mr. Thorn, I suggest you look the other way."

"I have to leave anyway. The layout for the stories we have is done, and I'll have to wait for the rest of the stories. Would you like me to look for a new space?" he said.

Ellen shook her head. Finding the right space was something she must do herself -- as soon as she felt better. Right now she couldn't even bear to think of it.

After he left, Ellen opened her blouse so the babe could suckle. She had not realized how tired she was, for she dozed off along with little Hester. A knock on the door awoke her. She placed the sleeping baby on the sofa and buttoned her blouse while Carlotta hurried from washing diapers to answer the door.

"May I help you?" Carlotta asked.

"Hello. I'm here to see Ellen," a female voice said gaily.

Ellen's head jerked up. She knew that voice. It was Hattie Garrett, Ellen's former employer from her days as a lady's maid. The last thing Ellen wanted was company. But a moment later a rosy-cheeked young woman in a dark teal day dress and matching hat with black feathers sauntered into the room.

"Ellen," she squealed. Then she stopped in her tracks. "Oh! Whose baby is this?"

"'Tis my own," Ellen said, lifting the sleeping infant.

Hattie Garrett stepped closer to look at the baby. Her eyes shifted from Ellen to the baby and back.

"She's beautiful. But I didn't even know you were married," Hattie said.

"Didn't last long," Ellen said. The baby's milky eyes fluttered open. Ellen placed the child on her shoulder so she could burp her.

Carlotta stood in the doorway.

"Want me to take her?" Carlotta asked. "Whilst you two catch up?"

"Whatever we're paying you, it's not enough," Ellen said to Carlotta and handed over the child.

"Oh, it's plenty. I'd take care of this *bambina* for nothin'."

Hattie's eyes bulged as Carlotta left the room, bouncing Hester in her arms.

She turned to Ellen.

"I did hear about your inheritance. That must have come as quite a surprise."

"I'll say." Ellen fingered the fringe of the baby's blanket.

Hattie glanced around the small, shabby parlor.

"Why are you still living with Louisa and her mother? You could afford to live anywhere, couldn't you?"

"I've been wondering the same thing," Louisa said, entering the parlor. She sat in the armchair chair underneath the family portrait.

Louisa may have lost her fortune, Ellen thought, but she'd always have an aristocratic bearing. Hattie attempted it, but Louisa was born to it.

"What a lovely dress, Hattie," Louisa said. "The tea-length is so fashionable these days."

"Oh, Louisa, it's lovely to see you again," Hattie gushed. "I haven't seen you since..."

"Since your exquisite wedding. Your mother spared no expense. And how is married life?"

"It's full of surprises." Hattie blushed.

Gin-gin leapt onto Louisa's lap. Louisa stroked the cat's back, inducing a rumbling purr.

"But you wouldn't know about that," Hattie said. "You've never been married. Not like Ellen or I."

Ellen saw Louisa hide a smile. How Hattie assumed that Louisa lived the pristine life of an old maid could only be chalked up to naiveté, Ellen thought. She could name two men who'd been with Louisa on an intimate basis. Forrest Calloway and Reggie Grant. And why shouldn't she experience the pleasures of love? After all it was 1916, and Queen Victoria was long dead.

Hattie was oblivious.

"Ellen, I've missed you. I wish I could find another lady's maid like you. Two quit and I had to fire a third. Now Mother has foisted Smith on me."

"Smith? That old sourpuss," Ellen said. "Why are they quitting on you? I don't remember you being a hard task master."

"I'm not. I'm as sweet as pie. But one of them got a better offer from a department store and the other one left to get married. I had to fire the third when I caught her beating the scullery maid."

"I'm sorry, Hattie. Unfortunate as it is, I can't come back to work for you. I'm busy publishing a magazine."

"I know! I read the first issue. Isn't it funny? Louisa now works for you."

"I work *with* her," Louisa objected. "With. Not for."

"That's nice, Louisa," Hattie said. "I bet you miss the society beat. We're so busy these days, doing charity work to raise money for the war effort."

"The women I'm covering now also do important work," Louisa said. "Though I'll admit their canapés are sorely lacking, and they never serve champagne."

"I adore champagne," Hattie said. She turned her attention back to Ellen. "I just wanted to say, Ellen, if any of your country women come to you and they're looking for work, please send them to me. I want to return Smith to Mother as soon as possible. Where do you get your help from?"

"Well, the only one who helps around here is Carlotta, and we found her in a brothel."

Hattie burst out laughing.

"Oh, you're as funny as ever. Tell me something, Ellen." She leaned forward, head tilted. "Why would a rich heiress leave all her money to you?"

Ellen glanced at Louisa, who pursed her lips and gazed up at the ceiling.

"I believe," Ellen said in a measured voice, "that she trusted me to do something good with the money. She was a believer in reform and progressivism. And she knew I would honor her wishes."

Hattie seemed satisfied with the answer.

"I wish I had control over my money, but my husband has the final say on everything." Hattie looked wistful. The thought that she would always be beholden to a man rubbed Ellen the wrong way.

The cat jumped off Louisa's lap and capered away with a meow, interrupting the moment.

"It was lovely to see the both of you. I've a million things to do today," Hattie said and gathered herself together to leave. Then she stopped and gazed at Ellen. "You should get some rest, Ellen."

Even Hattie could tell that she wasn't doing well.

Once Hattie was gone, Ellen turned to Louisa. Louisa's remark about why Ellen hadn't gotten a place of her own had not been lost on her. Did she really want Ellen and the baby to leave? The shadow tightened around her. She couldn't give into it. She couldn't let Louisa see how terrified she was.

"Should we hire some help?" she asked. "You shouldn't have to cook. And between taking care of the baby and your helpless mother, Carlotta does have her hands full."

"Don't you even think about it." Carlotta entered the parlor and sat on the sofa. "I don't mind the work. It beats the hell out of laying on my keister with my heels to heaven." Louisa's eyebrows lifted. "Besides Mrs. Delafield's not so demanding. And I like taking care of the little un. Baby's napping, by the way."

"No more servants," Louisa said. "The place is already too crowded." She ran her index finger over the side table next to her chair and examined the dust. "We can all clean a little more, and I don't mind cooking."

It was just as well. Ellen hated the idea of having servants.

"It was lovely to see Hattie," Louisa said.

"It was," Ellen said. "I only wonder whose life her rascal of a brother, Hugh, is ruining these days."

"He's married now," Louisa said. "I'm sure he's behaving himself."

"Ha!" Hugh Garrett had shown himself to be an utter scoundrel and still somehow Louisa thought he would revert into her childhood friend.

"That Hattie sure is a fancy one," Carlotta said. "What's wrong with her brother?"

Louisa and Ellen shared a look.

"Three years ago, Hugh Garrett got Ellen's friend, a young housemaid named Silvia, pregnant and would have sent her to a brothel if she had not died during an abortion," Louisa said.

"Don't forget, he bid on a chance to rape a woman," Ellen added.

Louisa had been the woman whose virtue was up for bid. Ellen had enlisted the help of Forrest Calloway, and they had saved Louisa from an unspeakable fate. Thinking of it even now sent a shiver of rage through her. Marriage didn't stand a chance in hell of reforming Hugh Garrett. What he needed was a bullet to the brain.

She sucked in her breath. Where had such a thought come from, she wondered. The violence in the air — from the war, from the whispers of Irish rebellion — it could infect a person like the germs nurses were always going on about these days. The seeds of that violence had been planted in her heart the day Hester French died in the bitter Irish Sea.

So many dark feelings roiled inside her. Maybe she should move out. And yet what would happen if she were alone with the shadow. What might happen to little Hester?

Chapter 9
Louisa

Louisa rode the crowded subway to the Village and then made her way to Mabel Dodge's Fifth Avenue apartment. She walked up the red-carpeted stairs and entered a white-walled, white-curtained drawing room. On the walls were photographs by Alfred Stieglitz and a portrait by Gertrude Stein. About a dozen people milled about the room, drinking cocktails. They were all chattering about this new play or that new novel. Among the guests were the poet, Edna St. Vincent Millay, a painter, a model, a political journalist, and a governor of the New York Stock Exchange named Mr. Halle and his wife, a dour-looking woman in black velvet. Mabel was trying to convince Mr. Halle, who regularly invested in Broadway plays, that he should spread his wealth to help some of the avant-garde theaters.

"The Washington Square Players are doing marvelous original plays. They truly deserve your support, Mr. Halle."

"Get me tickets, Mrs. Dodge, and I'll happily give them a look-see," he said.

Halle turned toward a tall, olive-skinned waiter and took a highball glass filled with an amber liquid and topped with a cherry from his proffered tray. Not the sort of drink that interested Louisa. The waiter's hands were rough with callouses, the nails dirty. He must be some sort of moonlighting laborer, she thought.

"Excuse me," she said. "Is there any champagne?"

"I will get for you," he said. He made a slight bow, and she noticed that his left ear lobe appeared to be missing. She unconsciously reached for her own earlobe and touched it as if to make sure it hadn't wandered off.

The waiter disappeared in the crowd.

Louisa's previous social set had been mostly vapid social strivers, who cared about wealth and status above all else. She wondered if these artists and Bohemians looked down on her for having been born to a stodgy blue blood family.

Then she saw just the person to make the trip worthwhile: Margaret Sanger.

"Margaret," Louisa said. "Do you have a moment?"

"For you, Louisa? Of course. I really don't have much to say to these Bohemian types."

"I'd like to interview you for an article in our next issue." Louisa handed her a copy of the first *Ladies' Lantern* magazine.

Margaret glanced at the cover and nodded with approval.

"I'd be happy to give you an interview, but we better do it tonight. I'm leaving town first thing in the morning."

Louisa looked around for the waiter with her champagne but he was nowhere to be seen. That was unfortunate.

Mabel directed Louisa and Margaret to her study, where the two women sat in armchairs beside a fireplace with a crackling fire.

"I'm in trouble for mailing diaphragms to women who want birth control," Margaret said.

"Diaphragms? I don't know what those are," Louisa said.

"They act as a barrier to prevent semen from reaching the ovaries. They aren't perfect. Nothing but outright sterilization seems perfect. But used in conjunction with a prophylactic, they can be quite effective. Of course, if you print any of this in your magazine, you will certainly be banned in Boston and possibly arrested for violating the Comstock Act."

Louisa knew there were perils in publishing any-thing about birth control, so she would have to be care-ful not to be too specific. And yet the thought of ending up in jail simply for conveying information was difficult to fathom. She wished she had that glass of champagne.

"I'll be circumspect," Louisa said. "I understand you're planning on establishing a birth control clinic. That should be a safe subject."

"I do plan to open a clinic in Brooklyn. My goal is to help poor women limit their family size."

"Why is that so important to you?"

"My own mother had 11 children and died at the age of 50."

Good heavens! Louisa thought.

Louisa broached a topic that had been on her mind. "As a journalist, I aim to stay objective, but as a woman I heartily approve of what you are doing, Mrs. Sanger, but I have a different sort of question for you. What do you think of a woman who has had intercourse several times and yet has never gotten pregnant?

"Did the man in question use any sort of prophylac-tic?"

"Not always." Louisa was thinking of a few careless bouts of passion with Reggie Grant.

The door opened suddenly and a man staggered weakly into the room. It was Mr. Halle, the theatrical investor.

Louisa rose and took his arm. "Are you ill, Mr. Halle?"

"My apologies, ladies," he said in a strained voice. "I'm feeling quite restless, and my jaw is stiff. I want to move, but my muscles ache so."

"Here, let me help you." Louisa led him to an over-stuffed chair with an ottoman so he could put up his feet.

"Thank you…" His breath came out in hard gasps as he sank into the chair. To Louisa's horror, as soon as he landed in the chair, his whole body convulsed. His jerking legs kicked the ottoman over on its side.

Margaret, a former nurse, hurried over and looked at the man. His body bent violently back and forth.

"What do you think is wrong?" Louisa asked, helplessly.

"Strychnine," Margaret said. "The effects can come on very quickly."

The poor man gazed up at them and groaned, holding onto his stomach.

"Why?" he asked, his eyes darting back and forth. "Why?"

"Is there an antidote?" Louisa asked.

"I'm afraid not," Margaret said, "but go get Mabel and tell her to get a doctor."

Louisa dashed out of the room. She looked around frantically. How did so many people fit into this room?

Their peals of laughter so absurd. There's a man dying, she wanted to scream. She stopped, took a breath, and composed herself. She saw Mabel smiling at a drunk man, who was gesticulating wildly. Probably ranting about the reviews of his latest play. As if that were the most important thing in the world. She shoved her way over to Mabel and leaned in so close she could smell her floral perfume.

"Is there a doctor?" she whispered. "Mr. Halle is quite ill."

"Not here," Mabel said, alarmed.

"Then get one," Louisa said and turned back to the library.

By the time Mabel's maid had fetched a doctor, Mr. Halle was dead, his eyes wide open, his face a gruesome visage, and his body frozen in an unnatural contortion.

"Rigor mortis has already set in," the doctor said. "I agree with your assessment, Mrs. Sanger. It certainly looks like poisoning by strychnine."

Mabel had managed to get most of the guests to leave except for the drunken playwright who had passed out on the sofa and Mrs. Halle. When Mrs. Halle saw her husband, she screamed and had to be sedated by the doctor.

"It could be accidental, but you will have to notify the police."

"Doctor," Louisa asked, "how could he have come into contact with it?"

"It's sometimes used as a pesticide and occasionally someone ingests it accidentally, but usually only children do that."

The police came, and a detective with an Irish accent questioned Mabel, Margaret, and Louisa while Mrs. Halle slept in Mabel's bedroom.

"Mrs. Dodge," the detective said, "do you know how Mr. Halle came to ingest poison?"

"I don't," she said, wringing her hands. "The building superintendent might keep poison, but I certainly don't."

"What about the caterers?" Louisa asked. "Perhaps they know something."

"Let's go to the kitchen and find out," the detective said.

The three women and the detective went to the kitchen while a coroner came to take the body away.

Of course, the caterers, a mother and daughter, and the waiters knew nothing. Louisa saw the look of panic in the mother's eyes.

"No, we don't use strychnine in any way, shape or form," she said. "I don't know he got it."

"It comes from the seeds of the *nux-vomica*," Margaret interjected.

"And that is…?"

"A tree. It grows in India, however, so I doubt he would have come into contact with any seeds."

The detective looked around and said in an exasperated voice, "Anybody? Anybody see anything?"

Louisa's eyes roved over the waiters. There were only three of them. And they were all Negros.

"Wasn't there an Italian waiter?" she asked.

The caterer shook her head. "Nope, just these three."

"I'm certain I was served by an Italian waiter," Louisa said. "He brought Mr. Halle his drink."

The detective sighed. "Did anyone else see an Italian waiter?"

"Not that I remember," Mabel said.

"Nor I," Margaret said.

Of course, the "help" was always invisible.

The detective shook his head, wearily. "Miss Delafield, I'll need you to come downtown with me so you can give me a description of this mystery waiter."

Louisa blew out a long breath. This wasn't the first time she'd witnessed a death by poisoning. Each time was more horrific than the last. She'd never forget the confusion in Mr. Halle's eyes. He knew his life was ending. He just didn't know why. She had a bad feeling the reason might never become known.

Chapter 10

Ellen

"Why don't you take a stroll with the baby? It's not so cold out this morning," Carlotta suggested. "I'll bundle her up and put her in her carriage."

"I don't want to," Ellen said.

"Look, I know I'm not the boss around here, but you've turned into an old sow. You never smile. You only work and sleep. Mrs. Delafield said you had some kind of baby blues, but you shoulda been over that by now."

Ellen hadn't been out of the house since before the birth. Perhaps, a walk would rouse her from her lethargy. Maybe all she needed was a little fresh air.

The snow had melted, leaving dirty clumps along edges of the sidewalk. She pushed the carriage a few blocks to Morningside Park where she found a bench to sit down. The baby didn't seem to mind the cold. She looked up at the world with wide eyes.

A couple of boys ran past her, yelling and throwing rocks at each other. Then a flock of pigeons descended on the sidewalk around her, cooing and bobbing and circling each other in their strange dance. She watched them, hypnotized by their movements until she saw a white pigeon, a single eye cocked toward her.

How did they see like that, she wondered.

To her surprise, the white pigeon flew up with a loud fluttering of wings and landed on the edge of the baby carriage. The bird tilted its head toward the baby and then toward Ellen.

"Sure, that's my very own baby," Ellen said.

The pigeon looked down at little Hester for a moment before lifting its wings to the wind and soaring away.

Ellen looked around to see if anyone else had been witness to this strange occurrence. But there was no one. She knew what her gran would say. She would say that the spirit of Hester French had come to check on the two of them. For a moment the shadow lifted from her heart. She could see a glimmer of light in the darkness that surrounded her.

"Fancy meeting you out here." Martin ambled toward her, hands in his pockets.

"Did you happen to be in the neighborhood?" she asked.

"Went by your house. The Italian girl told me where to find you. She's a looker. Too bad about the scar on her face."

"Good looks aren't always a blessing for a girl," Ellen said.

Martin sat down beside her.

"Ya know, Elleen, I was thinking about you and your new circumstances. You might find it in your heart to lend a bit of support to the cause yourself."

"Are you asking me for money, Brother?" She felt a wave of indignation. "It's not even my money."

"What are you saying, it isn't your money?"

"It's Hester's money. I wouldn't have it if she hadn't been drowned by a godforsaken German U-boat." Her voice cracked with bitterness.

"I'm sorry you lost your friend. But 'tis your money now."

"Martin, I must spend the money in a way that honors her. And Hester was a pacificist. I could never give her money for the purchase of weapons, and you know that's exactly where all that money is going — for weapons of war."

"How else are we going to get independence?" he asked. Then he said in a mincing voice, *"Oy, sirs, would*

you please take your feckin' arses out of our land?
Pretty please?"

Ellen shook her head.

"You're throwing good money after bad. Your leaders have no experience in battle. They're all poets and dreamers. And you don't have the people behind you like you think you do."

"They'll get behind us once they see we mean business."

"And then there's the Germans," she went on. "Look at what they did to poor little Belgium. They're no better than the English. Maybe worse."

"And look at what the Belgians did to the Congo. Cutting off of the natives' hands, they did. And for no reason. The Germans are just trying to defend themselves from the English and they need access to the sea."

There was no winning this argument.

"Martin, we were not born at the same time, but you are the twin of my soul. Don't ask me for money for the cause again. If you need money for yourself, then I'm more than willing to help."

"I'm just not sure whose side you're on," he said. He got up and walked away. She watched his broad back receding.

"Martin," she called out. He turned around.

"Don't say anything to your German friends about me," she said.

He tilted his head in confusion, but she said nothing else. She didn't even know if he was friendly with the Germans. She hoped to God he wasn't. And she hoped to God they had forgotten all about her and her promise to spy for them. That promise had gotten her into this fix what with a baby from a German officer. She had planned to be a double agent and get some measure of revenge for Hester's death. And the plan had worked. But now, would they be wanting their own revenge?

Hester fussed, so Ellen picked her up and held her warm little body close to her.

"Hush, now," Ellen said. "It will all be just grand, I promise you, wee one." It didn't hurt to comfort the little one. And maybe to comfort herself.

Chapter 11
Louisa

Louisa couldn't shake the image of the dying man from her mind. She hadn't been much help to the police. She only remembered that the Italian waiter was tall, his hands were calloused, and he was missing an ear lobe. The police weren't really interested in labeling Halle's death as a murder. And that feeling was verified in the morning when she read the newspaper accounts of the "accidental" poisoning of the wealthy man.

It was ten in the morning when she got out of bed. She dressed and wandered into Ellen's room where Carlotta was changing the baby's diaper. Perhaps it was the recent brush with death, but she found she was inexorably drawn to the baby.

Carlotta put the pins in the diaper and a fresh gown on her. Then picked her up and held her toward Louisa. Louisa looked at Carlotta in alarm.

"Oh, just hold her, Louisa," Carlotta said. "She won't bite. She doesn't even have teeth."

Louisa tentatively held out her arms for the tiny thing.

"What if I drop her?" she asked.

"You won't." Carlotta placed the baby in her arms. "Hold her head like this."

She positioned Louisa's hand so it cradled the baby's skull. What a helpless little thing she was, and yet so full of the force of life.

"I didn't expect her to be so heavy."

"She's a healthy one," Carlotta said, smiling down at the baby. "Ten days old now."

As Louisa looked into the blue-ish eyes of the child, her knees suddenly felt liquid.

"Oh," she squeaked. "She's precious."

Louisa stared, entranced, at the infant in her arms. She hadn't expected to feel this way. After all, it wasn't her baby. She wasn't prepared for the tears that sprang to her eyes and dropped onto the baby's blanket. Were they for herself, she wondered, or for the poor man she had seen die the night before.

"Please don't mention the poisoning. That's of no interest to our readers," Ellen said, as Louisa typed up her interview with Margaret Sanger in the dining room.

"Readers are always interested in murder," Louisa said and returned the carriage with a ding.

"The police aren't calling it a murder, are they?"

"They may not call it that, but I don't know how else it could have happened." Louisa was sure that the Halle family wealth had influenced the police decision not to pursue the case. A murder would cause a scandal, as Louisa knew only too well. And yet, ignoring what happened would not get justice for the dead.

"A rich man's death is not the focus of the story," Ellen said and sat across from her with a cup of coffee. She dropped in a cube of sugar and swirled the dark liquid with a silver spoon.

"Don't worry. I make no mention of the murder. Just birth control. You do know you can go to jail for publishing information about methods for limiting birth." She thought of Margaret Sanger's warning, which she brushed off, but which was actually worrisome. The suffragists and birth control advocates might be willing to go to jail for their causes, but Louisa had no interest in winding up behind bars.

"If I go to jail, I'll be in good company," Ellen said. "And I'll get an interview with Emma Goldman since you refuse."

"I don't care for that old anarchist. I do plan to write an article on the debate about whether or not to support American neutrality. The women at Heterodoxy are fighting tooth and claw," Louisa said.

"Whose side are you on?" Ellen asked.

"I don't want war, but I feel there is no other choice. If America doesn't enter the war, it will drag on forever, wiping out Europe."

"Ay," Ellen said. "I could never admit this to my countrymen, but I hope America throws off her cloak of neutrality and goes in full throttle. I've lost a brother and a lover to this war. And I'm bloody well tired of it."

Louisa glanced at her friend in awe of her righteous anger. It was a force to be reckoned with.

"If you ever go to battle, I feel sorry for your enemies," Louisa said.

That evening Louisa sat at her vanity while Ellen brushed her hair into a pompadour. Louisa wore a white chenille evening gown from Paris with a dark blue velvet overlay and sheer white sleeves. She justified the expense as a way to support the war. She situated a rhinestone head band with a white feather over her pompadour.

"Are you sure you should be going to the show tonight?" Ellen asked.

"Why wouldn't I go? It was Thorn's idea. He loves musicals, and Al Jolson is supposed to be marvelous as Crusoe's Man Friday," Louisa said.

"But *he* might be there, am I right?"

"I assume he will be in attendance," Louisa said, applying just a hint of rouge to her cheeks.

"I'm guessing you're over him anyway," Ellen said.

"Quite right."

They both knew that wasn't true.

Thorn picked her up in a taxi cab, which took them downtown to 50th Street where the Winter Garden Theatre occupied most of a city block. They entered the building and gazed around at the profusion of domes, curved walls, and Classical Roman motifs.

"The Adam style," Thorn pronounced. He had an eye for interior design that Louisa only discovered when he became editor of a woman's magazine. As the editor of *The Ledger*, he'd been stand-offish. Now he allowed more facets of himself to be visible. She suspected that the reason he had never married was not for lack of opportunity but because he wasn't interested in women that way.

The show itself was an extravaganza with a cast of more than 200 players supporting Jolson, whose face was painted black with a large white smile. Jolson had been a minstrel performer before he became a star, and old habits died hard. In this case, they didn't die at all. Louisa thought the painted-on smile was ridiculous, but his voice was sublime. Jolson and his chorus sang and danced their way through a silly plot — a millionaire has a dream that he goes to a desert island, complete with pirate girls, a crocodile, and a haunted forest. Jolson played the chauffeur who transforms into "his man, Friday."

Louisa tried to lose herself in the jaunty music and the elaborate spectacle, but throughout the show, she remained aware that in a box seat above her, Forrest Calloway sat with his fiancée, the widow Sadie Treadwell. She had a terrible urge, an overwhelming desire to get him alone and confess that she still loved him. She wanted to beg him not to marry Sadie and to give her one more chance.

But did she have the nerve to do such a thing, she wondered as Jolson sang "Yaaka Hula Hickey Dula." A voice in her head argued that Forrest ought to know she had changed her mind. It was only fair he have all the information before marrying another woman. But what if he was truly in love with Sadie? Well, then, she reasoned, he could tell her so, and she could gracefully concede.

The after-theater party was held in the Paradise Supper Club at Reisenweber's on Columbus Circle where a group of five musicians played something they called "jass." The lively music was unlike any music Louisa had heard before with horns blaring and drums beating. Louisa glanced across the room and saw Forrest at a table with Sadie and a man with mutton chop sideburns. Sadie wore an elegant evening gown of green silk and black lace. She smiled at something Forrest said and gazed at him like a smitten school girl.

Louisa downed one cocktail and then another. The alcohol dulled the ache inside.

"Shall we dance?" Virgil asked.

"I have no idea how to dance to this music," Louisa said.

"It's the one-step. I'll show you," he said. "You'll get the hang of it."

She laughed at the idea that Virgil Thorn, the man she had once thought so finicky and fastidious, was going to teach her how to dance.

It took a few minutes to pick up the quick, mincing movements, but Louisa got "the hang of it" and momentarily forgot her sadness until a few songs and a few drinks—later when she found herself in Forrest's arms, twirling around the floor. She felt dizzy from the drink, but also bold. She always behaved so properly, she thought, and look where it had gotten her. Single, poor, and possibly irrelevant.

"Congratulations," she said. "The show was certainly a success."

"All I did was pour money into it," he said.

"It paid off." She looked up into his mahogany eyes, sure she was about to make a fool of herself.

"We'll have to see how long it runs."

He did not hold her close; she felt the heat of his body nevertheless. His scent, desert and moonlight mixed together, washed over her. She remembered their first night alone together, how he had oh-so-tenderly kissed every part of her body so that she shivered with anticipation and then she thought of the moment when his hips sank against the insides of her thighs.

She shook her head to dismiss the memory. She saw Sadie dancing with the mutton-chop man.

"Something wrong, Louisa?" he asked.

"Nothing at all."

If he was remembering the same night, he showed no signs of it. It didn't matter. If she didn't disclose her feelings to him, she was afraid she would implode. She couldn't hold it in another second. She didn't expect it would make a difference. Once wedding invitations were sent out, there would be hell to undo it, but she had to tell him. The cocktails had given her the nerve. It was now or never.

"Forrest," she said, "there's something..."

A murmur passing over the crowd like a wave interrupted her. Dancers stopped in their tracks and the music faltered. Forrest turned to look for the source of the commotion.

"Somebody, help! She's fainted," a voice cried out. "Is there a doctor?"

Forrest's grip tightened on Louisa as he peered through the crowd.

"It's Sadie," he said in alarm. He immediately released Louisa and pushed through the revelers. Louisa followed him.

"Sadie!" he said and knelt beside her.

The maître d' knelt at her other side, waving smelling salts under nose. Above her the man who had been sitting with them at the table stood by, helpless. After a few moments, Sadie roused and looked around in embarrassment.

"Oh, dear. I'm so sorry to cause trouble," she said. She gazed up at Forrest. "And I'm sorry to ruin your celebration."

"Hush," he said. "Let's get you home."

He helped Sadie to her feet and held onto her as the two of them walked off the dance floor. Louisa's hands drooped at her side. Virgil came over and stood next to her.

"That puts a damper on the night." He sipped his martini.

"It does," Louisa agreed. "On the other hand, I may have been saved from utter humiliation."

She could not help but think that was an awfully convenient fainting spell Sadie'd had.

Chapter 12
Ellen

Before she died, Hester had urged Ellen to read the work of a man named Sigmund Freud, a doctor who worked with patients suffering from mental illnesses. Nothing she'd read in all those pages or in all his cases shed any light on the dark thoughts that besieged her since the birth of the baby. Sure, she had grieved the death of her lover. Sure, she had suffered nightmares from being locked in a box on a ship. But she had managed to keep those horrors at bay by working on the magazine and being around others.

She leaned over the wicker bassinet and watched little Hester wave a silver rattle that had belonged to Anna when she was a baby.

"It's not your fault," she whispered. "Something has gone off inside my head. But I don't blame you."

Louisa had made fish for dinner. Ellen had little appetite, but she forced herself to eat.

"It's not bad," Carlotta said.

"Not bad, but not exactly good either," Anna said. "The potatoes are lumpy."

"Well, if you can do better...," Louisa said to her mother, "you're welcome to the kitchen."

"I'm not complaining."

Ellen said nothing and ate listlessly.

"You're out of sorts," Anna observed.

Ellen sighed and put down her fork. She couldn't tell them that she felt she was back in the box on the ship. She couldn't tell them about the thoughts plaguing her—how she imagined walking into the ocean and never turning back. What she did tell them was true, but it was only part of the story.

"If I'm being truthful, I'm worried about Martin."

"Your brother?" Louisa asked.

"The one and the same," Ellen said. "He's gotten involved with John Devoy, publisher of *The Gaelic American* and founder of *Clan na Gael*. And now they're fomenting rebellion. Like our father, his blood is on fire."

"Rebellion against the British? Why, that's treasonous," Anna exclaimed, clutching her napkin.

"Is it any more treasonous than when your own ancestors overthrew the yoke of your British overlords?

Aren't *you* a member of the Daughters of the American Revolution?" Ellen said.

"I suppose you're right," Anna said. "But this is a time of war."

"I'm aware of that, and I'm no sympathizer of the Germans. But I do understand the logic. This may be the best time to get out from under the thumb of the English. Whilst they're distracted."

"It's dangerous for him, is it?" Louisa said.

Ellen nodded.

"What are their chances of success if there is a rebellion?" Louisa asked.

"I haven't the foggiest," Ellen said. "I can't blame him for being involved, but it keeps me up at night."

Louisa reached over and squeezed her hand.

"I'd like seconds please," Anna said.

"I thought you didn't like it," Louisa said.

"I don't, but I'm hungry."

Louisa heaped more food onto her mother's plate.

"Did you ever go offer condolences to your friend?" Anna asked.

"You mean Judith? I was going to, but got distracted by Mr. Halle's poisoning."

"You know, suicide brings a great deal of shame. Almost as much as murder." Anna sipped her sherry, which she had lately taken to having each night after dinner. "Many will shun her now."

Anna had become a pariah in society after her husband's murder.

"You're right, Mother. I'll go see her tomorrow." Louisa turned to Ellen. "Katherine Murphy called. She's coming over tomorrow with baby presents."

Ellen was puzzled. Why would Hester's sister show such an interest?

"I believe she may be unable to bear children," Louisa said, answering the unasked question. "And you know, you aren't the only one who grieves the loss of Hester French. Katherine was quite close to her sister."

While Hester was alive, Katherine seemed to be the most snobbish, provincial and silly woman, craving the attention of society and oblivious to the real relationship between her sister and Ellen. But she had no doubt the two sisters loved each other. She hated to think how her own heart would break if she lost her brother — a fate that seemed much too likely these days. So much Irish blood spattered across Irish land.

When the knocker thudded against the door the next day, Ellen and the baby were ready. Ellen forced the perpetual gloom into hiding as Katherine came into the parlor, carrying two large bundles. She set them down to remove her sable coat, which Carlotta took to hang in the hallway.

"Oh, let me see that darling baby," Katherine said. "May I hold her?"

"Of course," Ellen said.

The baby was fascinated by the double strand of pearls hanging around Katherine's fleshy neck.

"Why, look how beautiful she is." Tears sprang to Katherine's eyes. "I was four years old when my baby sister was born, but I'll never forget the first moment I saw her."

"What was she like as a baby?" Ellen asked, perking up at the mention of her lost love.

"She was a good baby, from what I remember. Mother complained that I was a fussy thing, but said that Hester was born an angel."

"She was, indeed, an angel." Ellen stifled a sob that wanted to leap from her lungs.

Katherine looked at her kindly.

"Ellen, I know you and Hester were more than friends. I don't know how you wound up with a baby, but part of me thinks there's a little bit of our Hester in this baby."

Katherine poured the grief she felt over Hester's death into love for this baby. If only Ellen could do the same, perhaps there wouldn't be this chasm in her heart.

"Since you're busy with your magazine, if you like, I could take care of Hester sometimes. Even this afternoon. There's a milk bank at the hospital where they sell bottles of breast milk so she wouldn't even go hungry. In fact, I purchased some just in case."

Ellen had not known there was such a thing as a milk bank.

"As a matter of fact, I do need to speak to someone this afternoon. If you could keep her for a few hours, that would be an enormous help."

Katherine beamed.

"I'm delighted. I'll have my driver take us to my home, and then you can borrow him instead of taking a taxi."

After taking Katherine and the baby to her Central Park Avenue apartment, Katherine Murphy's driver dropped her off in the financial district.

Ellen had been to the offices of *The Gaelic American*, New York's top newspaper for all things Irish, a couple of years ago, but she'd never actually met the famous, and some would say infamous, John Devoy. She did know he'd been in an English prison years ago and had only been released if he promised to leave the country, which is how he wound up in New York City — a mistake on the part of the English for he could make ever so much trouble for them over here.

She had called before her arrival and dropped Sir Roger Casement's name to get an appointment. She assumed that Sir Roger was still attempting to get German weapons for an Irish uprising. And if he was, there was one person who would be financing his efforts: John Devoy, the publisher and editor of *The Gaelic American,* the man the Irish called Sean Fear, or the Old Man.

The newspaper was located in a tall stone and brick building on William Street. Ellen went inside and took an elevator to John Devoy's office. She wore a black silk dress and a pearl brooch. Money had a loud voice, and though she hated any show of ostentation, she must make an impression on him.

Devoy — or "Sean Fear" — had a white beard that jutted from his chin in a square shape. His cheeks had the deflated look common to many an elderly Irish man who had drunk their share of whiskey and plotted against the English their whole lives.

"Ellen Malloy," he said. "A pleasure to meet you. Where do you hail from?"

"The Claddagh," she said.

His eyebrows squinched together as he appraised her.

"You don't look like a girl from the Claddagh," he said.

"My life has taken a twist here and a turn there since I left our Emerald Isle."

He chuckled.

"You mentioned Sir Roger on the phone," he said. "How do you know my good friend?"

"I met him in Germany along with Joseph Plunkett. In fact, I went with them to speak to the Germans, who I will tell you had no intention of helping them in their silly scheme to get Irish POWs to fight for Irish freedom — not as far as I could tell."

"That scheme was a failure, I agree," Devoy said, stroking his beard. "But as for weapons, the Germans can still be useful. Casement has gotten a promise of enough rifles to support the uprising."

This was not welcome news.

"Mr. Devoy, my brother is now a courier for the Brotherhood. I would not like to see him harmed."

"And who is your brother?"

"Martin Malloy."

"I know him. Clever boy-o."

She leaned forward, hoping to convince him. "He may be clever, but he's made of flesh and blood, my own blood, and I'm asking you not to put him in harm's way."

"Miss Malloy, this is bigger than us. There will be a rising," he said. His eyes had a fanatical fire in them. "I canna tell you when. But it will come."

"And why can you not be satisfied with Home Rule?"

"Home rule? And remain a vassal of the English invaders? Never. As is all too obvious, the Anglo-Saxons can revoke home rule whenever they like."

Ellen inhaled deeply. Was there no talking to this man? It was like arguing with her stubborn old dad, God rest his soul.

"Mr. Devoy, once Ireland picks up the gun, I'm afraid there'll be no turning back. Decades of violence will be on your hands." She held her own hands out, willing him to see the trouble that was coming.

"And *you* must choose a side, my dear. What will it be? Are you Irish or no?"

"I'm an American now," she said.

His eyes narrowed and he leaned forward. "Tis the same hand that crushed the colonies that crushes our cradleland. Only a fool would believe that the leopard has changed its spots and now England is a friend to America. I ask again, whose side are you on?"

Ellen sighed and looked down at her gloved hands.

"I will always be on the side of Ireland."

"So be it."

He leaned back and clasped his hands over his belly. The old men were all for making martyrs of the younger ones.

"Tell me. Are you still in touch with the Germans?"

"What do you mean?" she asked.

"I heard tell of an Irish lass who worked for Herr Koenig at the Hamburg American shipping office. Would that have been you, by any chance?"

"'Twas. But I stopped last summer after an accident. I've my own business now. I want nothing more to do with them."

"The question, Ellen Malloy, is do they want anything more to do with you?"

"And what do you mean by that?"

"My dear, we will not be free from the English without foreign interference. You may be useful yet. I could use someone to deliver funds to von Igel now and again to pay for the rifles. A woman walking into his office, a woman not affiliated with us, wouldn't raise any suspicions."

"Are you truly asking me to be your delivery girl?" Ellen was flabbergasted.

Devoy's eyes widened and he said, "You want me to protect your brother, don't you?"

His Irish moniker of Sean Fear was just as appropriate in English as it was in Irish.

"After all, you worked for the Germans before," he continued. "What's the harm in it? You do want to see your country free of tyranny, do you not?"

She lowered her fists onto his desk and glared at him.

"You're a fool if you think siding with the Germans will do it."

"Now, now. Don't be rash, lass."

He had her in a tight spot. She wanted nothing to do with the Germans, but she would do anything to protect Martin. On the other hand, she had no faith that the fanatical rebel would keep his word, and she wasn't sure if the Germans would still trust her. She might go waltzing into some office and get her throat slit.

"I'll think on it," she said.

Ellen left the newspaper building, having accomplished nothing except perhaps getting herself into trouble.

She stepped over a pile of horse dung and made her way to the subway to go to the Murphys' residence to fetch little Hester. As she crossed the street, she noticed a man in a trench coat and a fedora on the sidewalk in front of a vegetable stand, watching her.

Devoy's comment about the Germans came back to her, and a shiver ran down her spine. He must have told them she was coming to see him. Did they know she was complicit in uncovering their secrets? And did Walter Nicolai, the spymaster, know he had a child born as an American?

Chapter 13
Louisa

Louisa had planned to see Judith that afternoon, but after a breakfast of poached egg and toast, she opened an invitation that had been sitting on the desk underneath a pile of magazine correspondence. The invitation was for tea that same day. Generally, Louisa loved an afternoon tea — sitting around with other ladies, nibbling on sweet cakes and hearing the latest gossip. Unfortunately, this invitation was entirely unwanted.

"Who is it from?" Ellen asked.

"Sadie Treadwell."

"The widow marrying Forrest Calloway?"

"I'm afraid so. I must make up an excuse."

"Don't be unkind, Louisa. She's not one of us," Anna said, pouring her second cup of coffee from the service on the coffee table.

"Mother, there is no more 'us.' The *nouveau riche* own Manhattan these days. The old guard is gone," Louisa said. "Besides, Sadie hails from a Bostonian Brahmin family. She's probably the great granddaughter of John Quincy Adams."

"But she married a New York banker! That's not what Brahmins do." If anyone knew the mores of the upper classes along the entire Eastern Seaboard, it was Anna Delafield.

"Probably to escape incest," Ellen chimed in.

Anna gasped. "Must you be so vulgar?"

"I'm only making the point, those Brahmins are an insular group. They let no one in their ranks. I bet they even look down on you blue-blooded Knickerbockers."

"And how do you know so much about them?"

"Because many an Irish immigrant chose the cheaper passage to Boston and now they're trapped there. I've spoken to one or two escapees, and they say there's no way to rise socially in Boston. Whereas here in New York, Irish have found their way into politics, policing, even in business. We won't be living in tenements a generation from now."

"Boston has an Irish mayor right now," Anna said.

"That may be so, but I betcha they don't invite him to tea."

"Stop squabbling, you two. Mother is right. It would be bad form for me not to go simply because Sadie is marrying the man I love."

Ellen and Anna stared at her in surprise.

"Well, I never thought you'd admit it," Ellen said.

"You had better forget about him. I won't have my daughter chasing after a man who's engaged to someone else." Anna threw Louisa a scathing look.

"Mother, please." Louisa dropped the invitation on the table and went upstairs to change clothes, burning with humiliation because chasing after Forrest was just what she had intended to do at the supper club the other night. She would have made an utter fool of herself if Sadie hadn't fainted.

The address for Sadie Treadwell was in the Park Slope area of Brooklyn. Many wealthy merchants had moved out to Brooklyn rather than absorb the expense of Manhattan real estate. In Park Slope one could have a mansion within shouting distance of Manhattan. They even had their own Fifth Avenue with a grand theater and their own Plaza Hotel.

Sadie's mansion stood on Garfield Place and looked enormous from the outside with striped awnings over lead-glass windows — a whimsical decorative feature. Louisa didn't want to like Sadie Treadwell, but she knew it would be impossible to dislike her. On the few occasions they had met, Sadie had always been kind.

She wondered if Forrest would move into this house after the wedding or if Sadie would move into his house on Gramercy Park. Maybe they would keep both places. She knew it was crass, but she couldn't help but wonder just how much money Sadie's husband had left her when he died.

A butler answered the door and showed her into an impeccably furnished parlor with gold and silver-patterned wallpaper, a marble fireplace, and two soaring windows that flooded the room with light. Louisa admired a Duncan Phyfe table with decorative dolphins for support. The gold-brocade sofa was adorned with carved, scrolled rails. A harpsichord occupied one corner of the room, and various Oriental carvings sat atop the mantel piece. A fluffy white cat slept in the middle of the sofa. Louisa couldn't help comparing the luxurious creature to her moth-eaten ginger cat. Perhaps she fared no better next to Sadie.

"Louisa, welcome to my home," Sadie said. She wore a silk wrapper dress with a ruffled skirt. Louisa assessed the statement the dress made — well-made but not showy. Sadie was no gauche snob. A truly upper-class woman never flaunted her wealth.

"What a lovely home," Louisa said.

"Yes, I'll miss it. I hardly know what to do with all this stuff," Sadie said in her upper crust Boston accent, which Louisa found somewhat annoying. She didn't envy Forrest having to listen to it every day when he became her husband.

"You'll be moving to Gramercy Park after the wedding then?" Louisa asked.

"Yes. I don't think I want my new husband to live in the same place my former husband built."

Louisa was about to ask for details about the building of the mansion, but just then a man who looked to be about forty in a smoking jacket entered the room. Louisa recognized the mutton chops. He was the same man who had been at the Paradise Supper Club with Forrest and Sadie.

"Louisa Delafield, may I introduce my cousin, Edgar Morton."

"Pleased to meet you, Mr. Morton," Louisa said, taking his hand.

"The family is so proud of Edgar — our own genius. He teaches mathematics at Harvard," Sadie said.

"Stop, Cousin. You'll make me blush," he laughed.

At this moment, Sadie's two young boys came storming into the room.

"Oh, goodness," Sadie said. "Where is Mrs. Braithwhite? What are you two monsters doing loose?"

Immediately, both boys raised their hands in the air as if they were claws. They roared and growled and ran circles around their mother.

"Boys, please, stop." But she seemed more pleased than put out by the display.

"Mother, we're monsters," the elder of the two explained.

"I know. And you're quite terrifying. But it's time to go back upstairs." She took the two boys by the hand and, with an apologetic look at Louisa and her cousin, said, "Do excuse me. I will return shortly."

Edgar Morton was a pleasant fellow, about Louisa's own height of five foot six inches. He sat down in one of the claw-footed chairs, and Louisa sat on the couch near the white cat. She tentatively reached out to pet it, but the cat had no interest in being social. It looked up, hissed and then resumed its nap.

"I suppose I'm too forward," Louisa said.

"Fluffers believes she's descended from Cleopatra's cats," he said with a grin.

He had bright, curious eyes and made small talk about the weather, asking Louisa about the New York opera, and opining that J.P. Morgan's efforts to help the Allies would turn the tide of American opinion. The war in Europe was never far from anyone's mind.

She wondered if he suspected, as she did, that the two of them were being set up by Sadie.

"So, you're a Delafield. Quite a distinguished name. When did your family come to America?" he asked.

"The Delafields arrived in the early 1800s, and Mother's family harkens back to the old Knickerbockers. What about yours?"

"In Boston, our families like to say we sent the servants ahead on the Mayflower to prepare the summer cottages."

"Oh, my," Louisa said and chuckled. Boston was even more snobbish than Old New York.

"The women in your family are all D.A.R. I suppose?" he asked.

"Of course. And my grandmother was an ardent abolitionist."

"A family of women rebels against the status quo then. I understand you work outside the home?" He looked at her with a bemused expression.

"I'm unmarried. What would I do with myself otherwise?"

"Quite right. I admire a woman who uses her mind."

Sadie returned and sat down.

"I'm so embarrassed to have fainted at the Paradise," Sadie said. "I hope you don't think less of me, Louisa."

"For fainting? Of course, not," Louisa said. "Women do it all the time. Our corsets are too tight." More women were switching to brassieres, but evening gowns were undoubtedly more flattering with a corset.

"You are kind. How is your magazine coming along?"

"It's not really my magazine. I'm but a lowly writer. I used to be a syndicated columnist..." She didn't finish the sentence, as it was clearly Forrest Calloway's fault for selling *The Ledger* that she had lost that vaunted title.

The maid came into the room with a letter on a tray for Sadie.

"Excuse me for a moment," Sadie said, slicing open the letter with an ivory-handled opener. Her eyes skimmed across the letter and her brow wrinkled.

"Is everything all right, Cousin?" Mr. Morton asked.

She gave him a tight-lipped smile and said, "It's nothing. Just another diatribe from one of my late husband's relatives. Louisa, have you seen any of those new dresses from Coco Chanel? I'm planning on buying some."

"I have. She's quite a genius. And buying her clothing is one way we women can support the war effort."

The rest of the afternoon passed pleasantly. It was impossible to feel any animosity toward Sadie Treadwell. She was gracious, stylish, and moderately well educated — also thoroughly unambitious. She would make an excellent wife for Forrest. She would stand at his side, and never steal the limelight. And she would provide him with the one thing he desired above all else: ready-made sons.

"Edgar can drive you home in his roadster," Sadie suggested when Louis asked if she could call a taxi for her.

"I couldn't put him out like that," Louisa said.

"Of course, you can," Edgar said. "I'd love nothing more than to take you for a spin in my new roadster."

"Do let him show off his motorcar, Louisa," Sadie said.

So Louisa went outside and stood on the street in front of the house to wait for Edgar to bring his car from the garage. He soon pulled up in a baby blue two-seater with black fenders. The butler opened the door for her, and she slid onto the red leather seat.

"Sporty!" she yelled over the sound of the motor.

She turned her big floppy hat into a motoring costume by tying it down with a chiffon scarf, lent to her by Sadie. Then they were off, driving across the Brooklyn Bridge, the Hudson glinting greenish-blue in the afternoon light. Lady Liberty in all her green glory upheld her torch for the huddled masses.

"You say you live in Harlem?" he asked when the wheels hit the city street.

"Yes, on the west side."

"You'll have to direct me. I don't know New York well."

"It's easy. Just go up Riverside Drive. That's the scenic route."

They drove along Riverside Drive. The bare trees made designs along the sky, making her think of cracked china.

"What is this beautiful sylvan glade?" he asked as they came alongside a densely wooded stretch.

"Riverside Park."

"Do you mind if we stop?" he asked.

"Not at all."

Edgar pulled the car to a stop along the side of the road, and they got out. This was one of Louisa's favorite walks. The long path curved around outcroppings and rock formations. Below them the river sparkled in the sun, and two sailboats with billowing white sails, raced each other.

When they stopped to look at the water, Edgar turned to her. His brown eyes were full of something akin to admiration. A breeze rustled in the trees above them. The water's surface gleamed like polished pewter, and the sun's rays glinted off the waves.

"Louisa, let me take you out while I'm here," he said. "We can go to the opera if you like. Or dinner at one of the rooftop gardens. I find you utterly fascinating."

Louisa wasn't sure what to say. She hadn't had a suitor in years, and she wasn't getting any younger. She was still in love with Forrest, but he was no longer in love with her. Should she give this man a chance, she wondered. What would it hurt? He lived in Boston, after all, and if it turned out they weren't compatible, it would be easy enough to let the whole thing drop. At any rate, going out with him would get her mind off Forrest and Sadie's upcoming nuptials.

"That would be nice. I do love the opera," she said. "And now I'd better get home. I have to make dinner."

"Make dinner? Is your cook ill?"

"We don't have a cook," she said. "We did, but she got married. Anyway, I'm enjoying learning how to make recipes. It's rather fun."

"You are full of surprises."

They went back to the motorcar, and he opened the passenger door for her. Then he cranked the engine and hopped in the driver's seat.

She directed him to her street. He turned down and looked rather mystified. She pointed to her brownstone, and his mouth dropped open.

He pulled in front and turned off the engine.

"This is where you live?" He could not disguise the incredulity in his voice.

"Yes. Is there something wrong?"

"I...I'm simply a little surprised. I thought you were from an 'Old New York' family."

"I am. My father was swindled out of the family fortune shortly before he... died," she said. She was ashamed to say he was murdered and then she was ashamed of her shame. "So, yes, this is what Mother and I could afford."

"Sadie didn't say anything..."

"Sadie is not a New Yorker. She wouldn't have known the history," Louisa said. "Did you think I was an heiress?"

"Well, not that it matters. You're a fascinating woman, as I said."

"A fascinating woman with no money," Louisa clarified. "Thank you for driving me home, Mr. Morton. I'll see myself to my door."

With that she pulled on the handle of the door and got out.

"I'd...I'd still like to go to the opera," he said.

"I'm afraid I'm too busy. I have to take in laundry so I can afford to eat." She turned and climbed the steps to the front door. She entered the house without looking back. The man was nothing but a gold digger.

Chapter 14
Ellen

In her dream Ellen sat at the desk in the parlor, making funeral arrangements for someone. The will stated there was to be no casket. How and where to bury the body then? Should they wrap it in a shroud? There was a cemetery outside the window and she needed to make a decision. Then she was in a small cold room with the body. When she went over to the pallet to look at it, she saw that it was herself. She woke with a start, wondering if the dream was a prediction of the future or a description of the present. Was she somehow dead inside?

The baby was already fussing, and Carlotta was not in the room. Ellen got out of the bed and tossed her long braid onto her back. She bent over and lifted little Hester under her chubby arms, discovering that her diaper was wet. After finding the stack of diapers, Ellen set her on the make shift changing table. As she took the soaked diaper off and wiped her down with a damp cloth, the dream returned to her. What if something were to happen to her? The wee girl had no godparents, no appointed guardians. What if the Germans decided to exact revenge for her double-crossing them? She didn't know what they knew about her actions the previous year.

She powdered the baby's bottom and pinned a clean diaper on her. She needed to find out what the Germans were thinking, and the only way to do that was to get in that brothel where Carlotta had worked. That's where they did all their plotting. But Carlotta would no longer be welcome there, and Ellen certainly couldn't walk in the place.

As she took the baby into the bed with her and opened the front of her flannel gown, it occurred to her that she did know someone who might have overheard what the Germans at Martha Held's brothel were plotting.

Ellen rode in the back of the taxi to the brownstone where Suzie now lived with Mr. Sweet. Little Hester snuggled in her arms. Suzie gasped at the sight of Ellen holding the baby on her stoop and then opened the door wide.

"Let me have a look at that precious child," she said.

"You can hold her if you like."

Ellen removed her coat and scarf.

Suzie's brownstone looked not much different from the brownstone where she and Louisa lived, except for the odor of pipe smoke that indicated the presence of a man. Also, it was cleaner. The tables were polished, the wood floor gleamed, and not a speck of dust could be seen.

"Is Mr. Sweet still working at Martha Held's club?" Ellen asked.

"Yep, he's upstairs sleeping. Doesn't go in 'til later."

"Do the girls still buy lingerie from you?"

"Oh yes. Business is good," Suzie said. "I've got quite the clientele now from ladies of the night to ladies of high society."

"I'm not sure there's much difference between the two," Ellen said with a wry grin.

She sank down in a comfortable chintz-covered armchair while Suzie paced the floor, bouncing the baby in her arms. Hester stared at Suzie's smiling face in fascination.

"How are Louisa and her mother doing?" Suzie asked.

"You mean, how are they doing without you?" Ellen responded, grinning. "We're all drinking tea because no one knows how to make coffee, but Louisa does try to cook. She made the worst cabbage and potato stew I've ever tasted the other night, but we all ate it out of politeness."

"Oh, no," Suzie said. "Can't Carlotta cook?"

"No, but she's been a lifesaver, cleaning, doing laundry and taking care of Louisa's mother and the baby. Especially taking care of the baby."

Suzie sat on the sofa with little Hester and looked at Ellen, concern in her deep brown eyes.

"What aren't you saying, Ellen?"

Of course, Suzie could see right through her.

"I'm saying I don't feel the way I'm supposed to feel." She sighed. She couldn't tell Suzie about the shadow or the dark thoughts, but she couldn't pretend that all was well.

"How are you supposed to feel?" Suzie seemed genuinely curious.

"You know. Like a mother. Like someone whose whole life revolves around their baby. The other day while I was working on the magazine, I forgot I even had a baby."

Suzie was silent for several minutes, staring down at Hester's face.

"I never had a child of my own, but I know this much. There's no particular way you are supposed to feel. There're things you're supposed to *do*, but how you feel is how you feel. It seems to me that when it comes to this baby, you are doing what you're supposed to do. Making sure she's fed and clean and warm. You don't have to feel anything."

"'Tis Carlotta keeps her clean," Ellen said. "I feed her but even that I'd rather not do."

"As long as someone is doing it, then that is what matters. Colored women have been raising other people's babies for generations. And some of them turned out fine. Maybe even better than if the real mothers raised them."

"But that was slavery," Ellen said. "I don't want that."

"That was reality. I wasn't a slave, and I raised Louisa," Suzie said.

"Did you love her?" Ellen asked.

"Not when she was a baby, no. But as she got older, I did grow fond of her. I always wanted the best for her. I still do. I'm proud of her, too. Even if she can't cook."

Ellen laughed. "Not everything she's made is bad. She's learning."

The baby clasped Suzie's finger and sucked.

"Oh my," Suzie said, smiling. "Honey, I don't think I really knew what love was until I met Mr. Sweet. And here I am, an old woman."

Ellen sighed. "I knew real love once, but I don't think I'll ever feel that way again. I want to though. I want to love my child."

"Give it time. I know you'll do right by this little one," Suzie said.

What *was* the right thing for her, Ellen wondered.

There was a knock on the door.

"Oh, that's the ladies for my committee meeting," Suzie said.

"Committee? What sort of committee?" Ellen asked.

"Well, now, stick around and find out."

The four women who filled the parlor that day, laughing and passing the baby back and forth among themselves, were working to get the men of the NAACP to take on the anti-miscegenation laws.

"I don't understand," Ellen said.

"You see the law forbids a white man from marrying a colored woman," Suzie explained.

"Do you want to marry white men?" Ellen asked, confused by the conversation.

"No. But the result of the law is to leave a colored woman in the lowly position of a dog as far as white men are concerned. He can do whatever he pleases and she has no recourse. As Mr. Du Bois says, 'As low as the white girl falls, she can still compel her seducer to marry her.'"

"I never thought of it that way," Ellen said. As someone who'd had a child forced upon her, she realized if she hadn't been well off thanks to Hester's largesse, she would have been in a tight spot trying to raise a child by herself.

"If one of you wants to write an article about this issue, I'll publish it in my magazine. If I don't know about it, then a lot of women don't," Ellen announced to the group.

"Aren't your readers white?" one of the women asked, tilting her head to the side.

"I hope that women readers of any race, any creed, or any color will find something of value in *The Ladies' Lantern*," Ellen answered. She took the fussy baby in her arms and asked Suzie if there were somewhere she might feed her in private.

"Oh, go ahead and feed her here," a large woman in a bright floral-print dress said and laughed. "Ain't nothing we haven't seen — or done — before."

So Ellen opened her blouse and the baby grabbed the proffered breast between her tiny hands and sucked greedily while the women in the room continued talking about their business.

After they left, Suzie invited Ellen to stay for dinner so she could talk to Mr. Sweet before he went to work.

"I'm cooking chicken á la king," she said.

Ellen's mouth watered, and she agreed to stay. She hoped to find out from Mr. Sweet if he had any news about the Germans who frequented Martha Held's brothel. If anyone one would know, it would be the invisible butler.

Mr. Sweet entered and grabbed Suzie around the waist, kissed her on the mouth and called her "Babycakes." To see these two acting like young lovebirds was as grand a thing as Ellen could imagine.

"And look who it is!" he said when he saw Ellen. "We missed you at the wedding. But we sure do thank you for your generosity."

"I'm afraid I was big as a house and wouldn't have fit in the pew," Ellen said. She showed him little Hester, and he oohed and ahhed.

"Look at these clodhoppers," he said, taking hold of the baby's foot. "She's gonna be a tall one like her mama."

Suzie served dinner and they all dug in. The sauce with peas and carrots was creamy with a hint of white wine. The chicken was tender with warm, flaky biscuits on the side.

"Mother of God," Ellen said, and sighed. "Your cooking is even better than I remember."

"That's 'cause she's getting some good loving," Mr. Sweet said, his eyes twinkling.

"Now, Mr. Sweet," Suzie said. "Don't you speak of such things at my table." But her eyes were smiling.

Ellen waited until Suzie had cleared the dinner plates and placed a fig custard pie on the table for dessert to ask Mr. Sweet about things at Martha Held's.

"I'm wondering if you've heard ... well, if there's been any mention of me? Or Carlotta?" She wasn't sure how much the Germans knew about her role in their exposure the previous year.

"Nope." He shook his head. "You'd think it would be quieter these days what with those two ringleaders, von Papen and Boy-Ed gone," he said. "But von Papen's right-hand man is still here. Name's von Igel. He's a snake waiting in the grass. And he don't go nowhere without his giant bodyguard."

Von Igel was the same man that Devoy had mentioned. Was it he who had been watching when she came out of the newspaper building?

"What about that count?" Ellen asked. "Some sort of ambassador, right?"

"Count Bernstorff still comes by when he's not in Washington. They haven't tossed him out of the country yet, but he's up to no good."

Ellen took a bite of the fig custard pie.

"Would you let me know if you overhear of any more sabotage plans? If they come after me, I may need to have something on them."

"Do you think they'll come after you?" Suzie asked.

"I really don't know."

Ellen hailed a taxi to go home. The little one slept in her arms, lulled by the movement of the motorcar. Ellen pondered Mr. Sweet's news about the Germans who gathered at Martha Held's brothel. The war was still going on, and they wouldn't abandon their plans to stop America from helping England any time soon.

The taxi turned onto the street for Louisa's brownstone, which reminded Ellen of another problem. She had been living with Louisa since her ordeal with the Germans landed her in a box in the hull of a steamship. Louisa had brought her back to the house, insisting she stay there so they could take care of her. And then Louisa had taken in Carlotta as well. Ellen had never stopped to think that perhaps she had worn out her welcome. Didn't Louisa say as much when Hattie visited and she asked why she hadn't gotten a place of her own. Louisa, in spite of the loss of her father and her fortune, had spent her growing-up years sharing a house with only her upper-class mother and Suzie, who had been her rock. Now Suzie was gone, and instead two women of lower class — there was no denying that, no matter how much money Ellen now had — occupied her house and shared her bathroom.

Ellen should start looking for another place to live. She'd take Carlotta with her and let Louisa and her mother have the house to themselves. She would have to shake the darkness that had overtaken her and muster the energy to do it soon. In fact, she would tell Louisa tonight that she would be leaving.

The taxi dropped her off and she entered the house.

"Ellen, a messenger just came by with this for you." Carlotta handed her a letter.

Ellen opened it and read, "Sister, I need you. I'm in a spot of trouble. I'm hiding out at McSorley's Pub on East Seventh Street."

McSorley's? What could he possibly have gotten himself into?

Chapter 15
Louisa

Louisa sat at the dining room table, staring at the open cookbook, but not reading a word. Forrest Calloway was going to marry someone else, and it was Louisa's fault. Her tea with Sadie had made that fact all too real.

Carlotta entered, carrying the afternoon papers.

"Is Ellen still gone?" Louisa asked.

"She came and left again. Got a message from her brother. The baby's upstairs napping." Carlotta sat down and opened up the paper.

"Well, I'm glad Ellen is getting out of the house. She's been much too morose lately. I can't help but worry."

Carlotta didn't respond. Instead, she seemed to be engrossed in reading the newspaper. Louisa hadn't known Carlotta to even care much about the news.

"Holey moley. Look at this story in the *Herald*."

Carlotta sat down on the bed and showed her an article with grainy pictures of two women and two men — and a stable on East 108th Street.

"A 'murder stable'? In Harlem?" Louisa asked, reading the headline.

Carlotta said, "The story says this stable is known for harboring stolen horses. They steal them in New York and then sell them in other places. The younger woman in the picture stabbed a man she said robbed her, then someone else shot the mother right outside the stable. And these two guys, they were both killed there."

"They're all Italian," Louisa observed.

"Yeah. One of the stable owners, a guy named Greco, was shot in the back a few years ago. He was a friend of my family. I remember him."

"You have a family?" She had always believed that Carlotta must have been an orphan.

"Yeah, I got family. In Brooklyn now but used to live in East Harlem. My poppa is a boss." There was pride in Carlotta's voice, and Louisa suddenly felt like a fool.

She took in Carlotta's dark eyes, the olive skin and the jet black hair.

"A boss? Does he own a business?" Louisa was more and more mystified by the exchange.

"A boss of the family."

"Well, he is the father, is he not?"

"Boss means something else in my family."

Carlotta glanced away as if she had revealed a deep secret. Louisa had heard of Italian crime families, and, if she was not mistaken, Carlotta was telling her that she was from one of those families. Maybe that explained the frisson of danger that Louisa had felt around the girl. And why Carlotta never seemed afraid of anyone.

"If they're in Brooklyn, why can't you go home?" she asked.

Carlotta shook her head.

"I dishonored the family name," Carlotta said, putting the paper down. "I better go wash some diapers."

She rose and walked to the door.

"Carlotta," Louisa said.

Carlotta turned and looked back at her, her face unreadable.

"Thank you. The murder stable story was just what I needed to distract me from self-pity."

Carlotta nodded. A beauty — even with her crooked nose and the scar that cut across her cheek and upper lip.

Louisa went into the parlor where Virgil Thorn sat at the desk. He was also engrossed in reading the news.

"Hello, Virgil," Louisa said.

"Hello, Louisa," he said. "I'm concerned that we haven't enough stories for this next issue. Even with the stories from the Heterodoxy ladies. And we need some poems."

"I am not a poet."

"No, but that woman you were going to interview is. Djuna Barnes?"

"I still haven't been able to find her to get an interview."

Virgil twirled a pencil in his fingers. "Perhaps, you should consider the idea I mentioned earlier of having someone cover the motion picture industry. That Theda Bara is changing the whole idea of womanhood."

"You mean to tell me that a woman who feeds on men — a vampire — should be a model for today's woman?"

"The vamp is the first woman on the silver screen to be fully in charge of her own destiny. I would expect you of all people could see that. One of her movies is playing right now. The characters she plays may be evil, but why do you suppose she is so popular with women viewers?"

Louisa had never seen a Theda Bara movie, but the whole world buzzed about the beautiful, exotic star with the hypnotic gaze

"You might be onto something," Louisa said. "I suppose I could go see a picture and write about it from a feminist perspective."

"No time like the present," Virgil said. "I need stories."

The marquee said that Theda Bara was starring in a film called *The Serpent*. Louisa paid her dime and went into the dark theater where she quickly became entranced by the wicked, larger-than-life face on the screen. The vamp character exuded cunning and confidence. She was only 10 minutes into the film when she heard a voice in her ear, "My God, you smell magnificent."

Her head whipped toward the speaker, eyes wide. "You!"

"Hello, Louisa."

Reggie Grant smiled at her, the same charming smile he'd had when she was naked and lying next to him. She scowled at him.

"Now, now, we parted on good terms, don't you remember?" His Australian accent felt like a caress.

They *had* parted on good terms. She did remember that. But she also remembered the intoxicating nights he'd spent in her bed, only for her to find out he'd been engaged the whole time he'd carried on an affair with her.

"You deceived me," she whispered.

"Come now, Louisa, you didn't love me. You never stopped loving Forrest Calloway. We both know that. It doesn't cheapen what we had."

"You're a heel. You know that, don't you? Why are you here?"

"I've missed you." Shadows flickered from the screen across his face.

An usher hurried down the aisle toward them.

"Folks, you need to leave if you want to have a conversation," he said.

Louisa glared at Reggie. He shrugged.

"Oh, for heaven's sake," she said. She got up and left the theater with Reggie in tow. When they got to the lobby, she turned toward him.

"Do you miss your fiancée?"

"Not much," he admitted with a smirk.

"You are not here for me. I know that much, Mr. Grant. You're working, aren't you?"

Reggie looked at her, his smirk gone, a hard expression on his chiseled face.

"Let's take a ride," he said.

Outside the theater, a shiny Rolls Royce was parked at the curb. He opened the passenger door for her, and she slid onto the black leather seat while he went to the front and turned the crank. Then he got in the driver's side. Off they went.

They didn't speak as Reggie drove uptown through Washington Heights and then over the long bridge crossing the Harlem River. Down below a paddle boat glided over the glassy water. Once they were across the bridge in the Bronx, Reggie turned down a winding street and parked by the waterfront. The noise of the engine died and they both stared out the front window.

Finally, he spoke. "Our boys are dying by the thousands, Louisa. And it isn't just the death toll. Men are losing their minds. This type of warfare has consequences never dreamed of."

"It's awful, but what can I do about it? I don't even work for a newspaper anymore. I'm writing interviews with suffragists and feminists of all sorts. And they don't care about your war. Many of them are pacifists who don't want America to interfere. They have a point. Why should our boys die, too?"

"Because the fate of Europe hangs in the balance here, Louisa. You know that as well as I do. If England and France lose to Germany, you don't honestly think America will be safe."

"We are an ocean away."

"It won't matter. If the Huns win this war, they will be cowed by nothing."

Louisa sighed. America would join the war eventually. There would come a tipping point. Already there were "preparedness" parades and marches.

"None of this explains what you want from me," she said.

"Ellen's brother, Martin Malloy, is in the country. I want to know why."

Louisa looked at him in surprise. How did he know about Ellen's brother? "For heaven's sake, Reggie, how would I know what he's doing here? And what does it matter?"

"He's with the Irish Brotherhood. If they start a rebellion in Ireland with the help of the Germans, it will take precious resources from the Western Front," Reggie leaned toward her, speaking fervently.

"And do you honestly think Ellen would betray her own brother?" Louisa asked.

"Ellen was a great help to us last year when she infiltrated the office of the Hamburg American Lines. She knows how duplicitous and dangerous the Germans are."

"She's had a baby since then, and her priorities have changed." The last thing Ellen would do was something that might leave her child an orphan, Louisa thought. Then almost immediately, doubt gnawed at her. Ellen would never forgive Germany for the sinking of the *Lusitania*, for the death of Hester French.

"I know all about the baby. Do *you* know who the father is?" He peered at her.

"Some German intelligence officer. That's all I know. I did not feel it my business to pry any further." Louisa didn't like the superior tone Reggie had adopted.

"His name is Walter Nicolai, and he is known as the Father of Lies for his propaganda efforts. He is one of the most effective and ruthless spies I have ever encountered. I imagine his behavior with Ellen was anything but pleasant." His jaw jutted forward.

"Please, don't," Louisa said. She did not want to imagine what had happened to Ellen.

"Oh, my dear, tender Louisa," he said. He slipped his arm over her shoulder. Even if he had betrayed her by not telling her about his fiancée, they had formed a friendship. His breath felt warm against her ear as he whispered, "There are so many horrors in the world right now. Please help me to stop them."

Almost against her will, she leaned into him and buried her face against his shoulder. She would never again be intimate with him, but she could allow him to comfort her.

"Ellen's been so different since the baby was born. I thought having a child to love would help ease her grief, but it only seems to have made her sadder."

"That happens to women sometimes," he said. "Best keep an eye on her. Women have been known to hurt their child or themselves after a difficult birth."

"How do you know this?"

"It happened to my mother. Killed herself after her last child."

Louisa gasped.

"It happens," he said with a shrug, but he couldn't hide his sadness.

"Poor you," she said and clasped his hand. "And poor Ellen."

Chapter 16
Ellen

The taxi pulled up to the curb in front of the red brick building where McSorley's occupied the bottom floor. She glanced up at the sign: "McSorley's Old Ale House. Established 1854." And not once in all those years had they let a woman quench her thirst in there. The bastards.

She went to the window and peered inside.

"Miss Malloy?" a voice with a German accent asked.

She wheeled around and saw a man of medium height with a sharp pointed nose, wearing a trench coat and a bowler hat. She'd seen him outside *The Gaelic American*'s offices. His face had no expression whatsoever.

"What'll you be wanting with me?" she asked.

"If you want to see your brother alive, you'll come with us."

Her heart sank and her legs weakened.

"What have you done with him?" she asked.

"He has not been harmed. You need not worry. Come with me. *Bitte.*" He pointed to a black Mercedes motorcar, its engine running.

"Oh, it's a request, is it? Doesn't sound like one to me," she said. She got in the back of the vehicle where an enormous brute sat, looking straight forward.

The first man got into the front seat and told the driver to go. The windows in the back were curtained.

"And where will we be going?" she asked.

The men didn't answer. They sat silent as statues, and stared ahead without looking at her. The enormous man had hands the size of dinner plates. Perhaps they meant to kill her. But why now? What threat was she? Koenig, the man she had worked for and spied on at the Hamburg-American Shipping office, was in prison. Von Papen and Boy-Ed had been summarily ejected from the country. She had no more involvement with any such skullduggery. Christ on the cross, she was simply trying to publish a magazine about women's issues. Couldn't they leave her in peace? She never should have bargained with the devil — pretending to be in cahoots with the Germans while she fed information to the British.

She struggled to hold her fear in check. But when the car rolled onto the ferry to cross the Hudson, her heart quickened. No one knew where she was. If she screamed, the big man could easily crush her neck and who would be the wiser? She hadn't even left a message at the house. No one would know she had gone to McSorley's. She took a deep breath and reminded herself she'd been in other frightening fixes. She had survived each time. But luck always ran out. Had hers? And what would happen to little Hester if it did?

She forced her breath to slow. To pass the time, she imagined she was in a meadow back home in Ireland. She thought of the stone walls, the sheep quietly grazing. The Claddagh, where she'd been raised, was a rocky spit of sand but she remembered traveling with her da and her grandda to Limerick and to other small towns in their old cart. The steady clomping of the mule's hooves on the dirt roads. She would watch the soft landscape pass by and an ineffable feeling of peace would descend up on her. She called on that peace now, but it hovered just out of reach, and it was all she could do not to collapse in terror.

An hour later they pulled up to a weathered two-storey country house. This must be Cedarhurst. Louisa had talked about visiting Count Bernstorff and his wife here the previous year. The ocean was within spitting difference and would make a convenient dumping ground for her body. Again, she thought of little Hester and chided herself for not making arrangements in case something happened to her.

The man with the fedora got out and opened the door for her. His eyes were utterly devoid of any feeling.

"This way, *Fraulein*." He pointed to the steps of the weathered house. She could tell by his coldly polite air he was no flunky. His clothes were expensive, and he smelled of spice-scented cologne.

He walked her up the porch steps while the big man waited below. The door opened and there stood a tall, balding man in a double-breasted jacket. His thick mustache curled up on either end. She'd seen his picture in Louisa's society column—Count Johann von Bernstorff, the German ambassador to the United States.

"Miss Malloy, we meet at last," he said and ushered her inside. He turned to her escort and said. "*Danke schön*, Herr von Igel."

The man with the dead eyes clicked his heels and turned back toward the Mercedes.

So that was von Igel, Franz von Papen's right-hand man. What good had it done to evict von Papen and leave his errand boy?

"Come, please," Bernstorff said.

Ellen followed him into a library. A suit of armor guarded the corner, and dust motes danced in the light from the window. Ellen's mind whirled in confusion. She thought she might retch, only she had nothing on her stomach. Instead, she sneezed.

"Forgive the dust, Miss Malloy. We haven't been staying here in Cedarhurst lately. My wife prefers society in Washington." He spoke with the perfect English of a man who had been educated in London, which she knew to be true from Louisa's account of him.

"What do you want with me, Count?" she asked.

"First, I want to apologize for that dreadful business at the pier last year. That woman who trapped you turned out to be a double agent. She tried to deflect the blame on you. Your mentor back in Berlin, Captain Boehm, has been worried about you." The count stopped talking long enough to light a pipe.

Ellen thought of Captain Boehm. He'd been kind to her. He and his wife had taken care of her in Germany. They had given her a place to live, purchased clothes for her, and taken her out for entertainment. He had believed her when she promised to spy for him. He had trained her. But he was also the one who had sent her to Nicolai's rooms. He'd known the kind of man Nicolai was, but said she must prove herself, must show that she was capable of doing the job, and the job might require her to have sex with men. She hadn't blamed him. His country was at war, and she'd been so numb with grief she'd let Nicolai do what he wanted to do.

"How did you find me?" she asked.

"That was a simple matter of following your brother. He's a good chap but has little training. Unlike you." He puffed on his pipe and gave her an admiring glance. "Once we found you, Captain Boehm sent me a cable, excoriating me for wasting such a valuable asset."

"I'm afraid I can no longer be an asset. It's too dangerous. And I've my own business to run now."

"Oh, yes, I know all about *The Ladies' Lantern*. You see, you can be quite useful even in that role. I understand the ladies of New York are in disagreement about whether your country should enter into war against my country. You should simply print the opposing side."

"The pacifists, you mean?"

"Just so."

"Why should I help you at all? I no longer need money. I have plenty of my own."

Bernstorff studied her with curiosity.

"And how did that happen?"

"A friend died and left me an inheritance."

He feigned interest in a statue on his desk. "And how did this friend die?"

She should lie to him. She knew it, but she couldn't. The full weight of her anger pressed inside her, demanding to be let out.

"She drowned when the *Lusitania* was sunk."

He stared at her.

"Did Captain Boehm know about this?"

She shook her head, cursing herself for a fool. It was time to change course. There was little Hester to think of.

"Well, we weren't close. I was using this woman for her money, and now that she's dead, I have it all." Ellen forced a smile to her lips.

Bernstorff returned the smile.

"If you don't need the money, why don't you help us for the sake of your country? Any help you give to Germany translates into benefits for Ireland, does it not? The enemy of my enemy and all that."

Ellen pretended to consider what he said. She glanced out the window and saw a seagull flying by, a reminder of the ocean nearby.

"I have no problem printing the point of view of the pacifists." This wasn't a lie. "But as for anything else..."

"There is one other thing," he said, stepping closer to her, his voice going soft. "You live with Louisa Delafield, do you not?"

Ellen hesitated. Obviously, he knew the answer to his question.

"I worked with Louisa before I even met Captain Boehm. He knew all about our association. And yes, I am at her place, temporarily."

"We believe she may have taken documents from us and given them to her friend, the British Naval attaché and spy, Reggie Grant, who then turned them over to a newspaper."

He had the details wrong, but the basic information was correct.

"So what if she did? It has nothing to do with me. She's now in my employ."

"I only ask that you keep an eye on her. Let us know if she and Mr. Grant meet. I believe she's harmless for the time being. Keep her that way."

Ellen's mind raced. He wanted her to spy on Louisa, but Louisa wasn't doing anything regarding the war — at least as far she knew.

"Not to worry. She's quite busy writing about women's issues now."

"Good. Then we have an understanding."

"You mean to tell me you brought me all the way out here just for this. My brother was never in any danger."

"Of course not. We're on his side, and I'd like to think he is on our side. Devoy certainly is."

And there was the rub. Martin and Devoy were in cahoots with these war-mongering men.

Chapter 17

Louisa

Louisa sat down on the divan in the parlor and gazed down at Hester's plump, pink cheeks, the steadfast blue eyes and the golden fuzz atop her head.

Ellen sat at the desk working.

"Are you feeling better, Ellen?" she asked. She'd been unable to get the conversation about Reggie's mother out of her mind.

"Yes, I believe I am," Ellen said, sounding surprised.

"I know it's been hard for you. You've had a terrible year and you weren't prepared for a baby…"

"Aye, it has been difficult. More difficult than I let on. I tried not to worry you," Ellen said.

"Oh, Ellen. You shouldn't…"

"And sure, it's been hard on you, too, what with having all of us underfoot. In fact, I'm looking at the classifieds now to see if I can't get us out of your hair. Carlotta can stay with me, of course. She likes taking care of the baby…"

"What? What are you saying?"

"I'm saying I know you're wanting your house back to yourself. It's not right all of us just living here like a bunch of free loaders."

"But you're not free loaders! And I don't want you to move out."

"But when Hattie was here, you said…"

"I was being flippant. I do think that it would be better if the magazine had its own space, but as for living elsewhere, why we would miss you, Ellen."

Ellen stared at her for a moment and then lowered her eyes. Was she crying? Louisa felt like such a shrew. How had she let Ellen think that she and the baby were unwelcome?

At that moment, Carlotta came in and took the baby from Louisa.

"Time for someone's nap," Carlotta cooed.

"Louisa, do you have any more ideas for stories?" Ellen asked, changing the subject.

"Not at the moment," she admitted. She'd been so busy trying *not* to think about Forrest and Sadie and their upcoming wedding that she could think of nothing else. "Remember? The last time I did an interview, a man died in front of my own eyes."

Ellen blew out a long sigh.

"There's something else I need to talk to you about, Louisa," Ellen said.

The tone of her voice pricked Louisa's curiosity but at that moment, Thorn came into the parlor with Anna following.

"I'm done for the day, I believe," Thorn said. "Did you write the Theda Bara article, Louisa?"

Guilt washed over her. Aside from the Inez Milholland and Margaret Sanger interviews, she hadn't turned in anything, and it was already March.

"Something came up, and I didn't get to see the whole movie."

"What about the Barnes woman?"

"I will try to catch Djuna this week."

"That would be lovely." He grabbed his briefcase and left.

She could tell he was a bit rankled. She'd never been one to miss a deadline.

Anna went upstairs for her post-lunch nap, and Louisa turned to Ellen.

"What did you want to tell me?"

"I took a little unwanted trip yesterday. To Cedarhurst."

"Cedarhurst? Where Count Bernstorff lives?"

"Yes, he wanted to have a conversation with me."

"Oh no. Do they still think you are one of them?"

"They do. He wants me to print anti-war propaganda. He also asked me to spy on you," Ellen said. "Wanted to know if you'd seen Reggie Grant."

Louisa put her hands over her eyes to collect her thoughts. Then she lowered them and looked at Ellen. "I did see him. That's what I meant to tell you. It's why I never wrote the article about the Theda Bara movie. Reggie wants me to spy on you."

They stared at each other.

"Spy on me?" Ellen asked.

"He was specifically interested in your brother and his activities," Louisa said.

Ellen was silent. Louisa wondered just how much Ellen knew about her brother's activities.

"Ellen," she continued. "If the Irish are working with the Germans to defeat the British, then we must do what we can to stop them. The only way to end the suffering caused by this war is to stop Germany. They've invaded Belgium and now France."

"You mean the way the English invaded Ireland?" Ellen asked. "Louisa, the English are just as bad. They're starving the civilian population of Germany. I saw it with my own eyes."

Louisa stared at her friend. She couldn't believe her ears.

"Are you on the Germans' side?" Louisa asked. "After what they did to the *Lusitania*? After they sabotaged ships at sea, killing all those men?"

Ellen sat back and shook her head. "I am not on Germany's side. But I am on Ireland's."

"And do you think the Germans will be better overlords than the English?"

"I do not," she admitted.

Louisa clasped her hands in front of her. A flood of sympathy engulfed her. Poor Ellen — torn between conflicting loyalties.

"Then you must help Reggie stop it if you can," she said.

Ellen looked up at her with thoughtful eyes.

"And you must get me more stories for the magazine."

Louisa went back to the motion picture theatre, watched the entirety of the Theda Bara movie. As she watched the film's story of a vengeful woman, for some reason, her mind traveled back to the poisoning of Mr. Halle. She wasn't sure why, but the idea of a connection pestered her. Had Mr. Halle done something that caused someone to take revenge?

Chapter 18

Ellen

As Ellen rode in the taxi with little Hester to the Murphy apartment, she realized with relief that as unsettling as her encounter with von Igel and Count Berstorff had been, it did seem as if the dark thoughts, which had been smothering her, had finally departed. Perhaps that was because now she had something real to worry about.

"Take as long as you need. I'm happy to have darling Hester's company."

Ellen looked up at the portrait of Hester French, Katherine's sister, her child's namesake — the large eyes, the gentle mouth, the delicate eyebrows. She had not been a beauty in the conventional sense, but she exuded a strength of purpose that Ellen had found devastatingly attractive. She would never love like that again.

John Murphy came into the room. He was a big Irish bear of a man with black eyes and large features.

"So you're off to the Irish Race Convention, are you?" he asked.

"I am, indeed. My brother is one of them that believes now is the time to strike for freedom," she said.

"And what do you believe?" he asked.

"I do believe in independence, on the one hand. On the other, violence usually begets more violence."

"And if there is no other way?" he asked, his big head tilted to the side like a curious dog.

Ellen sighed and gazed out the window at Central Park 10 floors below. "I have no answer for that."

Ellen pondered this conversation as she left. Katherine had never seemed to resent the fact that Hester had left her fortune to an Irish immigrant, who was also a former domestic servant. Perhaps, it was because her own husband was also an Irish immigrant, a man who had not forgotten his roots.

She found Martin waiting for her by the bandstand in the park.

"I see you decided to come with me," he said.

"I should be working on the next issue of my magazine," she replied.

"That magazine means a lot to you, does it?" he asked.

"It does." Publishing the magazine was the only thing that had kept her from drowning in grief. And it was a natural path for her. She'd spent her time as Louisa's assistant at *The Ledger* learning about everything from printing half-tone photographs to running a printing press. She had also briefly helped at *Mother Earth*, Emma Goldman's anarchist magazine, two years ago. That was when she had done something that she still could not think of without shame. She had slept with another woman, an editor named Lulu, behind Hester's back. Hester, angel that she was, had forgiven her though she still could not forgive herself.

They descended the stairs to the subway, paid their nickels and waited for the train.

Martin pushed his fingers through his cowlick. "They say this will be the greatest demonstration of unity among our race ever held on this side of the Atlantic. The time is ripe, Elleen. Ripe for revolution."

"Martin, have you been reading that Catholic propaganda again?"

"It's not propaganda," he said. "Think of how many young men, including our own brother Michael, have been led to the slaughter under the flag of our enemy. You don't know what it's like back home — the martial law, the stifling of free speech, the spies everywhere. They imprison Irishmen with no trial and then spread lies about them in their tabloids."

Ellen didn't doubt her brother. The English pretended to protect Ireland, but it was merely a ruse for their own imperialism.

"The stranger reaps our harvest, the alien owns our soil," Ellen said, quoting the poet Lady Jane Wilde, who wrote about the terrible injustice of England exporting Irish crops while a million people died during the potato blight.

"*An Gorta Mor*." Martin nodded. No Irishman or woman would ever forget the Great Hunger. "Since the war began, they claim to the rest of the world that the long feud between our two countries is over. It will never be over until Ireland is free."

"My fear, brother, is that you'll all die and Ireland will still be in bondage."

"At the very least we will die fighting." His lips tightened in an angry line.

A light shone down the tunnel, and the train thundered down the track, stopping in front of them with a screeching of wheels.

The convention was held at the Hotel Astor, an imposing building occupying an entire block in the middle of the city, big enough to hold the more than 2,000 delegates who came to celebrate their Irish heritage and declare their sympathies for one side or the other: the side that wanted rebellion here and now versus the side that believed with time and patience England would deliver home rule.

The convention took place on the ninth floor in a series of enormous rooms with glittering chandeliers hanging from the successive ceilings. Martin joined a group discussing the formation of the Friends of Irish Freedom. This group had no interest in waiting for England to end their suspension of home rule, and there was much talk of the importance of America remaining neutral in the war so as not to assist them. On that point, they would lose, Ellen thought. America would not stay neutral much longer. Louisa had told her that J.P. Morgan, one of the wealthiest men in the country, supported the war. He said that once Wilson won the election, the way would be made clear. Wilson would do the bidding of the real rulers of the country — the rich.

"This convention will prove to the world that Ireland can never be absorbed into the British empire. We must be granted our God-given rights. And if we aren't, we will never stop fighting until the yoke is destroyed," one man announced to an agreeing crowd.

In spite of her misgivings, Ellen couldn't help but get caught up in the fervor. She might not approve of the involvement of the Germans in the cause, but Martin and his comrades were right, the war was a poor excuse for the British rescinding home rule.

Ellen found herself drawn to a table draped with the banner: *The Irishwomen's Council*. It occurred to her there might be a story here for the magazine. She might find one of these women willing and able to contribute an article. It also occurred to her that Count Bernstorff would approve of the idea, and she felt guilty for having such a thought. She was not beholden to the Germans, she reminded herself. On the other hand, it wouldn't hurt to continue to fool them.

"And what is your function here?" she asked a seated woman with her hair knotted in a disheveled bun.

"We're drumming up support for the women back home. Not only have they been fighting for suffrage and independence, they're also battling the rampant poverty in our cities," the woman said.

Ellen thought of Hester and how she had dedicated her life to helping the poor. She would have sympathized with this group of women.

Next to the older woman, a pretty woman with jet black hair, pale skin, and eyes as dark blue as the North Sea explained the group's function to an eager listener. It took her a moment to recognize the pretty woman as the widow of her old friend Paddy O'Neill, the police detective who had saved her skin more than once.

"Paula," Ellen said, leaning over the table. "'Tis I. Ellen."

Paula looked up at her, and her eyes widened.

"Quite a long time since we've seen you, lass. You weren't at the funeral."

"And I'll regret that until the day I die. I wasn't in the country at the time, but you will recall I did check in on you and the boys when I got back."

"So you did," Paula said. "My memory from that time is a bit hazy. Grief will do that to ya."

Ellen glanced around before leaning closer and asking, "Paula, can we talk for a minute or two? Privately?"

Paula agreed and asked another woman to hand out her pamphlets.

They rode the lift up to the rooftop garden on the top floor. The restaurant was closed and so they had the garden to themselves.

"So, this is how the other half lives," Paula said, gazing at the array of flowers blooming under the gabled glass roof.

"Indeed," Ellen said, not wanting to mention that she was now part of that other half. "How are the boys?"

"They're hellions, but I love them. The little one doesn't even remember his da."

Ellen's heart squeezed in her chest. She had cared about Detective Paddy O'Neill like a brother. It had been such a comfort to have a friend from Galway when she was lost and alone in a strange country. They walked to the edge of the garden and looked out over the city with its jumble of buildings scraping against the gray sky.

"I never asked, Ellen. Why *were* you in Germany last year?"

"I was there on Brotherhood business. Thanks to Martin. They sent me there with a message for Plunkett and Casement. But it was all for naught. The Germans had no intention of helping them."

She didn't mention that while there, she had been recruited to help the saboteurs in America, and that had been a mistake on the part of the Germans.

"You must be proud of Martin. All the work he's doing for Sinn Fein." Paula's eyes smiled, and Ellen wondered how Paula knew about Martin. Then again, there were few secrets in the Irish neighborhoods.

"I am proud of him but also concerned."

"Concerned? He's in no particular danger as far as I can see." Paula said and pursed her lips. "And who are you to talk? You forget my husband got *you* out of trouble more than once."

"He did," Ellen said. "And when I came back from Europe, as it happens, I was in the family way myself."

"No!"

Ellen showed her the wedding ring on her finger.

"Did you get married?"

"I'm a widow like you," Ellen said. With the loss of Hester, she felt as much a widow as Paula was.

"Paddy was under the impression that you... Well, that you weren't the marrying kind."

"I was deeply in love," she said and once again the familiar ache nudged at her like a hungry beast.

"I'm sorry for you. Loneliness is a terrible thing, but at least you have your wee one."

Ellen didn't tell her that the wee one had not filled the hole in her heart. She looked at Paula and wondered how she was surviving without her husband's salary and with two little ones to take care of. Paula would never take charity from her, but perhaps there was another way to give her some money.

Ellen told Paula about *The Ladies' Lantern* and said, "Paula, I know you were always quite a reader. Would you be interested in writing a piece for the magazine, explaining the Irish cause for our readers?"

"I write our pamphlets. I guess I could turn those ideas into an article. There's a couple of other women can write as well. When I get back to my table, I'll ask around."

They went back downstairs, and Paula gathered some of the women together. When Ellen told the women at the Irish Women's Council about her magazine and asked for articles, they clamored about her.

"Interested? You bet we are. When the rebellion happens, we'll need all the support we can get. Women won't be sitting idly by, I can guarantee that," the older woman she had first met said.

Ellen chatted with the women and found one who promised to have an article for her about women's suffrage in Ireland. Another one offered to write something about the privations the Irish suffered under British rule, and a third said she'd get an interview about the cost of Ireland's involvement in the war.

"The English claim that Ireland would not be safe without the English navy, but we would surely be safer if our boys were home to protect us instead of fighting in France and Gallipoli! Not to mention our population is half of what it was 70 years ago."

"My mother lost her eldest boy in Gallipoli," Ellen told them. She had never been close to Michael, but she wasn't the least bit happy that he was dead, and she hated for her mother's heart to be broken for such a senseless war.

Another woman piped up, "Mr. George Bernard Shaw calls the Irish 'the mendicants of the world,' because we are so poor but he never asks why Ireland is poor. Might it have something to do with the 'tribute' of over a billion and a half dollars we've paid? Or the so-called administrative costs. Can anyone tell me why the Lord Lieutenant of Ireland, an Englishman, gets

150,000 per annum for his so-called services. It's a travesty!"

The women knew their facts, and with their Irish gift of gab, Ellen felt sure the articles would be powerful. Thorn, an Englishman, ironically, might have to fix the spellings and punctuation, but she was gratified that the next issue would be even better than the first.

Before she left, she found Martin standing with John Devoy, outside a conference room. Devoy had a shifty look on his face, and she wondered what he was scheming. When he saw her, he put on a friendly façade.

"I see your brother has convinced you to join us, Miss Malloy," Devoy said and patted Martin on the back.

"Is that so?" she responded.

At that moment, who should show up but von Igel and two other men. He smiled. She'd never seen him smile before and it made her blood curdle.

Without another word, the four men went into the conference room, leaving her standing there with Martin.

"I guess you aren't grand enough to know their secrets," Ellen said to him.

"Oh, I'll know eventually. After all, I'm the courier." He stuck his hands in his pockets and shrugged.

"'Tis the date of the uprising they're discussing, isn't it?"

"I wouldn't know," Martin said.

The door opened and Devoy called out, "Martin, lad, come in here please."

"Careful, boy-o," she whispered to him as he turned to go.

Ellen went to the dining room downstairs where they were serving Irish meals of beef tongue, mutton, carrots, and cabbage. In spite of the fact, she didn't like her brother being in that den of snakes, she ate heartily for the first time in weeks.

When she went back upstairs, Devoy's speech was just beginning. His words were designed to appeal to the Americans as much as the Irish.

"We demand, in the name of American citizenship and by the memory of the sacrifices and deeds of those who in other days guarded American interests and up-held American rights, that such acts must be stopped; our neutral rights must be respected and restored, and all the force and power of this Government must be used to uphold the freedom of the seas against British aggression, and selfishness, as it was against Barbary piracy."

She tuned out the rest until at the end, his voice lowered, and he glared out at the audience, his gray beard wiggling as he exhorted his listeners not to do anything rash.

"Let there be no imprudent action which will give the English government the pretext for drastic, repressive measures."

Ellen sucked in her breath. That was it. The uprising would be soon, and Devoy — Sean Fear — was warning his listeners not to provoke the English before the deed.

The consternation felt like a whirlwind inside her.

She found Martin and said her good-byes. He told her he'd be heading up to Boston in a few weeks to gather more funds. Boston had more Irish rebels than the old country itself, it was said. From Boston Harbor, he would take a ship home.

"I'll see you when I come back to New York, some-time after Easter," he said. "Perhaps we'll have a free Ireland by then."

"Oh, my boy-o, do not count your fishes before they're in the net, as Da used to say." She hugged him fiercely. Then she whispered, "Please don't break my heart. I love you like I love my own life."

She released him and hurried off.

Sometime after Easter, he'd said. He'd told her more than he realized. He'd told her the date of the uprising. She wished she hadn't figured it out for she couldn't tell what she didn't know.

Chapter 19

Louisa

Louisa moved her typewriter to her bedroom in order to write in a little peace and quiet. In the next room, Hester was colicky and crying while Carlotta tried to soothe her, and downstairs Ellen was on the telephone with the printer.

She had already written her story on Theda Bara, the vamp who punished men for their sins. Now she had enough material for a second article on women's attitudes toward the war. As she looked over her notes, she wondered if she should write two separate articles: one explaining the position of the activists who believed peace was most important and the other delineating the arguments of the side who believed that patriotism was more important.

She was several paragraphs into the story when she heard the knocker bang on the front door downstairs.

Most likely it was someone for Ellen. They had advertised for a copy editor.

Then she heard a knock on her bedroom door, and Carlotta stuck her head in.

"Louisa, there's a swell downstairs says he needs to talk to you."

"Does this swell have a name?"

"Stephens, I think he said."

Louisa stood up immediately. What was Billy Stephens doing at her house? They had become friendly when they both worked at *The Ledger*, she on the women's desk, and he as the police beat reporter. It had been Billy who'd helped her land her first story outside the society page.

She followed Carlotta downstairs.

"Ah, Delafield. Muckraking agrees with you," Billy said, standing at the bottom of the staircase, bowler hat in hand. He had the same insouciant smirk on his face that he nearly always had.

"Mr. Stephens, what a surprise."

When she reached the bottom of the stairs, he took her hand and squeezed it. Billy was no fancy fellow, so taking her hand was a sign of genuine affection.

"Have you come looking for a job?" she asked. "I'm sure we can find something for you to do. Can you make coffee?"

"Thank you, ma'am, but I'm quite happy at *The Evening World.* I'm here because I wanted to talk to you about something. Is there somewhere private?" He glanced around the hallway.

At that moment Carlotta came out of the parlor with the baby in her arms to take her upstairs for her nap.

"Cute kid," Billy said. "Are you running a nursery?"

"Not yet. Let's go to the dining room," Louisa said, knowing that Thorn would be in the parlor going over the layout for the next issue of *The Ladies' Lantern.*

Billy followed her down the hall to the dining room. They sat down at the table. A window was open, and a brisk breeze blew the curtains aside. Louisa shut the window, and poured them both a cup of hot tea.

"Sorry, I've no beer to offer you," she teased.

"Tea is fine," he said. "So how's the magazine business?"

"It keeps us busy," Louisa said.

"And having your former assistant as your boss?"

"It's more of a partnership," Louisa answered.

"You miss the society beat?"

"Not much. The Bohemian women and the feminists are far more interesting," she said and stirred some sugar into her tea. "Billy, I'm delighted to see you, of course, but why, exactly, are you here?"

His brow furrowed.

"You know that sport who shot himself in the Woolworth Building a couple of weeks ago?"

"I read your story about it. I didn't know the man personally, but I knew his wife in college," Louisa said, remembering with chagrin that she had never gone to see Judith as she'd planned. "Why?"

"Turns out he was an investor in a play called *Handsome Harry's Dilemma*. A real dog of a play apparently, but the star was a Miss Cora De Capezio. When the investors pulled out, it never got produced and Miss De Capezio lost her chance to have her name in lights."

"I never heard of her," Louisa said.

"Nor should you have. She's a no-name vaudeville performer but her boyfriend is a Sicilian mob boss. When the investors pulled out, word is that the mob boss was none too happy."

"Wasn't the shooter a suicide?" Louisa said.

"That's what I thought but then I found out something about Mr. Halle, the man who died of poisoning. I saw your name on the police report. Was he a friend?"

"He wasn't a friend of mine, merely an acquaintance."

"Whatever he was, he was an investor in the same play. Now I'm thinking that's quite a coincidence."

"This is all fascinating, Billy, but what has it do with me? I happened to be at the party where Mr. Halle died. That's all. I didn't know the man."

"There was a third investor in that play," Billy said, drumming his fingers on the table.

"A third? Who is it?"

"Forrest Calloway."

Louisa's breath caught in her throat. Forrest?

"Is he in danger?"

"I don't know." He stroked his chin.

Louisa's stomach tightened. Forrest may have been engaged to marry another woman, but she still cared for him deeply.

"Do the police know about this connection?"

"They're on the payroll of the mob, Louisa. They're saying the first death was a suicide and the second one was accidental poisoning."

"That was no accident," Louisa said. "I noticed an Italian waiter at the salon that evening, but he was gone when the police showed up."

"Sounds suspicious."

"Have you gone to Forrest to tell him about all this?"

"He's out of town, but supposed to be back tomorrow. To be honest, I thought you might want to look into it." He took a sip of the tea, lofting his pinkie finger in the air.

"Me?"

"If I recall, you were quite the investigator," he said and took a sip of his tea, lofting a pinky finger in the air.

She pondered the idea, and felt her blood quicken. She didn't know how she would even begin, but as with her investigations of the past, she had no doubt a little bit of prying might yield intriguing answers.

"I suppose the first thing would be to speak to Judith," she said. "The wife of the Woolworth man."

"Let me know if I can help," Billy said, setting down the cup in its flowered saucer. "Good to see you again, Delafield."

He stood up, and as she watched him walk down the hallway to collect his coat and hat, she felt a tingling in her chest. Yes, she was worried about Forrest. But she was also excited — something she hadn't felt in months.

Chapter 20
Ellen

Ellen boarded the Ninth Avenue El that would take her back to Harlem. Katherine Murphy had offered to send her driver and a maid to bring the baby back to her as soon as she got home. Her breasts ached and she felt the damp of leaking milk. I'm no more than a cow, she thought. Sitting on the rocking train, she realized her bones ached with fatigue. She'd been moving too fast to notice how the tiredness had crept up on her. Now, she felt it in her creaking neck, in her shoulders stiff as a wooden post, and in the throbbing behind her eyes.

She kept seeing in her mind's eye Devoy and von Igel slipping into the conference room to hatch their plans. She wished now she hadn't seen them, that she didn't know what they planned. She must not let the information slip to Louisa, who would feel obligated to tell her former paramour, Reggie Grant.

The train pulled up to a station with a clatter and the doors opened. The middle-aged woman sitting next to her groaned as she rose from her wicker seat and got off the train. Ellen turned to look out the window. They were coming up to "dead man's curve" where the train had run off tracks several years ago, and Ellen always felt an odd thrill of fear and anticipation as if surviving "dead man's curve" was a feat in itself. She felt the seat sink beside her but didn't turn to look until she heard a man's voice say, "Hullo, Ellen."

She jerked her head around and saw, to her dismay, Reggie Grant, gazing at her with penetrating gray eyes. Speak of the devil, she thought.

"Are you here as friend or foe, Mr. Grant?" she asked.

"A bit of both, I'm afraid." He leaned toward her when he spoke and she leaned away in reaction.

"That was a dirty bit of business you pulled on Louisa," she said. Louisa may have forgiven the man but Ellen didn't have to.

"Ah, Louisa." He sighed. "She stole my heart. But she wasn't in love with me. In fact, I'd wager she enjoyed the liaison as much as I did."

"You didn't have to lie to her."

"But I did. She has too much propriety to enjoy herself with an engaged man. By lying to her, I gave her the freedom to act on her own impulses. She forgave me."

"I don't know why."

"Because whatever I did, I did for the sake of saving lives. She understood that. As do you, Ellen."

"Your cause wasn't very successful, was it? America is still neutral. Thousands of British boys, and Irish as well, still die every day."

He was silent for a moment, staring straight ahead, and she noticed the lines etched on his handsome face. His title was British Naval Attaché but his real purpose in New York was to get America to renounce her neutrality and join the Allies.

"And more Irish will die, if they go forward with this rebellion," he said.

She was silent, and he continued, "Oh, yes, we know about it. We don't know when, but we're expecting something."

"So that's why you're sitting beside me on a train when you've got a Rolls Royce sitting in a garage somewhere," she said.

He leaned in toward her again, and she smelled the woody scent of talcum powder.

"The Germans murdered all of those people who died on the *Lusitania*," he said. "Including your beloved Hester."

"Do you think I've forgotten?" She turned to him, rage boiling in her blood. "I was in that icy water. I looked in the coffins for her bloated face. Then I came back and spied on German saboteurs, risking my life for your bloody cause."

To her surprise, he clasped her hand.

"Then help me stop the Irish rebellion, Ellen. If England has to fight a war on two fronts, the Germans will surely defeat us. Do you have any idea when the Irish are planning their uprising?"

He might have been right, but while Ellen could betray the Germans who planted bombs on American ships, she could not bring herself to betray her own countrymen.

"I canna do it," she whispered. She extracted her hand from his, stood up, and stepped past him to the aisle of the train. "My stop."

The train doors opened, and she got out and hurried along the platform to the steps.

"At least, help your brother for God's sake," he called out to her. "We can have the Americans arrest him, you know."

She turned around and saw him standing on the platform as the train doors closed and it roared away.

She marched over to him and hissed, "You leave Martin out of it!"

"It's not I putting him in danger. You know that, Ellen. It's the Brotherhood and the *Clan na Gael* and John Devoy and his newspaper." His voice went low as he leaned toward her and growled, "And their friends, the Germans."

She inhaled deeply, turned and strode away. As she hurried down the steps to the street, tears spilled from her eyes. Tears for her beloved Hester, her bones at the bottom of the Irish Sea, tears for her stalwart young brother, tears for the dead in an insane war, and tears for the darling babe she wanted so badly to fall in love with.

Chapter 21
Louisa

The apartment of Bernard and Judith Benson was located on the eighth floor of a fashionable brick building in the Murray Hill neighborhood. A maid showed Louisa into a parlor that smelled of lilies. Portraits hung on the walls and a fire crackled in a marble fireplace.

"Louisa Delafield," Judith said, rising from her armchair and taking Louisa's hands in hers. "Look at you. We all knew you were the most likely to succeed."

Judith was still pretty, her dark eyes a bit more somber than before. She wore a stylish tea-length black dress with a white collar and a sheer overskirt with black loops of Georgette crepe.

"Succeed?" Louisa asked.

"Well, of course. You had that wonderful society column in papers all over the country and now you're writing for a magazine that you founded with another woman. I so enjoyed that first issue. Your interview with Crystal Eastman was fascinating. Why, I would have joined the suffragists myself if I wasn't busy with two children."

Louisa was surprised that Judith had seen the magazine. She had never seemed like the sort of person who took life the least bit seriously.

"How are you faring, Judith?"

"Aside from being devastated, you mean? I'm fine. Really." Tears brimmed in her eyes.

"Oh, Judith. I can't believe this happened to you." Louisa thought of the happy young woman she'd known in college, who had performed in plays and skits and flirted shamelessly with the boys at Columbia until she'd snagged a husband.

They sat down on the settee and waited as the maid brought in a coffee service and some cookies.

"I'm so deeply sorry for your loss," Louisa said and nibbled one of the sugar cookies.

Judith gazed at a portrait of her husband on the wall before speaking. In the portrait he looked thoughtful, but there was a hint of amusement around his mouth. Judith would never have married a man who didn't know how to have fun.

"Bernard invested in Broadway shows. Some were flops, and sometimes he broke even. Once in a while, he did more than break even. We'd celebrate at Delmonico's with steak and champagne. Bernard enjoyed life. He seemed to not mind the roller coaster of investing. I simply can't believe he'd take his own life."

"It must have been quite a shock."

"Oh, it was. He had no reason to."

"The newspaper account mentioned some pawn tickets?"

"That's what really confuses me," Judith said, rubbing her chin in distress. "One of the pawn tickets was for a German wall clock, a Gustav Becker. But you see that clock is hanging here in my parlor."

Louisa looked and indeed there was a Gustav Becker clock on the wall.

"That does seem strange. Judith, do you think it's possible that something else happened to your husband?" She was beginning to think that Billy Stephens' concerns were justified.

"I believe he was murdered," Judith said, leaning forward, her small hands balled into fists.

"But who do you think would do such a thing?" Louisa asked.

"I'm not sure. When I heard that another investor in the same play died mysteriously, I wondered if there might be a connection. But the police aren't interested in theories."

"Tell me about the play. Why did the investors pull out?"

"*Handsome Harry's Dilemma*? A poorly written, overwrought melodrama. When Bernard realized how bad it was, he refused to invest another cent. I do believe that someone murdered my husband, Louisa. But I don't know how to prove it. But you do, don't you? I read about the murder you solved in Florida a couple of years ago. Something about stolen diamonds? Can you help me?"

Louisa took Judith's hand in hers and squeezed it.

"You are right. I do have some experience in investigations. I will do what I can to get to the bottom of this."

Judith brushed a tear from her pale cheek.

After her visit with Judith, Louisa took a trip to Chinatown to purchase a package of egg noodles and sauce for the American Chop Suey recipe she'd found in the beef section of Fannie Farmer's cook book. Next, she stopped at a meat market and purchased chopped beef. She had everything else she needed at home.

As she prepared the chop suey, she pondered her next step. She needed to inform Forrest that his life might be in danger. Would he believe her? Or would it appear to be a pathetic excuse to see him? She shook her head. It didn't matter what it looked like, she must warn him. Perhaps he would know who it was that was angry enough about the play's cancellation that they would kill the investors. Billy had mentioned a Sicilian mob boss. She wondered if the mob boss might be mollified somehow.

She dipped a fork into the mixture and tasted. It didn't taste much like the food she'd had in Chinatown restaurants, but it wasn't bad. She asked Carlotta to set the table and poured the chop suey sauce into a tureen.

"Something smells not terrible," Anna said, taking her place at the head of the dining table.

"Please try not to be so effusive in your compliments, Mother," Louisa said.

The front door opened.

"That must be Ellen," she said.

"I missed the baby today," Anna said.

Louisa went into the parlor to tell Ellen that dinner was ready and found her on the telephone.

"Yes, I'm here now. Please bring her over. And thank you for keeping her today."

Ellen hung up the phone and turned to Louisa. The little pouches under her eyes had grown even darker. Louisa felt a jolt of pity.

"Ellen, are you getting enough sleep?" she asked as they went into the dining room.

"She shouldn't be working!" Anna said. "It's bad for the baby's milk."

"Don't mention milk," Ellen said. "My poor breasts are aching so."

"Come and eat," Louisa insisted. "You can feed the baby as soon as she gets here."

Ellen was silent as she ate. Carlotta never had much to say so Louisa and Anna babbled about the weather which threatened violence.

"March comes in like a lion," Anna said. "You're lucky the storms waited until tonight, Ellen. Or there would be more soaked than just the front of your dress."

Ellen looked down at the wet spots on her chest.

"I'm too exhausted to be embarrassed," she said and devoured the chop suey greedily.

When the Murphy's maid arrived with Hester, Ellen took her upstairs and Louisa followed.

Louisa watched with curiosity and a bit of envy as the baby latched her mouth onto Ellen's white breast and suckled. Louisa wondered what it felt like, the baby's eager mouth on her nipple. After a few minutes the baby's eyes closed.

"She's tired, too," Louisa observed. She found looking at Hester endlessly fascinating and remembered with chagrin her utter lack of interest before she was born.

"You'll never guess who I ran into," Ellen said, adjusting the baby in her arms.

"Why don't you tell me?"

"Your friend, Reggie Grant."

"Where was he? Certainly not at the Irish conference."

"No. He followed me onto the train. As soon as the person seated next to me got up, he slid right in like a snake."

"He's not a snake," Louisa said. "You forget how helpful he was last year when we were dealing with the Germans."

"Well, now he wants me to spy on my countrymen." Ellen moved the baby to her other breast.

"I'm not surprised," Louisa said. "When I wasn't helpful, he must have decided to take matters into his own hands."

"I won't do it, and I told him so."

"I don't blame you. It's entirely unreasonable on his part to expect you to do something like that. Although I do understand his concerns...fate of the world and all that."

Hester drifted off to sleep and Ellen covered herself.

"May I hold her?" Louisa asked.

Ellen handed over the sleeping baby. Louisa gently rocked her and stroked the downy head with the tips of her fingers.

"You should be the mother in this house, not I," Ellen said with a hint of sadness.

Louisa ignored the jab of pain in her heart. She'd never be a mother. Not only did she not have a husband but she thought perhaps she was barren.

"If England has to fight the Irish as well as the Germans, it will be a catastrophe," Louisa said.

"I know that, Louisa. But I simply can't fight that battle. There are matters here in New York City that need our attention. Suffrage and poverty and the right for women to earn a decent living."

"Why is Martin in New York, Ellen?"

"Why do you want to know?" Ellen pushed her hair off her face and glared at Louisa.

"I know whatever he's doing, you're worried about him. This is a dangerous game they're playing."

"It is," Ellen said. "But Reggie threatened to have the Americans arrest him. I can't have that. Or something worse. For all I know, Reggie might have someone kill him."

"He wouldn't do that." Louisa said. At least, she hoped he wouldn't.

"And what have you done today?" Ellen asked.

Louisa was grateful for the change in subject. She didn't like being the inquisitor.

"I went to visit an old college friend whose husband was found shot dead in his office in the Woolworth Building. Police ruled it a suicide, but she believes it was murder."

Carlotta entered the room and moved some clothes off a chair so she could sit.

"Why would someone murder him?" Carlotta asked.

"He was an investor in a Broadway play. And when he took his money out of the play, he may have angered a mobster."

"Which mobster?"

"Billy Stephens thinks it's a Sicilian," Louisa said. "Of course, there are so many gangs around these days. Irish, Jewish, Italians. Who can keep up with them all?"

Carlotta combed her fingers through her long dark hair.

"You don't want to mess with the Italian mobsters. Believe me," Carlotta said. "If they got a vendetta against you, you're done."

Carlotta stood up, took Hester from Louisa's arms, and put her in the bassinette.

"So, you're being distracted from the magazine stories by another possible murder?" Ellen asked.

"This is important," Louisa said.

"Why?"

"Because Forrest Calloway has invested in this same play," Louisa said.

She saw the look of surprise on Ellen's face.

"Who's that?" Carlotta asked.

"The man Louisa is in love with," Ellen said, matter-of-factly. Louisa didn't bother to deny it. "Then I suppose you must do what you must do."

They were all silent for a while. Then Louisa said, "Don't worry. I'll still write something about Djuna Barnes' book of poetry if I can ever find her. I'll also collect the articles from the Heterodoxy women at the next meeting."

"It might be enough. I picked up a few more contributors."

"At the Irish convention?"

"Indeed. The Irish ladies have seen the worst of it."

Louisa was impressed by how Ellen kept finding new causes for the magazine. She might make a success of the enterprise yet. Unless this war or the Irish rebellion somehow derailed her.

As she prepared for bed, Louisa glanced at the window and remembered how Reggie Grant would show up in her bedroom last year when he wanted her help. If he showed up again, she would turn him away. Their affair had been a momentary infatuation. She was too heartbroken over Forrest and his upcoming wedding to embark on some lark. Now, she must ignore that broken heart and make sure no one killed him before he *could* wed.

As she lay in her bed, she wondered how she might discover whether or not Billy was right about the Italian mob. Was it a coincidence that the waiter who served Mr. Halle his drink was also an Italian? She suddenly sat up. She had a connection to the Italians right here—in the room next to hers.

Chapter 22
Ellen

Ellen hadn't asked Martin where he was staying, but she had a strong idea where she might find him.

That morning she used the skills she'd learned from her German mentor Captain Boehm to make sure she wasn't tailed. She went in one entrance of a department store and out another, hopped on a train and then hopped off right before the doors closed. When she was sure no one was following her, she made her way to a street north of the Bowery along the Hudson and knocked on the door of a narrow brownstone.

The door opened and Paula stared at her in surprise.

"I haven't written the article yet, if that's what you came for, Ellen."

"I need to talk to Martin."

"Oh, come on in then and have a cup. He's in there with little Sean and Davey."

Ellen followed Paula into the kitchen, where she'd spent many an hour, enjoying the familial warmth. The smell of rashers hovered over the room.

"Oy, look at these two young men!" she said. "They're so big."

Sean looked up and screeched in delight. Davey, the younger one, didn't recognize her, so he beat on the table with a spoon.

"Boys!" Paula raised her voice. "Stop it this instant."

"Hullo, Ellen," Martin said, looking a bit sheepish.

Sleeping with the widow, are you, Ellen wanted to say, but didn't. If Paula could find a spot of happiness, Ellen would not begrudge her. It was not easy to be alone especially with two young ones.

She sat down and Sean crawled into her lap. Just like old times. She felt an ache in her heart that Paddy wasn't with them. Paddy had been killed last year, and now her little brother was courting trouble.

Paula set down a mug of tea in front of her.

"Martin, you're needing to be careful. There's a British spy here, name of Reggie Grant. And he knows of your presence in New York. Knows your purpose as well, I'm sure," Ellen said, leaning toward him.

Martin scoffed. "This is America. What power do the invaders have over me here? None. America is neutral. God willing, they'll stay that way."

Ellen leaned back and took a sip of tea.

"I'm not here to fight with you. Just to beg you to be careful. The American and British secret services are thick as thieves. If they think you're taking money out of this country to foment a rebellion, they'll throw you in the clink. Frankly, I don't trust the English not to do something worse."

"I like games," Sean said, looking up at her, his blue eyes the spitting image of his da.

"I bet you do," Ellen said. "What's your favorite?"

"Jacks!" Sean jumped off her lap and ran into the other room, presumably to get his jacks.

"Don't you worry, Elleenie. I'm off to Boston soon," Martin said, he picked a rasher off the plate and chewed on it. "I only need a few more pledges."

"Pledges?"

"Money, you know. Speaking of money, you mentioned John Murphy the other day. You remember?"

"I do." Ellen didn't like where he was going with this.

"He's a millionaire, isn't he?"

"He is." She glanced over at Paula. Her eyes were on Martin. *Oy, she has it bad for him,* Ellen thought.

"And Irish."

"American," Ellen corrected.

"Irish-American. Would he be willing to give to the cause? We need more Irish-Americans to donate so we can purchase weapons from the Germans. Devoy insists we pay for every rifle. We won't be beholden to the Germans. Maybe you could get me in to meet Mr. Murphy?"

"Martin, I'll do no such thing."

"The sooner we get our funds, the sooner I can get out of New York."

Ellen leaned her elbows on the table. Martin wasn't safe in New York. But would he be safe in Ireland? She sighed. "Martin, if you go back to Ireland, can you promise me not to pick up the gun? You're doing enough by being a courier, aren't you?"

He shook his head. His changeable eyes had turned green like the grass in the month of May.

"I will do whatever my country needs me to do. You know that." He spoke with the calm assurance of one who has weighed the consequences and made his choice.

Paula stood up, grabbed the tea pot, and topped off Ellen's cup.

Ellen looked from one to the other. Martin bounced little Davey on his knee. Why couldn't Martin abandon the rebels and marry Paula, she wondered.

Little Davey squealed in delight.

Chapter 23

Louisa

Louisa stumbled into the dining room and found Anna eating crackers and cheese.

"It's past noon," Anna complained. "I'm famished."

"I'm sorry, Mother. I had terrible dreams all night and barely got a moment's sleep."

Louisa sat down and looked at the newspaper. After a cup of coffee, she slowly revived. When she heard Carlotta in the hallway, she got up and went to speak with her.

"Carlotta, wait, please. I want to talk to you," Louisa said.

"I was just about to walk the baby," Carlotta said.

"I'll go with you," Louisa said, throwing on her coat.

In the months since Carlotta had moved into the West Harlem townhome with Louisa, Anna, and Ellen, Louisa had treated Carlotta with kindness, and Carlotta had treated her with a certain deference. Louisa was born a blue blood and well educated while Carlotta had spent her teenage years as a prostitute. That class difference created a chasm that was difficult to cross.

Ellen, on the other hand, had never acknowledged such a difference. From servants to laborers to the highest echelons of society, Ellen regarded everyone as equal to her. No one above and no one below, which was how she had managed to wind up in the arms of a wealthy heiress.

Carlotta had come into their home as a charity case rather like the ginger cat. She wasn't much of a housekeeper or a cook and couldn't help much with the magazine except to run errands, but she'd made herself useful since the baby had been born.

They found a bench in the morning sun and settled down, Carlotta slowly moving the carriage to and fro. Louisa looked at the dark-haired girl, her ruined beauty, her large dark eyes. What secrets lurked behind those eyes?

"Carlotta, I hope you don't think I'm being intrusive, but a while back you mentioned that your family was Italian and I got the impression they were affiliated with the mob. I'm trying to find out who might be after these Broadway investors."

"How can I help?"

"I'm not sure. Perhaps you can tell me your story? In all these months of your living with us, I never did learn how you ended up in a German bordello."

Carlotta leaned back

"My last name is Morano. That name means nothing to you, but on Coney Island, if you are a Morano, then you are like royalty. My family originally comes from Naples. When I was little, we lived not far from here in Harlem on East 115th Street. But then we moved to Coney Island."

"Why?"

"Pop mostly sold stolen horses, but then he got arrested for murder. He swore it was self-defense and the police dropped the charges against him. Then he moved to Coney Island and opened a restaurant. From the restaurant he ran gambling rings, his men sold cocaine, and he ran a numbers racket."

Louisa could hardly believe what Carlotta was saying, but Carlotta was so calm she might have describing the contents of her closet.

"A numbers racket?" Louisa asked.

"You know. People bet on numbers. Everybody does it." Carlotta leaned over to check on Hester, who was happily gnawing on her fist.

"Not everybody. Wealthy people bet on horses," Louisa said.

"Everybody wants easy money. I did errands for Pop just to get candy money. Including going to stores and making pick-ups. The bags would have names, numbers and money in them. I was good with numbers and Pop let me help him add up the receipts. That's how I studied arithmetic. Even Martha Held let me help her with the books at the bordello."

"What happened? It's my understanding that Italian families are quite close knit."

"Oh, we are. We will die for each other. But more importantly we will kill for each other." Carlotta glanced up at her with penetrating dark eyes.

"I see."

"The problem started when I turned 12 and started to look like a woman. I still felt like a little girl but my monthly curse started and I had breasts. The man who owned the grocery store started giving me candy, asking me to stick around. One day he locked the door behind me. And I will not tell a lady like you what he did."

"Oh no, Carlotta," Louisa gasped. "You were still a child."

"Not after he was done with me." Her voice was flat, devoid of all emotion.

Hester whimpered. Carlotta picked her up and jostled her up and down until the baby laid her head on Carlotta's shoulder.

A woman in a servant's uniform came by with three children in tow. Pigeons swarmed on the sidewalk, and the sun edged through a cloud to spill a few rays on the field next to them.

"What did you do?" Louisa asked. "Did you tell your mother?"

"I couldn't. I was too ashamed. It happened again. And again. Then my monthly curse stopped. My mama paid attention to those kinds of things. One day when I came home, she took a horse whip and beat me until I was covered with slash marks. She didn't care what I said. That night, I took money from Papa's desk and ran.

"I wandered the streets for a few days. I was too young to rent a room somewhere. When I saw the beautiful ladies going into that house and I heard the music coming out of it, I was drawn like a moth to the flame. Miss Martha wasn't so bad. She took me in and let me live with her. I cleaned up after the girls. After a while, a year I guess, I started taking on clients and earning my keep. None of the girls there were forced to work. They could leave anytime. Some of them got married. I didn't want to get married. I didn't like men. I was happy when they gave me gifts and money, but I couldn't bear the thought of living with one of them."

Louisa mulled over this story. Carlotta had a hard lot in life. And yet she seemed so strong. She had an easy smile and a fearlessness that Louisa admired. To have her face marred by the knife of a German spy only served to make her stronger. That scar had saved her from a life of further degradation and the disease that came so often with it.

"What do you know about these Italians in East Harlem? Are they related to your family?"

"We're from Naples. The ones in Harlem now come from Sicily. And my family is at war with them."

"At war? How long has this been going on?"

A wind gust came along and tugged at Louisa's hat.

"A couple of years."

"But how do you know about it if you haven't seen them since you left?"

"My mama."

"Your mother? But you said she…"

"She is still my mama. Sometimes I go to church and meet her when no one else is around. She begged my forgiveness, and I have given it. Like you did with your mama."

Louisa wasn't sure how Carlotta knew Anna's secret, but it was hard to keep secrets in a house full of women. The two of them did have this in common: they had each forgiven the unforgiveable. She realized that Carlotta could be invaluable in helping her discover who was behind the murders.

"Carlotta, do you think it would be possible to meet with that Sicilian boss?"

Carlotta's dark eyes widened.

"You want to meet with a Mafia boss?"

"Would he harm me?" Louisa asked.

Carlotta shook her head. "I won't let no one hurt you, Miss Louisa. I will find a way to meet with him."

The distance between the two women had disappeared in the course of a single conversation on a park bench on a windy day.

Chapter 24
Ellen

Katherine Murphy took little Hester from Ellen's arms as they stood in the foyer of the Murphy's 18-room apartment on Central Park. So much room for two people, Ellen thought.

"A month old now. Did I see a smile?"

"It's just gas," Ellen said.

"It looked like a smile to me." Absolutely smitten, the woman was.

"Do you suppose I could talk to your husband?"

"John? What could you possibly want to talk to John about?"

"I'm after getting some legal advice. I'd like to create a trust for little Hester. And... to create a will that would appoint the two of you Hester's guardians should anything happen to me."

Katherine looked surprised, but Ellen knew that the woman coveted the child.

"He's in his study. I'll let him know you want to speak to him."

"Thank you."

John Murphy's study held an enormous mahogany desk. A painting of a wide tree-lined path with a large body of water hung on one wall.

"Is that Dublin Bay?" she asked.

"'Tis. As you can tell it's from an earlier century," he said wistfully. "Have a seat."

Ellen sat and took a deep breath. She had faced down gangsters of all sorts, but John Murphy — a big, black-haired man with a gruff voice — managed to intimidate simply with his imposing presence. Hester had explained to her how he had clawed his way up from office boy to president of the company and then worked for seven years to earn enough money to marry the boss's daughter, Katherine.

"I need advice on some legal matters."

"Legal matters? You know I'm not a lawyer, Miss Malloy. I'm a business man. A capitalist." He leaned back with his hands clasped over his belly.

"I know that."

"And I know about your political leanings." He pointed a finger at her. "You think capitalism is evil."

"Not always. Some capitalists have the good sense to earn their place in heaven by spreading their wealth. As your sister-in-law did."

"Hester had a pure heart," he agreed.

Ellen nodded. "She did."

He studied her. The love and affection that Ellen and Hester had shared must be mysterious to him, she thought. But at least he would never question the gap in their classes — a former domestic servant and an heiress — as he had been the son of a street sweeper himself and was now married to an heiress.

"Let's get down to business. How can I help you?"

John Murphy agreed to be the guardian of Hester should anything happen to Ellen, and he promised he would have an attorney draw up papers creating a trust for the baby as well as the guardianship.

"There's one other matter," Ellen said.

He eyed her curiously.

"My brother Martin is over here, representing the Brotherhood, and raising money for the cause. He wonders if you'd care to make a donation?"

John Murphy's expression grew dark, and Ellen feared she'd gone too far. To her surprise, the dark expression was not about her request.

"It's about time we turned the thieving scoundrels out of our cradleland. I will happily donate to the cause. Tell him to come by tomorrow night."

Ellen shook her head.

"I'm worried he's being observed. Instead, how about I collect it whenever it's ready."

John Murphy stood and opened a cabinet. Ellen's jaw dropped when she saw the safe inside. He quickly dialed the lock around first one way and then the other. The door swung open, and Mr. Murphy pulled out a stack of cash.

"Here's seven hundred and fifty dollars," he said, handing it over to Ellen. "That should buy them a few tommy guns. I wish 'em all the luck."

Ellen stared down at the money. She was crossing a line if she gave this money to Martin. Rebellion was a bad idea, and yet he was her brother, and he has asked her for this favor. And if an uprising was coming, at least the rebels should have a fighting chance.

Chapter 25
Louisa

The balmy daytime temperature had dropped quickly as the streaks of pink in the Western sky slowly faded. Louisa wished she'd brought a warmer jacket as she walked toward Gramercy Park.

Mrs. Kimura, Forrest's housekeeper, showed no surprise when she opened the door and found Louisa on the stoop.

"Miss Louisa, come in," she said. She showed Louisa into the parlor. There was no fire in the fireplace so she must have missed him. She would have liked to warm herself. "Mr. Forrest is not here. You like something to drink?"

"When do you expect him?"

"Mr. Kimura went to train station to get him. Back any minute."

"Oh, good," Louisa said. "I'll just wait for him then. Nothing to drink, thank you."

Mrs. Kimura started to leave.

"Mrs. Kimura, I wanted to ask you... How do you like the future Mrs. Calloway?"

Mrs. Kimura smiled broadly.

"She nice lady. Two boys." She held her hands out to indicate their sizes. "Rambunctious."

Louisa felt a gaping hole in her heart. Forrest had yearned for children and now he would have them. She looked around the parlor. On winter nights, she had sat here by the fire with Forrest, talking about her investigations or the newspaper business or whatever crossed their minds. Now he belonged to someone else.

Louisa heard the sound of a motorcar pulling up to the curb out front. She glanced out the window and saw Mr. Kimura open the back door. Someone was getting out when BANG!

Louisa stifled a scream as a body fell to the sidewalk. Fear tore through her as she ran toward the door, thinking she'd been too late! She threw open the door and flew down the steps to the sidewalk. She found Forrest leaning over Mr. Kimura's prone body. Sadie Treadwell sat, trembling in the back seat.

Louisa immediately turned and ran back into the house, passing Mrs. Kimura on the way.

She rushed to the telephone hanging on the wall of the foyer and lifted the receiver.

"Please, operator!" she yelled over Mrs. Kimura's loud keening. "Send an ambulance to Gramercy Park. East 15th Steet near Second Avenue. A man has been shot."

She hung up and dashed outside. Forrest had his hands pressed against Mr. Kimura's shoulder to staunch the bleeding.

"I've called an ambulance," Louisa said.

"Thank you," Forrest said, glancing up at her. "Please, will you take Mrs. Kimura and Sadie inside?"

"Of course."

Louisa led first Mrs. Kimura into the house and then went back to get Sadie. A crowd had gathered and the clanging of an ambulance gong could be heard. Louisa opened the back door on the other side of the car.

"Sadie," she said in a gentle voice. "Come with me. Let's get you inside."

Mrs. Treadwell and Mrs. Kimura sat side-by-side on the sofa in the parlor while Louisa found a wool blanket to take outside for Mr. Kimura.

"Thank God you're here, Louisa," Forrest said as she draped the blanket over Mr. Kimura.

The ambulance pulled up and two hospital orderlies ran over with a gurney. They gingerly lifted poor Mr. Kimura and hoisted him onto a cot in the back of the vehicle. Forrest gave the driver his assurance that he would pay for Mr. Kimura's treatment, and off they went with one of the orderlies beating the gong, hanging off the side of the vehicle.

As soon as the ambulance left, a police wagon arrived. Louisa had a flashback to the first time she knew she was in love with Forrest, when he had rescued her from a house of ill repute where she'd been held captive. She remembered how they'd stood outside surrounded by the cacophony of police vehicles. He'd taken her hand and a sense of calm had descended upon her. This time he did not take her hand.

A police officer questioned Forrest about the shooting, but Forrest had no answers as to why someone would want to kill him. Louisa thought it best to share her own suspicions with him alone and let him decide what to tell the authorities.

"A detective will be by tomorrow," the officer said, before getting in his wagon and driving away.

Finally, Forrest turned to her.

"How did you happen to be here, Louisa?" he asked.

"Ironically, I came to warn you that your life may be in danger," she said.

"Whoever tried to kill me wasn't a very good shot," he said. "Let's go inside."

A doctor came and gave Mrs. Kimura a sedative. Mrs. Treadwell asked for something to help her sleep as well.

"To hell with propriety," she said. "I shall sleep in your guest room, Forrest. Good night, Miss Delafield."

"She didn't even ask why I was here," Louisa said after the woman ascended the staircase.

"She's a most trusting and honest woman," Forrest said, his voice filled with admiration.

"You must love her very much," Louisa said.

Forrest hesitated for just a moment. "I do love her. It's different. Perhaps not quite as fiery as... Well, one can get burned if the fire is too hot."

His words bore a hole in her.

"Tell me, why do you think that someone wants to kill me," he said.

"You're an investor in *Handsome Harry's Dilemma*, are you not?"

"I was. The other two pulled out," he said. "And so I got most of my original investment back. Some of it was gone, but that's the risk you take."

"Well, the other two are dead," she said.

"What? I heard that Benson killed himself over his debts, but Halle's dead, too?"

"You didn't know? Where have you been?"

"We've been in Boston, meeting Sadie's family. I had several business meetings as well."

"Benson's widow claims he didn't commit suicide. She believes he was murdered. And Mr. Halle was poisoned with strychnine. When Billy Stephens told me you were the third investor, I began to do some digging. Did you know that Benson borrowed money from a Sicilian mobster for his investment? Not only that, the mobster's girlfriend was to have the leading role in the show."

Forrest looked grim.

"I did wonder about the woman they chose. Beautiful but no serious acting experience. I did not know about any connection to Italian gangsters."

"I've learned a bit about them. These are men who are not to be trifled with. Apparently back in Sicily, they carry on feuds for hundreds of years."

"I see. Well, if it's money they want, I can pay them off. But I don't even know who they are or how to contact them," he said.

"You leave that to me. My assistant Carlotta is Italian and she's trying to arrange a meeting."

"Carlotta? What happened to Ellen?" he asked.

"Ellen inherited money and is publishing a magazine for women. Didn't you know?"

The expression on his face made Louisa smile ruefully.

"How did I miss that news?" he asked.

"You were too busy planning your nuptials," Louisa said. She grew serious and placed a white-gloved hand on his arm. "I'll find out what they want. Forrest, I couldn't bear it if something happened to you."

"But what about you? You should not meet with mobsters."

"Don't worry. I will be in a public place. And I don't think they'll want to kill me if I'm offering you're your money."

They stared at each other for a moment. His Adam's apple bobbed as he swallowed. If only there were some way to simply shut off one's feelings, she thought. But she would do nothing to interfere with his happiness.

"I'm so pleased that the shot missed you," she said. "I'll see myself out."

She opened the front door and stepped into the night.

Chapter 26
Ellen

At Paula's house, Ellen let Carlotta introduce herself and little Hester to the two boys, who were fascinated by the baby. Carlotta took the three children to the kitchen while Ellen hung back in the parlor to speak with Martin. She reluctantly handed over the cash.

"I don't approve of it," she said. "But I told you I would ask Mr. Murphy for a donation, and here 'tis."

"You're a good sister, you are," he said.

"When will you be leaving for Boston then?"

"In a week or so. I promise. In the meantime, I've got a parade to go to."

He swept the top hat off his head and waved it. He was going ahead to the St. Patrick's Day parade without them because he had a choice seat in the parade itself.

"Lass, I'm off!" he called out to Paula, who was in the kitchen. He bowed extravagantly to Ellen and then marched out the door.

The toddler Davy ran toward the door crying, but Paula scooped him up.

"Come in the kitchen and have a bite of lunch before the parade," Paula said. "Your friend says you haven't been eating enough. Something about not having a cook?"

Ellen followed Paula into the cozy kitchen where Carlotta sat holding Hester. The two boys were staring at the baby in fascination.

"Grab yourself a bowl," Paula said, uncovering a pot of steaming stew.

"Is the baby coming to the parade?" Sean asked.

"No, she'll be staying here at the house with Carlotta and your little brother whilst the three of us go," Ellen said.

"Why can't Davy go?"

"He has a cut on his foot and I can't be carrying a four-year-old child around," Paula said. Then her voice softened. "That's a mighty sweet little baby you have, Ellen. Lookit the hair."

"She's a very good baby," Carlotta said. "It's a special day for you Irish, isn't it?"

A sad smile crossed Paula's face.

"My own Paddy was in it every year, wearing his uniform with every brass button polished," she said.

"I wonder how Martin managed to get himself invited as a guest of the Ancient Order of Hibernians," Ellen said. "He's fitting in here like a regular New Yorker. Maybe he should stay, not go back to Ireland at all."

She glanced at Paula, who shook her head.

"You're the one who wants him to leave," Paula said.

"Only because he's involved with those *Clan na Gael* rebels. If he were to stay here and get a job on the police force, then he wouldn't be in any danger at all."

"I suppose I wouldn't mind that," Paula said and smiled, brushing a strand of dark hair off her face. "Carlotta, I'm mighty grateful you staying here with little Davy and the baby."

"I don't mind," Carlotta said and winked at Davy. Ellen had thought he'd throw a tantrum at not being able to go the parade, but he seemed to have fallen under Carlotta's spell and he didn't utter a single complaint as Ellen, Paula, and Sean left to go to the St. Patrick's Day Parade.

As a police officer's widow, Paula and her family were given a prime viewing spot on the steps of the cathedral. Thousands of people had gathered all along the street. American flags waved from the buildings. Ellen stood next to Paula and held Sean's hand. In his excitement, he kept trying to tug away from her. Even in their spot, the crowd was at least six deep.

"Did you see that the Cardinal isn't coming?" Paula said over the noise of the crowd.

"He's no supporter of the Grand Marshal," Ellen said.

"Then he's no Irishman," Paula said. "And as for the 69th Regiment, the so-called Fighting Irish, they're a lousy bunch of turncoats for not marching today."

Ellen wondered how the rebels could possibly expect to expel the British from Ireland when they couldn't come to any sort of agreement among themselves.

In spite of the infighting among various factions, the parade would be as grand as they come. The papers said that 9,000 workers had been hired to clear the streets of old snow. The city had promised to make the street "shine like a mirror."

The parade started promptly at three o'clock at 42nd street. They would march down Fifth Avenue all the way to 120th street before turning east to Madison Avenue and then north again to the Harlem River Park.

"I can't see!" Sean complained, so Paula lifted him in her arms and squeezed through the crowd to get to the front. Ellen tried to follow but she could only get so far.

First came the platoon of Mounted Police, followed by a military band playing fifes and drums. Then the

Grand Marshal, followed by aides and escorts. Men in suits wearing white gloves carried flags, both the American and the shamrock. Next came the Spanish War Veterans, followed by the Boy Scouts Military Band and on and on with battalions and county associations from Limerick to Ulster. The guests of the Ancient Order of Hibernians came in a carriage and there were John DeVoy and Martin waving at the crowd. Sean screamed and waved at Martin. He was already a father figure to Paula's boys, Ellen thought.

The crowds clapped and hooted, everyone dressed in their best hats and coats. The temperature never reached above freezing but luckily there was no snow and not a cloud in the sky.

When the Battalion of Eccentric Firemen marched by, Ellen felt goosebumps along the back of her neck before she even realized someone had sidled next to her in the crowd.

"Miss Malloy. I would like a word." He was so close she felt his breath on her neck.

She turned and saw the large, unblinking eyes of Herr von Igel, staring at her. She tried to shrink back but the crowd was too thick.

"Oh, would you? Why don't you bugger off?" She didn't need these goons bothering her now. She looked around. "Where's the big man?"

"You mean, Rupert? My bodyguard? He's at the good widow's house. Your nursemaid and baby are there, aren't they? He'll make sure nothing happens to them."

Panic shot through Ellen like a spear.

"What are you trying to pull, von Igel?" she hissed.

"I just want to talk to you. My car is just around the corner."

"You're vile," she hissed at him.

This only made him laugh, a grating unpleasant sound.

"It will only take a minute. Your friend won't even know you're gone."

She looked over at Paula, holding Sean up so he could see the fife and drum band passing by. An enormous woman in what looked like a bear-skin coat stood between then.

Ellen cursed under her breath, but followed von Igel in a serpentine path through the crowd. As soon as they got off Fifth Avenue, the crowds disappeared. She followed him down the block where they turned another corner. A motorcar with a driver sat rumbling by a lamp post. He opened the door. She got in. The German man followed and shut the door. He lit a cigar. It was no warmer in the car, and there wasn't even a blanket to cover her.

"I apologize for taking you away from the festivities. But I have an assignment for you."

"I don't take orders from you," she said and waved cigar smoke from her face. She trembled and it wasn't only from the cold.

"I know you don't. But my bodyguard does. Don't worry. Nothing untoward will happen as long as you listen to my request."

"Spit it out then," Ellen said, tamping down her rage. "What do you want?"

"Tell me, has Miss Delafield been seeing Mr. Grant, the British Naval Attaché?"

"She hasn't said anything to me about it if she has." She rubbed her arms, grateful for the thick wool coat.

"We must keep the Americans out of the war, you know," he said. "It's for our interests as well as Ireland's."

He rolled down the window and flicked the ash from his cigar.

"You might as well try to stop the tide," Ellen said. "The Grand Marshall of the parade is riding a horse named 'Preparedness,' for crying out loud. It's only a matter of time."

He cleared his throat and paused before speaking again.

"We want you to tell Mr. Grant, the date of the uprising. Or rather, we want you to let Miss Delafield know the date so she can tell Mr. Grant. Better if it comes from her."

"You mean Easter weekend?" She had not forgotten Martin's comment that he would return to New York after Easter.

Surprise lit up von Igel's usually dead eyes.

"How did you know?"

She realized her mistake at once. They would not take kindly to Martin slipping up and letting her know the day.

"Devoy told me. He knows I can be trusted."

"I see. Well, you must not give that away. As far as you know, the uprising will be in June. At least, that's what you will tell Miss Delafield. June 18th. Father's Day."

"Do you think Grant will be fooled that easily?"

Von Igel blew out a long plume of smoke.

"I got a cable from Captain Nicolai asking after your health." The smoke from his cigar stung her eyes. "I neglected to tell him about the child."

His bushy mustache curled up at the ends like a smile, and Ellen was paralyzed by a murderous rage. She forced herself to breathe and look away. Never show them how you feel, she told herself. But someday, she thought, this man will pay.

"Why should you mention my child to Captain Nicolai? He had nothing to do with it."

"Oh? I must be mistaken then." He forced his lips up in a toothless smile.

"If you must know, I have kept the paternity a secret as a kindness to Joseph Plunkett's fiancée. Now, if we're done, I should like to return to the parade," she said and opened the car door.

"You haven't said what you will do. If the English discover the actual date, they will have gunboats in the harbor when the rebellion happens. Your brother will most likely die."

She closed her eyes. England was far more powerful than Ireland. They had more weapons, more men, and more experience in war. The element of surprise was the only advantage the Irish might have. But von Igel was demanding she deceive her one true friend, Louisa. She gazed down at her gloved hands.

"I'll let it slip somehow," she said, resigned. "Now, you need to go get your goon away from Mrs. O'Neil's house and away from my child. The New York City Police won't take kindly to a detective's widow being harassed by your people."

She got out and slammed the car door. As she hurried back to the place where Paula and Sean watched the parade, she wondered how von Igel had managed to shut down any human feeling. That could be a useful skill, she thought. Especially if one's feelings tended to be nothing but fear and anger.

While all of New York's Irish celebrated the parade, she felt the smothering darkness return. How would she convince Louisa that the rebellion was going to be on Father's Day? And what would happen to their friendship once Louisa knew the truth?

Chapter 27

Louisa

Louisa cringed as she read the article from 1902: the body of a 30-year-old man was found with his throat slit, his beaten body stuffed into a "pair of potato sacks." She wondered if the sacks had been placed at either end of the poor man's body or if the body had been cut into two pieces.

As she sat at a sturdy table in the New York City Library perusing articles, she came across more recent articles, detailing how the Mafia had been involved in various counterfeiting schemes, and the "boss" of the family was sentenced to 25 years in prison in 1910. The newspaper gleefully reported that this hardened criminal fainted when his sentence was pronounced. The most recent stories centered around the murder of a poultry dealer shortly before Thanksgiving Day of 1914.

"Someone was unhappy with their turkey?" Louisa asked aloud.

A patron at the next table shushed her.

Louisa whispered an apology and continued reading. No, it wasn't an unhappy customer who killed the man; the poultry industry was apparently rife with corruption, including "poultry trusts" to squelch competition, and the murdered man had been trying to create a monopoly of trade. One of the murderers had been caught and now, he had "broke," the newspapers said and was informing on the rest.

Although this was all fascinating, none of it pointed to the murders of Broadway investors, but at least she had an idea with whom she was dealing.

It was afternoon before she left the library. She couldn't resist stopping at the poultry market and looking around as if there might be a dead body stuffed into potato sacks. When she saw nothing suspicious, she bought a chicken. Surely Fannie Farmer would have an idea what to do with it.

As Louisa and Carlotta set the table for dinner, they discussed their progress.

"I spent the morning reading about the Italian Mafia," Louisa said. "They seem to be as violent as the Irish gangs."

"I had an interesting visit myself," Carlotta said.

Ellen came in, followed by Anna, who sat at her usual place at the head of the table. Anna shook out the napkin, placed it on her lap and asked, "What is the Mafia?"

"It's a club, Mother, for Italians," Louisa said.

"Some sort of fighting club? I understand that boxing is all the rage these days," she said.

"Will you be writing an article then on this salubrious topic?" Ellen asked.

"No, I'm trying to find out what's happening to Broadway investors. Someone took a shot at Forrest last night," Louisa said.

Ellen's head jerked up. "I didn't see anything in the morning papers."

"The story will be buried somewhere in the back, and his name will not be mentioned. If they write anything, it will be about a random shooting, in which a chauffeur was injured. That's all."

Anna put down her fork and said, "This is not a matter for discussion at the dinner table."

Louisa agreed.

"How was the parade?" she asked.

"I'm afraid that isn't a matter for the table either," Ellen said with a rueful glance at Carlotta.

Oh, dear, Louisa thought.

Carlotta volunteered to help Louisa with the dishes after dinner.

"What did you find out about the mobsters?" Louisa asked, rinsing soap from a china plate.

"Plenty. I got us a meeting with the head of the Morello family." Carlotta took the plate from her and dried it in quick circular motions.

"Is that the 107th Street Gang?" Louisa had read about them in her research and handed her another wet plate.

"The very same. Nicolo became boss a few years ago when his brother was sent to prison for counterfeiting."

"Oh, I read about that!" Louisa said.

"He's been trying to unite the families, but that's like asking cats to be nice to each other." Carlotta put the plates up in the cabinet.

"How did you get us a meeting?" She rinsed the silverware and stuck it in the drainer. "You can just leave these."

Carlotta leaned against the counter. "I went to the Venezia Restaurant on 116th Street around lunch time. Nicolo's sister, Salvatrice, eats there most days. Her husband, is in the federal pen in Atlanta, and she's lonely. I asked her if I could join her for lunch. With old women like that, all you have to do is ask about the old country or about what things were like when they were young, and they'll talk your ear off."

"How old is she?"

"Almost forty."

"That's not old," Louisa said.

"Old enough. Especially when your husband and your brother are in prison and scary fellas want to wipe out the rest of your family."

Louisa shook her head, unable to imagine such a violent life.

"Anyhow, I finally stated my business. I told her that my employer, a Miss Louisa Delafield, would like to meet with Mr. Morella, concerning a delicate matter. How would we go about arranging such a meeting?"

"Did she ask why?"

"Nope. The women in these families know it's better not to know. She said she'd handle it and gave me her phone number. I'm to call first thing in the morning."

"What are you two hatching?"

Louisa turned and saw Ellen standing in the doorway.

"Carlotta's trying to get me a meeting with a boss in the Mafia," Louisa said.

"Why?" Ellen asked, arms crossed.

"Well, the police aren't doing anything. They've completely dropped Mr. Halle's poisoning, and they say that Bernard Benson was a suicide."

"I see. And the magazine?"

Louisa felt a pang of guilt. Ellen had been so distressed lately, and she wasn't helping her at all. She turned the faucet on and filled a pan with suds. She would let it soak overnight. When she turned around, Ellen was gone.

She found her upstairs, nursing Hester in the big armchair that they had purchased for this purpose. Louisa sat on the bed and leaned against the post.

"You know how I get when I'm investigating something," Louisa said.

"I do. I just wish you were investigating stories for the magazine," Ellen answered.

"But, Ellen, Forrest is in danger."

Ellen sighed.

"I know. I'm worried, too. About Martin. He'll be going back to Ireland soon."

Dread knotted in Louisa's stomach. "Oh no. Will there be fighting?"

"I suppose there will be. He finally told me they plan to take over Dublin on Father's Day. Can you imagine? I s'pose that's their way of honoring their dead Irish fathers. But I'm afraid it will only make for more dead."

Louisa gripped the wooden post as she registered this information. Should she tell Reggie, she wondered. Would that be a betrayal of her friend's confidence? And did it matter when so many lives were at stake?

"Well, goodnight then," she said. "I need to get my beauty rest. I have a date with the Mafia tomorrow."

Chapter 28

Ellen

Carlotta pushed Hester back and forth in the baby nest, a contraption that Mr. Thorn had brought, while she sang an Italian lullaby.

"Our little Hester shouldn't be lying around all day," he'd said as he hooked a spring to the top of a tripod. A cloth "nest" with holes for the baby's legs hung at the bottom of the tripod. Ellen was skeptical, but the motion calmed little Hester. And it meant one didn't have to hold her all the time or worry about her falling off the sofa.

Louisa came into the room in a pinstripe suit, pulling on leather gloves.

"Good morning," she said, but there was nothing cheery about the way she said it.

"Off to consort with hoodlums, are you?" Ellen asked.

"I am. Shall I order an assassination for you?"

"I can think of a couple of Germans who would make for delicious fish food."

"What on Earth are you two going on about?" Thorn asked.

"Someone made an attempt on Mr. Calloway's life," Ellen said, "and Louisa is after finding out why."

Thorn was shocked.

"Someone attempted to kill Mr. Calloway?" he asked, shocked. "How?"

"Someone shot at him but missed. Hit the chauffeur instead," Ellen said.

Ellen turned to look at Carlotta as she stood up from the sofa.

"Don't worry. I won't let nothing happen to Miss Louisa," she said.

"You're going, too? But who will look after the baby?" Ellen said. "I've got pages to lay out, and a member of Suzie's committee came by with their editorial, which I need to type up."

"Sorry. Can't help out today."

Louisa and Carlotta gathered their things to leave.

After they left, Ellen looked at little Hester. Why did this child seem like such a burden? Why couldn't Ellen love her? And what if the dark thoughts with their deadly urges came back? She stroked the child's plump little leg. So helpless. So vulnerable.

"When might you get the stories from the Irish ladies?" Thorn asked. "And do have any idea the exact number?"

"I don't have an answer for you, Mr. Thorn," Ellen said.

Little Hester whimpered and then worked herself up into a full-on wail. Ellen took her out of the nest and held her.

"I s'pose you'll have to get on without me until I get her settled," Ellen said to Thorn.

"I'll manage. Perhaps Mrs. Delafield and I will work on getting more subscribers this morning. How does that sound, Anna?"

"I'd love to," she said.

Little Hester was finally napping when the telephone in the hallway startled Ellen with its insistent clang. She picked up the receiver quickly.

"Hello?"

"Did you tell her?" a voice with a heavy German accent asked.

"Yes."

"Good."

"Don't call here again," Ellen said. She hung up the phone and turned to see Anna looking at her curiously.

"Who was that?"

"Someone trying to sell something," Ellen said.

The phone rang again, and Ellen spun around to snatch up the receiver.

"I told you we're not interested," she said.

"Ellen? It's me. We've got your stories," Paula said. "Can you come get them?"

"Oh, Paula. I would, but there's no one to watch Hester right now."

Anna went back into the parlor.

"There's another reason I'd like you to come. Bring the baby with you."

"What's so important?"

"You'll find out when you get here."

That sounded suspicious. She wondered if Martin had gotten into trouble.

"All right. I'll figure out something."

She hung up and went into the parlor where Thorn and Anna gossiped about things that happened sometime in the last century.

"I don't suppose you two could watch the baby?" Ellen asked.

Thorn and Anna looked at each other and then back at her.

"There's a bottle of milk in the fridge." Ellen had purchased a new-fangled pump to extract milk from her breasts.

"Will we have to change her diaper?" Thorn asked.

"I won't be gone long. But it would be a kindness if you could change it if it needs changing."

"Oh, go on. The baby will survive us," Anna said and waved her off.

Chapter 29
Louisa

Louisa and Carlotta walked briskly south toward 116th Street and then turned east. A couple of inches of snow had fallen overnight and their boots made prints in the pristine white. It was late March, but winter seemed in no hurry to get out of town.

"It's not far," Carlotta said.

"Oh, I know that. Almost every Saturday I go to East Harlem."

Carlotta gave her a puzzled look. "You go to Italian Harlem every week? Why in God's name?"

"For the cannolis from Luigi's Bakery." Louisa smiled with pleasure.

"Cannoli? The pastry?"

"My guilty pleasure. I adore the crunch of the pastry and then the taste of that divine filling, so silky and soft on the tongue. Not to mention the chocolate drizzle on the outside."

Carlotta barked a laugh.

"You know the Italians over there also sell cocaine," she said.

"Who wants cocaine when you can get cannolis? Besides, any group of people who make food as delicious as the Italians can't be all bad. It's too bad you didn't pick up the skill."

"I picked up other skills."

Their bodies warmed as they strode down the street. As soon as they crossed Park Avenue the stores began to advertise Italian goods, street vendors called out in mellifluous Italian to housewives braving the cold to get supplies, and dark-haired children threw snowballs at each other.

"Nervous?" Carlotta asked.

"Not at all," Louisa said, her voice fading as they turned the corner on East 108th Street and found a ramshackle collection of structures made of sheets of iron, packing materials, and wreckage, all held together by advertising posters. All around this patchwork collection of "businesses," the walls of five-storey tenements advertised Gold Medal Flour and Fletcher's Castoria. It seemed the city was trying to swallow its past but some parts were simply too vile to go down.

She stopped and stared at the grim scene. For years she had read news stories of brutal murders committed in these neighborhoods. The only consolation was that their victims seemed to always be rival gang members or "stooges." Not a single victim had been a lady journalist. Of course, there was always a first time.

"Is *that* where we're going?" she asked.

"Yeah," Carlotta said. "We're s'posed to go to the stable next to the junk shop next to the theater. That looks like it."

"A stable?" Louisa asked. She had imagined they would meet at the restaurant. "Good heavens. Is this the 'murder stable'? The one in the newspaper article?" She quickly looked around for suspicious characters.

"The one and the same, but we won't be getting murdered here," Carlotta assured her. "It's just where they keep the stolen horses."

"Well, that's a relief."

Carlotta opened the door, and they stepped inside. To her left Louisa saw a collection of carts in various stages of repair.

"Stolen," Carlotta whispered. "They chop them up for parts."

Louisa's breath left her for a moment as she tried to hold onto her courage.

A scrawny stable boy glared at them as they passed the stalls, a pitchfork in his hand. Vapor steamed from the nostrils of the horses. The aroma of hay and horse flesh momentarily transported Louisa back to her youth, as she remembered the two big bays they had kept in a carriage house behind the mansion. She'd spent hours there, currying the horses or feeding them treats of apples and carrots. This stable was nothing like that.

"This way," Carlotta said.

Louisa observed that these horses were healthy, good-looking beasts that had fortunately been spared shipment to Europe for the war effort. Their rightful owners were probably frantic right now if they'd indeed been stolen. At the far end of the stable was a door, which Louisa assumed led to an office. Carlotta gave the "shave and a haircut" knock, and a blousy-looking woman with rouged cheeks opened the door. Staring at the buxom woman in her gaudy pink dress, Louisa lost her tongue.

"Coco, there's two dames out here," the woman said.

The terrifying gangster's nickname was *Coco*?

"Let them in," a silky voice said.

The woman stepped out of the way, and Louisa saw a handsome man about her own age with prominent ears, a bemused smile, and a square jaw. The one un-settling aspect was a pair of dark, sunken eyes.

"Pauline, go feed a horse or something."

The woman harrumphed and left, slamming the door on her way out. The room was warmed by a wood stove burning in the corner, and Louisa welcomed the relief from the cold.

"Mr. Morello, I'm Louisa Delafield and this is my helper, Carlotta. Carlotta spoke to your sister, I believe."

"Won't you have a seat, Miss Delafield?"

"Thank you."

She sat in a wobbly chair across from him. Carlotta had no choice but to stand as there was nowhere else to sit.

"How can I help you?"

"I'm here on behalf of a gentleman who believes there may have been a misunderstanding," she said. "You see, he's an investor in Broadway productions."

"Broadway? That's not exactly in my territory." He leaned back.

"He invested in a play, titled *Handsome Harry's Dilemma*, a play that he believes you may have an interest in?"

"Oh?" the man said. He seemed to have no inkling what she was talking about.

"He is concerned that the play's failure may have inconvenienced you somehow."

Mr. Morello's dark eyes shifted from her to Carlotta and back.

"I don't follow," he said.

"Well, there's a young woman named Cora, who was supposed to have the lead. Don't you have an interest in her career?"

"You mean Cora the Blonde? She's last week's news."

"I see." Louisa got the distinct feeling she was barking up the wrong tree.

"So you don't care whether or not the play gets made? I thought..."

"Look, one of the investors borrowed some money from me. He's a gambler and he was already in debt. But I'm not stupid, Miss Delafield. I had collateral. Sure, he went and shot himself. I'm still in the clear. Before his demise, he signed over the deed to his house. Nice place, I hear."

Louisa's stomach tightened, but she managed not to gasp audibly. If this were true, then Judith and her children would lose their home. She let his words sink in. He had the look of a man telling the truth, but mobsters were probably good liars. Then again, why would he lie?

"My friend is willing to pay for any losses you may have incurred," she said, treading carefully.

"Lady, while I'm always happy to take money from a chump, I don't intend to be in any man's debt. Tell him to keep his dough. Invest in another play."

If he wasn't interested in Forrest's money, perhaps the Italian gangster had nothing to do with Benson's "suicide," Halle's poisoning, or the attempt on Forrest's life. The room suddenly felt too small, and Louisa couldn't wait to get out of it and away from this man with his dark, deep-set eyes.

"I apologize for taking up your time," she said.

"I don't mind. You're a pretty lady. I always like to talk to a pretty lady. But I do have other business to attend to," he said.

Louisa hesitated and then said, "I have one other question if you don't mind."

"Shoot," he said with a sardonic grin.

"I was at a party and there was an Italian waiter, a man with broad shoulders and calloused hands. He had a high forehead, a smallish chin, and one of his ear lobes was missing. Could he possibly work for you?"

"You sure he was Italian?"

Louisa nodded.

"No idea," he said. Then he looked at Carlotta and said something to her in Italian.

Carlotta's face showed no expression.

Then he stood and Louisa stood as well.

"*Buona giornata*, Miss Delafield."

"Thank you," she said.

She had just opened the door when he said, "Make sure to stop at Luigi's Bakery. There's a box of cannoli with your name on it, compliments of a friend."

The breath staggered out of Louisa's lungs as she thanked him and hurried out, followed by Carlotta.

"What did he say to you?" she asked Carlotta.

"He said to ask my own people. He knows who I am." Carlotta visibly shuddered.

"How did he know about the cannoli?" Louisa wondered.

"They know everything that happens in their territory."

They walked toward the bakery.

"I don't think the mob is involved in these deaths," Louisa admitted.

"You may be right. The whole thing isn't their style. I asked Salvatrice if her brother went to the theater and she looked at me like I was crazy. 'Coco doesn't care about that kind of stuff. He runs card games and numbers rackets and a sporting house.' So I said I heard he was looking to get into some legitimate business, and she just laughed."

Well, if it's not the Sicilian mob, then who is it? Louisa wondered.

Chapter 30
Ellen

Ellen took a taxi to Paula's house in the lower eastside. When she entered, she found Paula sitting on the sofa in the parlor with another woman.

"Here ya go." Paula rose and handed her a stack of hand-written articles. "We don't none of us have a type-writer."

"I have one," Ellen said.

Paula motioned to the other woman, whom Ellen recognized from the convention. She had a round face with a sharp little chin and gray-streaked hair. Her plain chambray dress and boots looked new, and she wore a fashionable if modest hat.

"Ellen, I want you to meet Maeve. She's got something to talk to you about."

"Nice to meet you," Maeve said.

"Nice to meet you as well. How can I help you, Maeve?"

"There's a terrible misjustice going on."

"Anything in particular?" Ellen asked.

The woman leaned forward. "Indeed. If you go into any prison or jail for women, you know who you'll find? Irish girls. More of them than any other."

"Why do you think that is?"

"I don't think it's because they're born worse than any other girl," Maeve said. "Take my niece, Brigid, for example. She's pure feek as they come."

"Pretty, is she?"

"All golden hair and dimples. And she's a good girl, but her ma and da, they expect her to be meek and obedient all the time. They try to break the girl's spirit. When she finally rebelled and went off to have some fun with her friends, they had her arrested."

"Arrested? On what charge?"

"That of being stubborn," Maeve said. Her lips formed a thin, angry line.

"I didn't know that was a crime."

"It is if you're an Irish girl, apparently." The woman frowned in disgust.

Ellen pondered this information and then asked, "What do you want me to do about it?"

"I'm worried about Brigid. Why would they do that? Why would they kill her spirit like that? Is there anything you can do? What with all your money and your magazine and what not?"

Ellen's shoulders suddenly felt heavy as iron. She had a baby to feed, a magazine to publish, a friend who was off chasing the Mafia, Germans pestering her, and a brother who seemed bound and determined to get himself arrested or shot.

"I don't know," she said. "What can I even do?"

Paula gave her a puzzled look.

"What do you mean, Ellen? Didn't my own Paddy help you when you were after looking into one thing and another? And aren't you a mother yourself?"

Ellen looked down at the worn carpet on the floor. She thought of little Hester, who would grow up to be an Irish girl. Maybe she couldn't yet love the wee child, but she surely should do something for this Irish girl whose parents had no idea how to look after her.

"I suppose I can look into it. What's the girl's last name?"

"Rafferty."

"Do you know what jail she's in?"

Maeve shook her head.

"Well, has she been sentenced yet?"

"Not that I know of."

"Can you help, Ellen?" Paula asked.

Ellen shrugged. If only Paddy were alive, he would know what to do. Then again, Ellen knew a couple of police matrons. They might be able to help her at least locate the girl.

"I'll try," Ellen said, reached over and squeezed Maeve's hand.

Ellen called the Harlem Precinct and learned that Detective Mary Sullivan was expected to return to the station at 11 p.m. So she planted herself outside the precinct at 10:45 and waited.

"Detective Sullivan," she said when Mary approached the station at nearly midnight wearing a sequined evening gown. "I see you've been painting the town."

Mary recognized her, grinned, and said, "Look who it is! Ellen Malloy. Wait for me to get in some normal clothes, and we'll go have a pint."

Mary's work entailed going into nightclubs and gambling establishments and finding girls who had been procured for illicit purposes. Ellen had helped her a few times in this work in the past.

After Mary came out in her civilian clothes, the two of them strolled down to a pub a few blocks away. The bartender knew Mary and brought them each a pint of Guiness.

"It's good to see you, Ellen," Mary said. She was a broad-faced, good-looking woman with a ready smile and eyes as sharp as ice picks. "I heard about that business at the dock last summer. What were you doing, mixed up with the Germans?"

"I wasn't on their side, but that's about all I can say."

Mary took a long drink and wiped the foam from her lip. "Captain Tunney said you and that society writer helped expose their sabotaging of American ships. Dangerous stuff."

"'Twas indeed. But so far, the Germans don't know about my role. I need to keep it that way."

"I always thought you'd make a good police matron," Mary said.

Mary had told Ellen that same thing once before, but Ellen knew that as long as she was breaking the law simply for who she was, she would not be welcome among the police.

The bartender brought over a bowl of peanuts and Ellen popped a handful in her mouth before bringing up the subject of her concern. "Mary, is it true that the majority of girls getting knicked these days are Irish?"

Mary picked peanuts out of the bowl one at a time and nodded as she chewed.

"Unfortunately. Our girls are the willful ones."

"Well, I've heard tell of a girl going to jail for the crime of being stubborn. Doesn't sound fair to me." Ellen leaned back and looked over at the police woman.

"I'm not saying it is. The rules for women are always harsher."

"Then I'm here to ask you for a favor."

"Which is...?"

"Can you help me locate a girl named Brigid Rafferty? Her aunt says she's in the jail but that's all she knows."

Mary wrote the name down.

"I'll do what I can."

"And you'll telephone me with any information?"

"That I will. Now, tell me about this ladies' magazine, won't you?" Mary raised her half-empty glass. "Do you want another?"

"No, I'm nursing a baby. One is probably enough." Ellen was only halfway through her drink.

"A baby?"

"Long story," Ellen said. She held up the hand with the wedding band.

Mary raised an eyebrow. Ellen knew that Mary assumed she was an 'invert' — a person who preferred members of their own sex. And Mary did not approve, so there was no need to go into the details of how she happened to become a mother.

"Our goal in the magazine is to point out the injustices that women face today. As well as the progress we're making."

Mary shook her head and leaned forward.

"Did you know that our women officers don't get any sort of training? Only the men. Our police matrons, for we are never called 'policewomen,' are paid less than the patrol men, have no opportunities for promotion and get a very low pension compared to the men when they retire."

Ellen took a sip of her drink. "I'd never even thought about it," she admitted.

"Well, maybe you should."

Mary walked over to the bar and had the bartender refill her glass. She came back to the table and raised her glass. "Sláinte."

They clinked glasses, as Ellen realized there was no end to the stories she could publish about women and their fight for a place in the world.

A heated argument erupted at a table in the middle of the room. Her countrymen were going on about which side to support — those who wanted to work within the British government or those who wanted to destroy it. The voices grew louder, the curses more profane, and before she knew it a table overturned — a signal it was time to go home.

Chapter 31

Louisa

As Louisa strolled down the street, contemplating how she would tell Judith that not only had she not found her husband's murderer but that Judith was most likely going to lose her house, she passed a motion picture palace and noticed the marquee advertising a new Charlie Chaplin movie, called *The Pawnshop*. She was tempted to step in and see it. She could use a laugh, and the funny little man with the silly mustache and the twirling cane always provided a few. She was about to dig into her handbag for a coin when she remembered that the police had found several pawn tickets in Bernard Benson's desk.

She dismissed the idea of going into see a movie. It was time for another conversation with her old pal Billy

Stephens. She took the subway to 34th Street and came out at Herald Square. On her way to the news building, she took a moment to gaze at the bronze statue of Horace Greeley, seated with a bronze newspaper forever clutched in his hand.

She took the elevator to the newsroom, stepped out and was slapped with a wave of nostalgia. Conversations hummed, men guffawed, typewriters clacked, and someone bellowed, "Copy boy!" She inhaled deeply. It smelled of wool and smoke with the occasional thread of after shave. It smelled like heaven. She sometimes forgot how much she missed it. Working out of her house just wasn't the same.

She found Billy at a desk on the far side of the room, engrossed in typing a story. His eyes widened in surprise when he saw her.

"Delafield! What are you doing here? Did Malloy's magazine go bust already?"

"No, it's floating along quite nicely. No danger of going bust." She pulled over an empty chair and sat by his desk.

He leaned forward. "Must be awkward being on the payroll of your former assistant."

"Not at all," she lied. Ellen not only paid her a salary as the chief writer for *The Ladies' Lantern*. She also paid the utilities bills and bought all the food for the household. The fact that Ellen had become an heiress and Louisa's blueblood family had nothing but a shabby townhouse in Harlem was one of life's ironies.

"Billy," she said. "Do you know the name of the pawnshop that Bernard Benson used?"

He opened his desk drawer, which was crammed with narrow reporters' notebooks. He took one out, flipped through it. He flipped through another and another and finally said, "Got it. It's on Third Avenue between a curiosity shop and the Fat Men's Store. That's according to the police. I didn't go there myself."

"Not even to purchase a suit from the Fat Men's store?"

"Hey, now. I may have put on a few pounds but I'm not a customer there. Yet."

"Billy, do you still believe there's something suspicious about Benson's death?"

Billy shrugged. "Look, I know he got a loan from the mob. He might have shot himself once he realized he couldn't pay it back. Or he might have had help. It's the Halle murder that made me suspicious."

"Well, I found out that Benson had signed over the deed to his house to a mobster."

"Oh, boy. I guess he'd rather do himself in than tell his wife she'd be living on the streets. So maybe he did do the deed of his own accord, but that doesn't explain why Halle also died under suspicious circumstances."

"Or why someone shot Forrest Calloway's chauffeur in front of his Gramercy Park house a few days ago," Louisa said.

He leaned forward. "I didn't hear about that."

"Forrest squelched the story. He still has friends in the newspaper business."

"Why?"

"He's getting married. He doesn't want any scandal. And since it was a servant who got shot, the police are willing to look the other way."

They were silent for a moment. Then Billy asked, "How are you? I mean with him getting married and all."

Louisa smiled wryly and said, "I'm over the moon for them."

"I bet you are," Billy said. He squeezed her hand. "You're a good kid, Delafield. Too good for the likes of him."

She was grateful for the sentiment, but she knew it wasn't true. She was neither too good for Forrest Calloway, nor was she a kid.

She found the pawnshop next to the Fat Men's Store and went inside. On the walls hung coats and hats. *How desperate did one have to be to pawn his coat?* In glass cases, jewels and pocket watches gleamed. A separate case held guns and ammunition.

A gargantuan man in a fez stood behind the counter.

"Can I help you find something?"

"I'm looking for a clock," she said.

"Over on that wall." He pointed across the room.

Louisa perused the clocks and then she saw it. A Gustav Becker.

"Can you tell me about this clock? Who was the owner?"

"Some guy with a lotta debt," he said with a shrug.

Louisa stared at the clock and knew she'd be making a visit to her friend.

Chapter 32
Ellen

Ellen took the trolley down Franklin Street. She looked up at the Bridge of Sighs between the Tombs and the rust-colored courthouse. She'd crossed that bridge herself two years ago, when her employer had falsely accused her of theft. Now, that was an article she should have in the magazine, the abuse of domestic servants by the self-designated lords and ladies of society. She stepped off the trolley and looked with dread at the triangle-shaped building. At least she knew what to expect.

Mary stood outside the building, wearing a plain dark suit and a boxy hat.

"There she is," Mary said when Ellen approached. "Did you get your press credentials?"

"I did," Ellen said, "but will they let a reporter interview an ordinary girl?"

"Nope," Mary said. "But you'll never guess who's in the cell across from Brigid."

"Who?"

"Your old friend, the anarchist, Emma Goldman. I got you an appointment with her."

Ellen followed Mary into the building and through heavy barred doors into the prison proper. Ellen couldn't believe her luck. Emma Goldman had received a sentence of 15 days for the crime of trying to help women limit the size of their families.

Mary handed Ellen over to one of the matrons and whispered something to the matron, who merely nodded before walking her up the metal steps, flight after flight, then down a long corridor. The noise of the place was truly deafening as every assorted waif and criminal was housed in the cells for 22 hours a day. And the smell! Awful. Like a sewer.

"Here she is," the matron said when they got to a cell at the end of the dark corridor.

Ellen looked in and saw Emma Goldman sitting on a cot. Nowhere else to sit. Ellen wasn't allowed inside the cell. Like all the other visitors that day, she had to stand at the door, a crosshatch of metal bars.

"Miss Goldman?" Ellen said. "It's Ellen Malloy. Do you remember me?"

The older woman looked up, her eyes full of keen intelligence behind a pair of spectacles.

"Ellen! Of course, I remember you. You were Lulu's special friend, weren't you?"

"I was."

"Then that terrible accident in her apartment. We never saw you after that. They never should have been building a bomb. I told them over and over that violence doesn't work. But they all believed in the propaganda of the deed." Emma stood up and slowly approached the door as if her bones ached. Her gray hair was twisted in a bun at the back of her head.

"You believed in it, too, at one time," Ellen said.

"I did, and then Sasha, the love of my life, spent fourteen years in prison for attempting to murder one of the robber barons."

Ellen had met Sasha along with the other anarchists in Emma's circle. They all meant well but they were not particularly competent in their efforts.

"I've come into some money and started a magazine of my own," Ellen said. "It's called *The Ladies' Lantern.* A magazine for thinking women."

"All women think, Ellen, They just don't always think the right way," she said.

"We've only had the one issue so far. I'm working on the second issue now. And that's why I'm here. I'd like to include an article from you. About your situation here, and what we need to do so that women can get the information they need to stop having so many children."

"When do you need it by?"

"We're going to press in just a few days."

"Then I'll have to dictate it to you as I'm not allowed any writing or reading material. You do know I'm the 'most dangerous woman in the world,' don't you?"

"I've heard it said."

Emma cleared her throat and began to dictate. "When a law has outgrown time and necessity, it must go and the only way to get rid of the law, is to awaken the public to the fact that it has outlived its purposes and that is precisely what I have been doing and mean to do in the future."

When Ellen had enough material for her article, she cleared her throat and leaned forward.

"Emma, I'm also looking for an Irish girl. I've learned she's in this jail and her cell is near yours."

"An Irish girl? The pen is full of them. What's her name?"

"Brigid Rafferty."

"There's a Brigid in that cell over there," Emma said and pointed across the hall. Trust Emma Goldman to know the name and story of every woman or girl in the place. She may have been an anarchist but she had a heart as big and warm as a meadow in summer.

"Thank you, Emma."

"Don't thank me yet," Emma said. "I need a favor from you."

"Anything that's within my power. You know that."

"Take that letter you just wrote to the office of Mother Earth so they can print it," she said and waggled a finger at Ellen's notebook.

"But I was going to print it in my magazine," Ellen objected.

Emma gazed at her and blinked several times. "But your magazine will take too long to come to print and you don't have enough readers. Yet. Mother Earth has readers all over the country."

"All right."

"Make sure you give it to Lulu."

Ellen felt she'd been tricked but she hadn't been exactly forthright either.

The matron was dozing off in a chair at the end of the hall. She crossed to the cell that Emma had indicated. Inside, she saw three women. One of them was a streetwalker, her breasts bulging from her bodice. Another lay on the floor, snoring. The third was a young woman — or rather a girl — with blond hair, wearing a prison dress much too big for her.

"Are you Brigid Rafferty?"

She looked up, startled and said, "That's me."

"Hello, Brigid. Your aunt Maeve asked me to see if there's some way I can help you. Is it true your parents sent you here for stubbornness?"

"Ay, they did." The girl got up from the floor where she'd been sitting and came over to the barred door. She was a petite thing, and under the jail grime, quite pretty. "Who are you?"

"I'm Ellen Malloy, a friend of your aunt's. What happened? Why can't you get along with your family?" Ellen asked.

"What do you think? Da drinks too much, and Ma keeps having babies. There's eight of us now all living in that filthy place. This isn't even my first time in jail. They sent me to the House of Refuge two years ago for going to the fair after they said I couldn't go."

"Why did you disobey your parents like that?" she asked.

"They never let me go anywhere. I'm always in charge of taking care of the little uns. But my brother can go out and do whatever he pleases. They wouldn't even let me go to school."

Ellen shook her head. It wasn't just a man's world. It was a boy's world, too. A rat scurrying by her foot.

"When do you go to court?"

"I'm going to Night Court on Thursday. I'm scared. They told me I could go to prison for an 'indeterminate' sentence. I don't even know what that means."

"Means they can keep you as long as they like," one of the other girls in the cell interjected.

"Unless someone takes me on as a servant," Brigid said in a confiding voice.

"A servant?"

"Indentured is what they call it. For three years. I don't think I'd mind that so much. They don't pay you but you get a place to sleep and food."

Ellen rubbed her forehead. Was there nothing the rich wouldn't stoop to in order to get free labor from someone else's hands?

"When do you go to court?" she asked again.

"Next week. Thursday night."

"Then I'll be there."

"Ho, you there!" the matron yelled from the end of the hall. "Time's up."

Ellen emerged from that dark hell into the clean light of day and took a deep breath of air. It was April and the trees were budding with new life. How could the world be so vile and so sublime at the same time?

At least this girl's problems had made her temporarily forget her own problems. She wondered if Louisa had spoken to Reggie Grant yet about the date of the coming uprising. The lie still sat in her belly like rotten food—hard and indigestible.

Chapter 33
Louisa

"Judith, you lied to me," Louisa said. "Your husband *was* depressed. And he did pawn those items, didn't he? Did you purchase another clock just to fool me?"

Tears leaked along Judith's pale cheeks.

"There's a suicide clause in the insurance," she whimpered. "I just thought if we could cast some doubt."

"You mean, someone might have gone to prison or even been executed for a crime they didn't commit."

"No! I wouldn't let that happen."

Louisa didn't approve of Judith's scheme, but she understood the desperation behind it. She had children to support, and no means to do it.

"Your husband signed over the deed to the house to an Italian mobster. What will you do now?"

Judith twisted her intertwined fingers nervously.

"I'll have to leave New York. I have family in South Carolina. I'll take a teaching job. At least I have some college."

"You might marry again," Louisa suggested.

"Who's going to marry the widow of a man who committed suicide, a woman with two young children?"

Louisa thought of Forrest, his upcoming marriage to a widow with two children.

"You'd be surprised."

Louisa had no doubt that with her beauty and vivacity, Judith would land on her feet like a pretty Persian cat onto a parquet floor.

That answered the question of the Woolworth suicide, but who had killed Mr. Halle, Louisa wondered as she took the subway home. She thought back to her first conversation with Billy. He had said that a mob boss was angry because Cora de Capezio had lost her chance at Broadway stardom. And according to Carlotta, there were at least two Italian mob bosses in New York — the Sicilians in East Harlem and the Neapolitans in Brooklyn. It was possible that Bernard Benson had killed himself over a debt to the Sicilians, and also possible that another Mafia boss was angered over the cancellation of the play.

The one person who could answer that question was "Cora the Blonde" as Nicolo had called her. He had said she was "yesterday's news." Did that mean he had been involved with her at one time?

Louisa sat in a coffee shop and perused the Vaudeville ads in the local entertainment paper. Finally, she found a small ad for a burlesque show on Staten Island that featured Miss Cora de Capezio — a far cry from Broadway. Ticket prices ranged from 15 to 75 cents. And showtime was 8 p.m. She'd have to make dinner early.

Instead of making dinner, she purchased a pound of roast beef from a delicatessen and left it along with left over salad on the table.

"This is dinner?" Anna asked.

"For tonight. I'm going out," Louisa said.

"Another Broadway show?" Ellen asked.

"Vaudeville actually," Louisa said.

"Oh, heavens," Anna muttered.

Louisa took the ferry to Staten Island and then a taxi to the Palace Theater. She had no intention of actually going into the theater where men would be gathered, drunkenly hooting at glimpses of female flesh. Instead she knocked on the stage door, and a lug of a man answered, looked her up and down and said, "You're a right school marm, aren't you?"

Louisa had never been described as a school marm, but she had dressed in plain dark clothes to avoid garnering unwanted attention, and she wore no rouge or lipstick and certainly no eye makeup.

"I'm here to see Miss de Capezio."

The man stepped aside.

"End of the hall," he said and pointed.

The hall was narrow and stained with the smoke of gas lamps. A woman with an enormous sequined bosom brushed past her, their bodies rubbing against each other despite the fact that Louisa had constricted herself to the diameter of a broomstick.

At the end of the hall, she knocked on a door, its paint peeling. Nothing.

"Miss de Capezio?" she called.

"Just go on in," a wiry little man said in passing.

Louisa decided timidity would get her nowhere, so she opened the door and went inside a cluttered room that smelled of floral perfume mixed with sweat. And lying on the floor was the body of a woman with her throat slit, a puddle of blood spooling from her neck like a red scarf in the wind.

She went to the door and called out for help and then everything — the cheap smell of perfume, the racks of sequined outfits, the dead body — faded away.

When she came to, the room was filled with people murmuring. The wiry little man waved smelling salts under her nose and the big man who'd greeted her at the stage door was ordering everyone else away from the room.

"Get out, now! All of youse!" he yelled.

The wiry man helped Louisa up. But she was still woozy. She sank down on the pink cushioned seat in front of the vanity and willed her stomach to settle. She didn't want to, but she forced her eyes to gaze upon Cora de Capezio. The dead woman wore a gold sparkling gown with a slit to show her long shapely legs. Even in death, she was a stunning creature, slender and elegant as a flame.

Louisa turned away and noticed at the edge of her fingertips — a necklace. At first she assumed it was paste, but on second glance, her breath caught in her chest. This was no piece of costume jewelry. She recognized it as a Cartier design and those stones were no rhinestones. They were rubies and diamonds. Someone had given Cora an incredibly expensive gift, something no mere showgirl could afford on her own. Before she even realized what she was doing, she reached for the necklace and slipped it into her bag.

"Come on," the wiry man said. "I'm the manager. Let's get you to my office while we wait for the fuzz."

She sat in a dingy office with posters of half-naked women on the walls.

"What was you doing in Cora's dressing room?" he asked.

"I came to ask her about something," Louisa said.

"About what?"

"About a murder, if you must know," she said.

There was a knock on the door and the big man stuck his head in. "Cops are here, boss."

"All right. Don't go nowhere," the manager said and left her in the room.

Louisa squeezed her hands to keep them trembling. That poor woman, she thought. She closed her eyes, but couldn't get rid of the sight. She thought of the necklace in her purse. She should turn it over to the police. And yet, she didn't trust them. Would the necklace simply disappear? Would they claim it was fake? What if the police were under the thumb of the mob?

After about 20 minutes, the door opened. She thought it would be the police, but instead Billy Stephens entered the room.

"What are you doing here?" she asked.

"I was curious about the dame who instigated a murder so I came to see her show," Billy said. "Then I saw the cops and asked them what had happened. What are *you* doing here?"

"I was also curious about the dame who instigated a murder," she said.

Billy sat beside her and crossed his foot over his knee. "Louisa, the detective's gonna want to ask you some questions since you found the body."

"What will I say?"

"The truth, I guess." He gave her hand a reassuring squeeze.

A lanky detective from Staten Island came in to talk to her, and Louisa explained about the deaths of the two Broadway investors and the attempted murder of a third. Billy told him about the rumor that Cora, who was supposed to star in a canceled Broadway show, was a girlfriend of a mob boss.

"Did you see anybody suspicious?" he asked Louisa, a cigarette wedged between razor-thin lips.

"No."

"Ain't that funny? No one else did either," the detective said. "Seems there was a steady stream of admirers coming in and out of the dressing room before you got there. But no one remembers anybody unusual."

"Could there have been an Italian man? Tall and rather handsome?" Louisa asked.

"Nobody saw or if they did, they're not saying. Lady, leave the investigating to the cops next time, would you?" he said and blew a column of smoke over her head.

"I make no promises," she said.

"Suit yourself," he said and left the room.

Billy offered to make sure she got home safely. They took the ferry back to Manhattan and Billy apologized for getting her involved in this mess.

"No, you were right to tell me," Louisa said. "Someone did try to kill Forrest, and I plan to find out who."

"Fine, kiddo, but don't let anything happen to yourself in the meanwhile," he said and squeezed her arm. "That wouldn't make me too happy."

He leaned against the rail of the ferry, his fedora pulled over his brow.

"Thanks, Billy. I'm glad you were there tonight." She pulled her coat tight against the chill.

His Model T was parked at the dock, and he drove her home. The house was dark. Everyone was asleep. She took off her boots downstairs and carried them upstairs with her. Placing them by her door, she quietly crossed the hall and opened the door to the room Carlotta and Ellen shared. She peeked inside. Carlotta's bed was empty. She stealthily made her way over to Ellen's bed, which had once been Suzie's, and saw both women asleep with the baby between them.

She gently tapped Carlotta on the shoulder. Carlotta shrugged her off, so Louisa gripped Carlotta's arm and whispered, "Carlotta."

Carlotta's eyes opened. She stared at Louisa in confusion. Then she looked down at the sleeping baby.

"Come," Louisa whispered.

Carlotta carefully removed the covers and slipped out of the bed. She wore only a chemise and a pair of bloomers. Louisa looked around and took a robe off a hook and handed it to her.

"What happened?" Carlotta asked once they were in Louisa's room. "Why'd you wake me?"

"Cora the blonde was murdered," Louisa said.

"What? How do you know?" Carlotta sank onto Louisa's bed and rubbed her eyes.

"I found her body. Her throat was slit..."

Carlotta's eyes opened wide. "This is bad."

"Yes," Louisa agreed. "The murder could have been ordered by the Mafia. I read a news story earlier about how they slit a man's throat. Did you find out anything?"

Carlotta shook her head.

"No, I asked my mother if anyone in our family knew Cora. She said, no. She doesn't even think Cora is Italian."

Louisa sighed. She looked down at her hands. They were trembling again.

"What about the waiter? I think if we can find him, we might get some questions answered."

"Men like that don't talk," Carlotta said.

"They will if they're facing the electric chair," Louisa said.

The next day Ellen asked Louisa about the articles from the Heterodoxy women.

"They have a meeting today," Louisa said. "I'll go get any articles they have ready. It might get my mind off what happened last night."

"What happened last night?" Ellen asked.

Louisa didn't want to think about it, but it was futile to try to keep it from Ellen.

"I found a body. A murdered woman. I think it may have something to do with the attempt on Forrest's life."

"And I thought my life was getting queer."

"How so?"

"Aside from getting pestered by Germans wanting me to feed false information to Mr. Grant and trying to get an Irish girl out of jail and worrying about my brother and his cronies, everything is dandy."

"Then let's make sure we put out another issue of the magazine," Louisa said.

Louisa went back to Polly's restaurant. To her relief, three of the women who had promised articles had already written them, and another two said they could finish theirs by the end of the week. Mabel Dodge surprised her by turning in a profile of Gertrude Stein.

"Mabel, may I ask you a question?" Louisa said. "It's about the salon I attended at your place, the one in which poor Mr. Halle died of poisoning. Whom did you hire to cater that night? Do you remember?"

"Certainly. There's an oyster bar on Wall Street with a couple of colored cooks who do catering on the side. Colored people make the best cooks. I use them whenever possible."

Louisa didn't know about that, but she could vouch for at least one Negro's talent in the kitchen — Suzie's.

Louisa found the restaurant and asked if she could go in the kitchen to speak to the cook. The manager pointed his thumb to a door at the back of the restaurant.

A woman in her fifties and another in her thirties — they looked to be mother and daughter — shucked oysters on a metal table. Louisa introduced herself and explained her purpose for coming. They kept shucking, sliding their small knives between the lips of the shells and twisting the knives to pop them open and reveal the delicious gray blobs.

"Go ahead. Ask your questions," the older one said.

"Do you remember an event you catered for Mrs. Dodge's salon on Fifth Avenue."

"How could I forget? That man died of poisoning and they wanted to blame me. Good thing no one else got sick or I'd be in prison now."

"Do you remember if you hired any Italian waiters?"

"No, ma'am, only Irish boys and Negros."

"Do you know why there was an Italian waiter there?"

"I do not. But I reckon he was there to poison that man."

"I reckon you're right," Louisa said.

She thanked the woman for her time and left.

This was beginning to seem like a Herculean task. Three people were dead and all three were connected to the same play that Forrest had invested in. But none of the pieces fit.

Louisa sat in Captain Tom Tunney's office. A picture of Teddy Roosevelt hung on the wall from his days as Police Commissioner. The smell of a recently eaten ham sandwich hung in the air.

"I'm here to confess to a crime." Louisa clasped her hands and gazed at Captain Tunney. He was the one member of the police force, in whom she had utter faith.

"Are ya now?" he asked and stroked his walrus mustache.

"You see, I found a piece of evidence at a murder scene and rather than turn it over to the Staten Island detective, I secreted it in my purse. It's quite an expensive piece of evidence."

"And is it in your possession as we speak?"

"It is." She pulled the necklace from her purse and poured it into a pool of glimmering light onto the desk in front of him.

"Great cats!" he whispered and held the strand of jewels in the light streaming in from the window. "Perhaps you should start at the beginning, Miss Delafield."

So she reiterated the whole story, beginning with Halle's poisoning and moving on to Benson's supposed suicide.

"I actually believed that Sicilian gangster when he said Cora was 'old news,' but now that I've seen this necklace, I think we can prove he was still enamored with her."

"Why would he have her killed?"

"We'll have to ask him," she said. "If you'll allow me to keep possession of it for just a while longer, I believe I know where this piece was designed. I should like to confirm the identity of the purchaser."

Captain Tunney leaned back in his chair and examined the necklace before handing it back to her.

"I'll have one of my men follow you. Once you've discovered the purchaser, you can give it to him, and he'll bring it to me where I can keep it safe. Of course, I can't let Mrs. Tunney know about it, or it'll never get to trial." He laughed, and Louisa smiled politely. It wasn't a particularly funny joke.

Louisa headed straight to the horse's mouth, Cartier's Rue de la Paix in the 700 block of Fifth Avenue. Just last year Pierre Cartier and his wife Elma had returned from Europe, where Pierre had driven a colonel around France during the war. Louisa had written extensively and effusively about the Cartiers' efforts in the war back when she was writing society news for *The*

Ledger, and Elma had sent her a lovely thank you note upon their return. She could use that as leverage to get into see him if necessary.

A clerk took her up to his office.

"Mademoiselle Delafield," he said. "What brings you into see me? I know my dear wife would love to have you over for dinner. She has not forgotten your kind words about our work in France."

"Thank you. I will happily accept her invitation. I'm actually here to see you...," she stopped and stared at what looked to be blueprints on his desk. "What is this?"

"This shop is no longer big enough," he said, a smile plastered on his gaunt face. "I have purchased two magnificent townhomes in the next block and these plans show the conversion."

"You must be excited."

"*Vraiment*! Now the Cartier New York store will be the most recognizable jeweler in the world." He positively beamed in delight.

Louisa was glad she'd found him in such a good mood.

"Speaking of jewelry. I have a necklace I want to ask you about," she said.

She pulled the necklace from her purse and handed it to him.

"Ah! How did this come into your possession?" he asked.

"I'm afraid it's part of a murder investigation. A young woman is dead. I need to know who gave this to her."

"I do recognize the piece, but let me look in my records to be sure," he said. "Please wait here."

He left her alone with the architectural drawings. She knew the building. She'd been to several soirées there before the lady of the house died. The old money must be livid that the area was turning into a commercial center.

He returned with a somber expression. She waited for him to reveal the identity of the mobster who had purchased the necklace.

"A Mr. Mark Halle bought it. I remember the sale. He said it was for his wife. Is it his wife who was murdered?"

The blood drained from Louisa's face.

"Mark Halle? The ... Broadway investor?"

"Yes," Mr. Cartier said. Then he gasped. "Mon Dieu, he died of poisoning, didn't he? I read about it in the paper. I'd forgotten he was a customer."

"He did indeed."

Louisa assessed what this new information could mean. Mark Halle had been involved with Cora de Capezio. If she were also involved with one of the gangsters, that could provide another motive for his death.

Ellen found Tunney's man waiting for her on the sidewalk. She handed over the necklace and took the Ninth Avenue El back to Harlem, staring out the window at the buildings rushing past. New ones popped up every day. The seat beside her sank down, and she turned to find Carlotta next to her, eyes ablaze with excitement.

"I found out something interesting," Carlotta said.

Chapter 34
Ellen

"I don't know how long I'll be gone," Ellen said as she stood in the foyer. Louisa and Carlotta watched her from where they stood in the doorway to the parlor.

"From what I understand some of the younger members of society like to go to Women's Night Court for entertainment," Louisa said.

"Slumming, are they?" Ellen asked, not bothering to hide her disgust.

"You'll wanna take a taxi home," Carlotta said. "Else the hoodlums'll be slooping after you with their knives in their teeth."

"You have such a colorful way of expressing yourself, Carlotta, dear," Louisa said.

"I'll take a taxi, not to worry."

"Ellen," Louisa said as Ellen reached for the door. "There's a woman attorney who's been working the Night Court for years. I met her at one of the Heterodoxy meetings. She may be helpful. She's upset about the way the women are treated in the Night Court. Her name is Miss Moskowitz."

"Thank you," Ellen said and stepped out into the night.

The Jefferson Market Courthouse looked even more Gothic and imposing at night than it did in the day. And Louisa had been right. Outside, a group of society's finest, dressed in sequins and plumes, having most likely left some club, laughed and flirted as they waited for admittance.

Ellen found Maeve outside and they went inside to find a seat.

When all were seated in the cavernous room, a man she assumed was the district attorney rose and said in a loud voice so all could hear: "This is not a court for fines and punishments. We are here to give moral support to the people who are brought in and a moral lesson for the public."

The seats were indeed tiered to provide spectators a perfect view of the parade of women "miscreants." A prim woman sat in front of Ellen in a high-necked black dress with two girls on either side of her. The girls looked to be about 13 or 14. Ellen couldn't imagine why the woman had brought them to such a scene, until she heard her say to them in a voice, dripping with smugness, "See, girls. If you don't behave yourselves like proper young ladies, you will wind up like them." *Moral lesson, indeed.*

The first woman to come before the judge was charged with "common lewdness." She stood before him in a cheap satin dress and complained, "I've not three cents to my name, sir. This man, this so-called detective, has been pursuing me, offering me fine meals and a warm place to stay. What is a woman in my position to do? It was him that came after me."

The judge looked down at her and sneered, "How can I accept the word of a painted and obviously vicious strumpet against the word of police detective?"

Ellen's scoffed audibly. These women didn't stand a chance, she thought. More women came forward. Their crimes included public drunkenness, prostitution, vagrancy, and disorderly conduct. One woman had been arrested for wearing pants.

She noticed then a stirring over on the side of the room where the wealthy slummers had gathered. A man had come in. Even from across the room she could see his bright blue eyes. She shrank into herself so he wouldn't see her. What was Hugh Garrett, doing here, she wondered, dressed in his navy suit and silk cravat.

She'd never forget his behavior from her time as Hattie's maid. He had destroyed a girl in his selfish quest for pleasure.

Two more defendants came before the judge. They were represented by a small, well-dressed woman, whose cogent points didn't have much sway with the judge. *That must be Miss Moskowitz,* Ellen thought.

Finally, Brigid's turn came. Unlike the others with their sallow complexions, she fairly gleamed in the electric light with her blond hair and her milky skin. She'd been cleaned up for her appearance. Hugh Garrett straightened and stared at her intently. For Ellen, it was like watching a wolf's ear prick up when he's picked up the scent of his prey.

"Your honor," the district attorney said. "We ask that you not sentence Brigid Rafferty to prison at this time but rather to a period of three years indentured servitude. As she is young, it is believed that in the proper environment she will learn the feminine arts and will someday make a proper wife or nursemaid."

You vile creature, Ellen thought, watching her former employer. He would be doing to this girl exactly what he did to Ellen's friend.

"Miss Moskowitz, does your client agree to this arrangement?" the judge asked.

"She does," the attorney answered. "We certainly don't want her in prison for the crime of being stubborn."

As soon as the judge agreed to the deal, Hugh Garrett slipped out of the room. He had gotten what he came for. Ellen had also seen enough.

"That's good, isn't it? Better than prison," Maeve said.

"I wouldn't be so sure about that," Ellen told her.

She found Miss Moskowitz, a petite woman with lines across her forehead and bright alert eyes, outside the courtroom.

"Miss Moskowitz, my name is Ellen Malloy. I publish a magazine for women, and Louisa Delafield, one of our writers, mentioned your name to me. I wonder if I might have a few minutes of your time."

Miss Moskowitz touched Ellen's arm in a reassuring gesture.

"I have one more client to represent and then I'll be right with you."

After Ellen promised to find out what she could, Maeve left.

While Ellen waited in the hallway, she wondered what to do about Hugh Garrett, one of the wealthiest and most powerful men in the city. The police couldn't touch him. Louisa had believed that marriage would cure him of his profligate ways. She was wrong, and Ellen was not surprised.

After a quarter of an hour had passed, Miss Moskowitz came out of the courtroom.

"Thank you for waiting." She exuded kindness and intelligence. Ellen wondered how she kept from losing heart in such an unfair system. "Let's go to my office."

Her "office" was a converted broom closet with two chairs and a wobbly table.

"I came here to see about Brigid Rafferty," Ellen said.

"What's your interest in Brigid?" the attorney asked.

"Well, for one thing, putting her as an indentured servant in the house of Hugh Garrett is doing her no favors. He's an incorrigible womanizer."

"But, Miss Malloy, if I hadn't agreed to the arrangement she could have gotten an indeterminate sentence on Blackwell's Island. This is much better. At least this sentence has an end date."

Ellen leaned forward.

"Hugh Garrett is no friend to poor women. Three years ago I was a servant in his house, and I saw his shenanigans first hand. He seduced a young woman, a servant, and she died of an abortion as a result."

Miss Moskowitz frowned and rubbed her cheek.

"Oh my. I'm afraid it's too late. She'll be released to him tomorrow afternoon."

Ellen sighed, wondering how she could possibly get Brigid out of his clutches. "Thank you for speaking to me."

"I'm sorry. I had no idea..." Miss Moskowitz said.

Ellen stood up to leave. Then she turned and asked, "I don't suppose you'd be interested in writing an article about your work here for my magazine, *The Ladies' Lantern*?"

Miss Moskowitz sat up straight. "An article for a magazine? Yes, I would be happy to do that."

"You know when I first decided to publish my magazine, I wondered if there would be enough material to fill the pages. It turns out there's more injustice and oppression than even I could have imagined."

Miss Moskowitz nodded sadly.

Chapter 35

Louisa

After Ellen left for the Night Court, Louisa and Carlotta conferred in the parlor.

"I went to St. Michael the Archangel Church and waited for my mama," Carlotta said in an excited voice. "She cuts the church flowers and arranges them. I asked her, 'Mama, you know of a man with a big forehead, a small chin and might be missing part of his ear?' She couldn't think of anyone right away. But she asks some of the other ladies and one of them says sounds like Mrs. Costello's husband. Lost his lobe to a rat when he was a kid."

Louisa sucked in a breath.

Carlotta continued. "So, I asked where I might find Mrs. Costello, and that lady says she does sewing for a tailor in Bensonhurst. Then I go over to Bensonhurst and I find the tailor. He gives me the address of Mrs. Costello."

"Did you speak to her?" Louisa asked.

"She didn't want to talk to me at first. Said she was busy. Said she hadn't seen her husband and what did I want with him anyway. I got the feeling that maybe Mr. Costello had a reputation with the ladies. I told her I never met him, but that someone wanted to hire him to be a waiter. She look at me like I'm crazy. 'A waiter? He's a gardener for some rich family in Washington Heights. He stays up there.' I could tell she wasn't happy about that. I asked the name of the family, but she wouldn't tell me nothing after that. That's all I know."

Louisa sat back. If the "waiter" were actually a gardener that would explain the calloused hands.

"Let me just look at something," she said. She went into the hallway where she left her purse on the credenza by the door. She opened it and took a slip of paper back into the parlor. "Carlotta, Mark Halle's address is in Washington Heights. Could Mr. Costello possibly be the Halle's gardener?"

"Wouldn't Mr. Halle know him?" Carlotta asked.

"The only thing to do is go up there and see for myself." Louisa folded the receipt for Cora's necklace.

"Need company?" Carlotta asked.

"Not this time."

Louisa rode the train as far north as it would go and then took a taxi to the address of the Halle estate. Louisa was astonished at how close this woodsy area was to the skyscrapers and cranes of the city and yet it seemed a world away. The huge white Federalist-style mansion, situated on a bluff overlooking the Harlem River, was spectacular.

She strode down the long driveway toward the house with its four pillars reaching to the top of the second storey. Along the way, bright yellow daffodils nodded, heralding the coming spring and evidence of a gardener in residence. Next to the house a greenhouse stood.

Louisa had decided against calling first so she might have the element of surprise. She knocked on the door, and a butler opened it, his ruddy face a mask of indifference.

"Hello," she said. "Miss Louisa Delafield to see Mrs. Halle, please." She handed him a calling card.

"I'm sorry, Miss, but Mrs. Halle has left for her home at the shore."

She felt a stab of disappointment.

"Would you like me to have the chauffeur take you to the train station, Miss? I'm sorry you came all the way up here for nothing."

Louisa looked around before answering. She saw a small white cottage in the distance.

"What is that?" she asked and pointed to the cottage.

"That the gardener's residence, Miss," he said.

She wondered if even now the gardener was there.

"He does a good job," she said. "The gardener, I mean. The heather is quite lovely. I wonder if I might look in the greenhouse."

The butler's eyes narrowed.

"I'm afraid not, Miss. I'll have the chauffeur bring the car around." He shut the door.

As she stood in the driveway and waited for the motorcar, heat crept along the back of her neck like a spider. She turned to look up at the house and noticed a curtain flutter closed in the corner room of the second floor. Someone had been watching her.

An image flashed in her mind of Mark Halle's body jerking, his face in a ghastly grimace. She didn't care what the butler said. She was going to look inside that greenhouse.

She marched along a path that ran beside the house toward the glass house. The door was locked, which seemed odd. Who locked the door to a greenhouse? She peered through the window and saw rows of flowers and herbs. And in the back, stood a small tree with orange fruit.

Several hours later, Louisa entered the Harlem brownstone, took off her jacket and gloves, and went into the parlor. Carlotta sat on the rug with the baby while Ellen worked at her desk.

"What have you been up to and don't tell me you've been working on stories for the magazine." Ellen looked up and pursed her lips.

"I have not been working on articles, no," Louisa admitted. "I'm still trying to discover who might want to kill the men who invested in *Handsome Harry's Dilemma.*"

"And what have you learned?"

Louisa sighed and sank down onto the worn divan.

"Bernard Benson's suicide was just that. A suicide. Not a murder staged to look like a suicide."

"Then what is the problem?" Ellen tent-poled her arms and rested her chin on her knuckles.

"Then there's the poisoning of Mark Halle. I thought that might have been a Mafia hit. That's what they call it when they kill someone — a hit."

"You're learning all about the Italian criminals from your new accomplice, I'm guessing." She pointed her chin at Carlotta.

"Ellen," Louisa said. "You're a mother now. I can't have you risking your life. Carlotta knows the way these families work."

"Not to mention you have your magazine to publish," Carlotta added.

Ellen grimaced. "Continue."

"Now, there's another wrinkle. Halle was having an affair with Cora de Capezio, or Cora the Blonde, who is now dead. And his gardener was at the party pretending to be a waiter where Halle was poisoned."

"Wait a minute," Ellen said. "Wouldn't Halle have recognized his own gardener?"

"I wondered the same thing. I don't have an answer for that one." Louisa drummed a finger on the arm of the couch.

"Louisa, you're jumping to conclusions. The poisoning could have been accidental for all you know."

"Maybe, but wouldn't someone else at the party have gotten sick?"

Ellen shrugged. "All right, so what is your plan?"

"I don't believe Mrs. Halle is out of town. I think she's there in the mansion. I want to go back tonight and get her to confess to me."

Ellen barked a laugh. "You've lost your mind! If the gardener is a murderer, what makes you think he won't murder you?"

"I don't know, Ellen, but I've got to find out. I've got to figure out what sort of plot this is." Louisa rose from the divan.

"Then I'll go with you." She stood up.

"No, you won't," Carlotta said. "I will. You're a mother now and you can't be risking your life."

Ellen stared at the two of them and then said, "Fine. I'll do you one better. I'll send Martin up with you."

Martin was young and strong. Louisa wouldn't mind having his help at all.

"Thank you, Ellen," Louisa said. "There is one other thing you can do."

An owl hoot-hooted as the oars of the boat sloshed water in a steady rhythm. The little rowboat had been right where the fish monger said he would leave it a short walk through Fort Washington Park, and they'd found it, smelling of fish and mud. Louisa and Carlotta sat on the benches while Martin rowed, his breath matching each stroke.

"It won't take us long," Martin said. "The current is flowing in the right direction."

As he hewed close to the shore, Louisa saw the bright shining eyes of some sort of nocturnal animal. A raccoon perhaps. Or a skunk.

Louisa thought of the conversation she and Carlotta had that afternoon with Mrs. Costello. Once the gardener's wife understood that her husband might leave her for a wealthy widow, she was quite forthcoming.

In 20 minutes they reached the boathouse belonging to the Halle estate. The dark house stood on the bluff.

They beached the rowboat and made their way in the moonlight along a path to the bluff where Louisa pointed out the gardener's cottage. Firelight flickered through a window. They crept closer.

Louisa peeked through a window into the parlor. She gasped. Mrs. Halle lay on the divan, eyes closed, breasts bared, skirt hiked up around her hips, the gardener hovering over her, pumping between her thighs.

Carlotta sidled up beside her and snorted when she saw the amorous couple.

"Shite," Martin whispered, joining them.

None of them looked away. Mrs. Halle's cries grew in intensity as the man's thrusts came quicker and quicker. Louisa held her breath. Then with a loud grunt, the man collapsed forward.

The three of them ducked down and looked at each other, eyes like saucers. Carlotta clamped a hand over her mouth. Louisa slid her head up and peeked over the sill.

Mrs. Halle took a gold cigarette case from the table and pulled out a cigarette. The man lit it for her and then lit one for himself. They said nothing, just stared at the fire. Then Mrs. Halle stood up, buttoned her blouse and adjusted her skirt. She kissed him on the forehead before leaving through the front door.

Louisa beckoned the other two away from the window.

"Stay here and make sure he doesn't go anywhere," Louisa said.

Martin pulled a pistol from his pocket and said, "Not to worry, Miss."

She'd expected the gun, but then a large knife appeared in Carlotta's hand.

"We'll take care of him," she said.

"I see," Louisa said. "Then I'm going to have a conversation with Mrs. Halle."

Louisa followed a path toward the mansion. She saw Mrs. Halle enter through a back door. Most people this far out in the wilderness didn't bother to lock their doors. Mrs. Halle wasn't most people. The door knob wouldn't turn for Louisa. And yet there was an open window not far away. So much for safety precautions.

Louisa hiked up her skirt and crawled through the window. She tumbled into a large kitchen. The moon's light illuminated the room. She found her way to the hallway. Footsteps fell on the stairs. She followed them. When she reached the top of the stairs, a bedroom door at the end of the hall closed. She didn't hesitate.

She opened the door and found Mrs. Halle with her shoes off, unbuttoning the front of her dress.

"Maggie, I do not need any help..." she stopped when she saw Louisa. "Who the hell are you?"

"You know who I am. We met at Mabel Dodge's salon, and you watched me from your window today," Louisa said.

"What are you doing in my house?" The corners of the woman's mouth twitched. "I'll scream."

"I wouldn't do that," Louisa said in a quiet voice. "You poisoned your husband, didn't you, Mrs. Halle? Or I should say the two of you together did. You and your gardener, Mr. Costello."

The woman's fists clenched. "You have no proof."

Louisa felt an ounce of pity for the woman, but it disappeared quickly as she walked around the room, running a finger over the marble table, gazing at the gilt wallpaper, the satin canopy, the carved walnut cabinet.

"And then poor Cora. Your lover slit her throat, didn't he?"

"Get out of my room." The woman advanced toward her, pointing her finger at the door.

Louisa stopped in front of the vanity to inspect the necklaces and bracelets, spilling from a jewelry box.

"I saw the necklace your husband gave Cora, Mrs. Halle. Did you know about that? Was it the final straw?"

Mrs. Halle's face grew pale and tears sprang to her eyes.

"He was a cheating bastard."

"Was he going to leave you for her?" Louisa looked at Mrs. Halle's reflection in the mirror. She couldn't hide her anguish. It was in the flare of her nostrils and the roving of her eyes.

"Of course not. She was a passing fancy. Nothing more. You have no proof of anything."

Louisa turned to face her.

"I wonder what the police will find in your gardener's greenhouse. Perhaps some specimens of the *nux vomica*?"

"What are you talking about?"

"The strychnine tree. The seeds are quite poisonous, aren't they?"

The woman's shoulder slumped in resignation.

"What do you want?"

Louisa turned back to the jewelry box. She lifted a diamond bracelet. The stones glittered in the lamplight.

"It depends."

The woman snorted. "Money? Jewelry? You can have that bracelet if you want it. And I have some cash in the safe."

"Cash?" Louisa said.

"Then will you leave me alone?"

"Happily."

"The safe is in the closet," Mrs. Halle said.

Louisa sat on the vanity chair while Mrs. Halle entered the large walk-in closet. It occurred to Louisa that the woman might come out with a weapon. She breathed a sigh of relief when instead Mrs. Halle came out with a handful of cash, which she thrust at Louisa.

Louisa thumbed through the cash and glanced at the window.

"Mrs. Costello is more than willing to testify against her husband. Apparently, she didn't mind being married to an assassin until she realized he was leaving her for a wealthy widow," she said.

"Testify? You said you would leave me alone if I paid you."

"Yes, I'll leave you alone, but the police won't. Look out the window."

Headlights shown through the black panes. Ellen had done her part.

"I had a friend call Captain Tunney for me. That'll be him now."

The widow ran to the window and looked out. She cried out in panic and then yanked on the sash to throw it open. Louisa leapt up and ran to grab her. She spun her away from the window and shoved her to the floor where she sprawled like a broken doll. Louisa was surprised at her own strength.

She leaned over the prone figure. "Mrs. Halle, you have to pay for the death of your husband and for that young woman."

The doorbell rang. Mrs. Halle laid her head on her arm and sobbed.

Chapter 36
Ellen

Ellen had stayed up late, worrying about Louisa and Carlotta. When they came back flush with victory, she turned her worrying in a different direction: Brigid Rafferty.

By the morning, she had her plan for rescuing the girl. She fed little Hester in bed and then handed her over to Carlotta and put on the plainest gray dress she had in the wardrobe — not that anything she wore was particularly fancy.

"Where are you off to?" Carlotta asked, patting Hester on the back.

"I'm off to make sure a lady gets her breakfast."

The baby burped and Carlotta said, "As long as you're back in time to make sure this lady gets her lunch."

Ellen sighed. "I'll be back with two jugs of milk."

"You still don't care for it? Being a mama?"

"I'm doing my best, girl. Doing my best."

Ellen stopped by Louisa's room on her way out and found her in bed with the newspaper. "Reading about your latest adventure, are you?" she asked.

Louisa put down the paper. Her dark hair hung in a thick mass over shoulders.

"I am. It turns out that the gardener did indeed grow his own strychnine tree and concocted quite a potent blend from the seeds. Mr. Halle left the supervising of the servants to his wife and that's why he didn't recognize the gardener at the party. He probably wasn't home that much anyway."

"I am glad you've solved the mystery of the dead investors, Miss Sherlock. Perhaps now, you can help me fill the pages of our magazine." Ellen leaned against the side of the doorway.

"Don't you have enough for the second issue?" Louisa asked.

"Except for your promised story on that poet, the one that writes those strange poems about women's thighs."

"Djuna Barnes. I'd almost forgotten about her. I'll look for her. Maybe tonight at the Knickerbocker."

"That's a grand idea," Ellen said. "Now, I have my own problem to solve. I'm after getting a poor Irish girl out of the clutches of an old friend of yours. I told you marriage wouldn't tame Hugh Garrett."

She was at Louisa's door about to walk out, when Louisa said, "Ellen. Speaking of the Irish."

"Yes?" Ellen said.

"We couldn't have done what we did last night without Martin's help. I wanted to let you know that your secret is safe with me."

"Secret?"

"About the date of the uprising. I thought of telling Reggie, but I couldn't live with myself if the British knew in advance and something happened to your brother."

Ellen blew out a breath. Von Igel's little scheme had failed.

"That's good to know," she said. With that she left Louisa to her newspaper and went downstairs where she didn't even bother with a cup of coffee. She walked to the subway station. She could, of course, afford to take a taxi. In fact, she never needed to ride a train again, but she enjoyed being immersed in the great mix of humanity like a fish in the midst of a school. The rich isolated themselves like sharks. No wonder they were so unhappy.

She stopped at a bakery on Fifth Avenue and bought a coffee cake, which the baker placed in a white box with string.

Hattie had moved with her new husband into a home on Carnegie Hill in the Upper East side. It was an impressive brick and granite townhome with wide concrete steps, but Ellen wasn't going in the front door. Instead she found the service entrance. She didn't bother to knock. The kitchen would be busy in the morning and the cook and her assistants would be annoyed to no end if they had to interrupt their work. So she opened the door, and popped her head in.

"Hello," she said in a cheery voice.

The cook stood over the stove. The smell of bacon filled the air. Her assistant arranged a couple of roses and some baby's breath in a vase on a tray.

"What can we do for you, Miss?" the cook called. "If you're selling cherries, I've got my fill."

"I've brought something for you," Ellen said. She entered and placed the coffee cake on the long butcher-block counter.

"Did the missus order that?"

"No, it's for you and the rest of the staff. From me."

The cook turned off the fire under the pan and wiped her hands on her apron.

"For us?"

Ellen opened the lid of the box, and the cook peeked in.

"Well, it'll be much appreciated, Miss...?"

"Malloy. I used to be Hatt…I mean, Mrs. Tremont's personal maid. She was Miss Garrett then."

"What are you doing here?" The voice had a tone of accusation.

Ellen turned and saw her old nemesis, Smith, standing in the doorway.

"I've come to give you the morning off, Smith. I'm seeing to the lady this morning." Ellen smiled cheerfully.

"You will do no such thing." Smith planted her fists on her hips.

Ellen took a deep breath and leveled hard eyes on the older woman with the permanent sneer etched on her granite face.

"Don't you stand in my way, Smith. You know how Hattie feels about her dear Ellen." Ellen intentionally used Hattie's first name to remind Smith of the closeness of her relationship with her former employer.

"Of all the gall," Smith muttered.

Ellen smiled and handed her an envelope she had prepared for just this moment.

"You could use a new hat, couldn't you, Smith?"

Smith looked in the envelope, and her countenance changed.

"Don't make a habit of this, Malloy." She stuffed the envelope into the pocket of her uniform.

"I don't intend to."

Smith turned and left. The cook and her assistant chuckled.

"You sure know how to manage the old crow." The cook broke off a piece of the coffee cake with her fingers and popped it in her mouth.

"Mmm, tasty," she said. "Here's the missus' tray, Miss Malloy. Enjoy your visit."

With practiced hands, Ellen lifted the tray.

"Where's her room?" she asked.

"Second floor, third door on the right."

Ellen went up the back stairs, walked down the hall, entered the third room, and placed the tray on the bedside table. Then she went over to the windows and pulled the curtains open. Hattie groaned.

"Top of the morning, girleen," Ellen said.

Hattie sat up in the bed with a jolt. She wore a pink negligee, and locks of her hair were tied in white strips of cloth to induce curls.

"Ellen? Ellen Malloy, is it you? Have I died and gone to heaven?"

"Not yet," Ellen said with a laugh. She set down the tray, unfolded the legs of the bed table and put it over Hattie's lap, then placed the tray on the table.

"It feels like it. Sit with me, Ellen. Please. Like you used to." Hattie patted the bed.

Ellen sat down and picked a berry from Hattie's tray. If Hattie's mother had ever caught them being so familiar with each other back when Ellen was a servant, she'd have had a fit, but Ellen had been more like a big sister to Hattie than a servant.

Hattie immediately launched into a recounting of her evening the night before. A dinner party. Who was there. What they ate. "The ambrosia was simply divine."

"Hattie, I'm over the moon that you're having such a grand time and eating so well. But I'm here for a reason."

Hattie leaned forward.

"Oh, do tell me. Are you on some sort of investigation?"

"Something like that. When you came to visit, you expressed the desire for an Irish lady's maid. And I know you'd like to send Smith packing back to your ma. I've found someone who is willing and available, and I think the two of you would get along like a couple of kittens."

"Really? Oh, Ellen, you're a lifesaver! Who is she?"

"Her name's Brigid Rafferty, and she's a bit younger than you. She might need some training but she's smart and willing to work hard. And I get the sense, she's....fashionable. She'd know how to do your hair in the latest styles unlike old Smith who can barely manage a bun."

Hattie clapped her hands.

"Send her to me. Today."

"It's not that simple. You see, your brother has already claimed her as an indentured servant."

"Hugh got an indentured servant? Isn't that like slavery?"

"It is, indeed. Only difference is that there's a time limit for indentured servitude." Ellen gazed down at the plush satin bedspread, and ran her index finger along the stitching. "The thing is that she's very pretty. Like Silvia was."

She looked up to see if Hattie got her drift. Hattie leaned back against the padded headboard.

"Oh."

They exchanged a long look. Hattie loved her brother, but she was aware of his behavior with Silvia, and how the young Italian girl had died because of his indiscretion.

"But he's married now," Hattie said. "He wouldn't do ..."

"Oh, sweet Hattie. That doesn't stop some men. In fact, sometimes they are worse after marriage. Think of his poor wife."

Hattie's brow crinkled.

"What...what do you think I can do?"

"You? Probably nothing. But your mother is a formidable force. She's the only one who can stop him from sullying the reputation of the family. I'm suggesting you enlist her help. But you have to do it right away. They'll be releasing Brigid to him at noon."

Hattie removed the table from her lap, and flung back her covers.

"Oh, where's Smith to help me get dressed?"

"I'll do it, girleen. I bet you have a pretty frock in here somewhere," Ellen went to the huge walk-in closet where Hattie's dresses hung and found a chenille day dress with a silk sash. "This will bring out the color of your pretty eyes."

After she left Hattie, feeling somewhat hopeful, she took the train downtown to the Jefferson Market. Her breasts ached and she knew she should go home to feed the baby, but Carlotta could make do with a bottle and some sugar water.

Who should be coming down the wide courthouse steps but the diminutive attorney, Miss Moskowitz, herself?

"There you are," Miss Moskowitz said, reaching into her briefcase. "I stayed up all night to write your article." She handed Ellen two sheets of paper.

"You're a saint," Ellen said. "And you even typed it!"

"I'm just happy to have the opportunity to let the public know about this travesty of justice," Miss Moskowitz said. "You know, most of the girls who wind up here dropped out of school after the fifth grade. Then they're thrust into the world with no education and no prospects for marriage. They have no choice but to turn to prostitution in order to survive. We don't protect our girls. We feed them to the wolves."

Ellen thought of her own baby girl. Could she really protect the child?

"I'm hoping that Brigid will not be a meal for one particular wolf. I've enlisted his sister's help. But I'm worried she won't have enough time to get her away from him."

"I'll delay her release as long as I can," the attorney said. "Excuse me. There's the prosecutor, and I have to convince him to let a 13-year-old girl go home to her parents."

Ellen watched as Miss Moskowitz hurried off and stopped the attorney from the night before. She spoke earnestly to him, leaning in and gesticulating with one hand, her briefcase tightly gripped in the other.

Aren't you a warrior, she thought. The world needed more just like her.

"Hullo, Ellen," a voice said.

She looked up. Reggie Grant stood next to her. Her heart hammered. Had Louisa spoken to him yet?

"I understand your brother was involved in some police work last night," he said.

"You know everything, don't you?"

"Almost everything. I don't know when he plans to go back to Ireland," he said. "Do you? Do you know when they are planning their little party?"

This was it. This was her moment to plant the lie. It was right there on her tongue. *He'll be back for Father's Day.*

"Sorry," she said. "I don't know a thing."

Chapter 37
Louisa

Louisa strode through the extravagant lobby of the Knickerbocker Hotel. The chandeliers glimmered above groups of people gathered in the sitting areas, surrounded by hydrangeas in vases and statues of athletic nudes.

She didn't actually expect to find Djuna Barnes there. This wasn't the Bohemian "scene," but she did find Forrest Calloway in the barroom, his favorite Friday night haunt. Above the bar, Old King Cole watched the proceedings from a mural on the wall. The tiny king had become the symbol of New York nightlife.

The famous and the fatuous filled the room. Enrico Caruso, Mary Pickford and Douglas Fairbanks, the film director Frank Powell and several of Broadway's finest, clustered beside the bar. Forrest chatted with a conductor from the Metropolitan Opera when Louisa made eye contact. He excused himself and came over to her.

"You look lovely. Black velvet suits you," he said. "Are you meeting someone here?"

"Actually, I came to see you. I thought it better to speak here than at your house."

"Of course. Let's sit down. Would you like something to drink?"

"A glass of red, please."

They found a table for two by the window. Light shone from a wall sconce above. Louisa sipped a robust Bordeaux, and felt a glow beneath her skin.

"How is Sadie?" she asked. "I hope she recovered from the shock of the attack on you."

"She did. She's gone to Boston. An aunt recently died, and she had to go up for the funeral," he said.

"I don't think you should be out in public like this, Forrest. The next time they might not be such a bad shot," she said.

"There's been no sign of danger since that night. I believe it may have been some random attempt at robbery."

She looked at her glass, entranced by the shards of light glimmering in the deep red liquid. Melancholia welled inside her.

"Is anything wrong, Louisa?" he asked.

"No," she said and set down her glass. "I'm just rather stumped. I can't figure out who would try to kill you or why. I told Mr. Morello, the head of the Sicilian gang, that you were willing to compensate him for any inconvenience as a result of the play's cancellation. He said he hadn't ordered any hits on anyone, and didn't intend to be in your debt. Apparently, the mob boss doesn't care about the play or about Cora the Blonde, who is now dead by the way."

He leaned forward, his brow furrowed in concern.

"I saw something about that in the paper. Who did it?"

"A gardener, we believe. He also killed Mark Halle, your fellow investor, at the behest of Mrs. Halle."

"I see," he said. "Why?"

"Apparently, Mr. Halle was having an affair with Cora."

Forrest frowned and shook his head. "How awful. The poor girl. Does this mean there is no plot to murder investors. If the first one was a suicide, and the second one a matter of revenge, was the shooting at my house was simply a robbery gone bad?"

Louisa tilted her head. She couldn't be sure of anything.

"Maybe. Still, you should be careful."

He swallowed the last of his whiskey. She had a sip of wine left in her glass, which she decided not to finish.

"It's getting late," she said.

"Let me see you home," he said.

"I'm fine. I can take a taxi."

"Mr. Kimura is right outside," he insisted.

"All right," she said. She did want to see Mr. Kimura and make sure he had recovered from the shooting.

"You seem to be doing well, Mr. Kimura," she said when he opened the back door for her.

"Thanks to you, Miss Louisa," he said with a slight bow. "The doctors were able to make me better."

Of all the servants she had met over the years, none was more dignified than the slight Japanese man.

"I'm sure Mrs. Kimura was happy to see you come home."

"Very happy, Miss."

Mr. Kimura drove the Packard north toward Harlem. She glanced at Forrest. An awkward silence ensued. His hand rested on the seat next to hers, but his expression looked troubled.

"What is it?" she asked in a quiet voice. "What's wrong?"

"When I'm with you like this, Louisa," he said. "My feelings are...unruly."

As were her own.

"Now that you're not in danger," she said, "I'll be out of your life. You'll soon be married to a lovely woman and there will be two little boys under your roof who need a father."

He nodded.

"Yes, the boys. I'm crazy about them already," he said. He reached over and took her hand. "Thank you for understanding."

"Of course, I understand." It seemed presumptuous of him to think her heartbroken when she was the one who had broken off the engagement. And yet with his hand holding hers, she regretted her choice more than ever. She *was* heartbroken to have lost him.

When Mr. Kimura opened the back door for her, Forrest got out of the other side to walk her to the door as any gentleman would do. She stepped onto the sidewalk and then stopped and stood stock still.

"Miss Louisa?" Mr. Kimura asked.

She stared at him. She understood something in that moment: the shooter had not been aiming for Forrest at all.

She wheeled around and looked at Forrest.

"Forrest, did you say Sadie is in Boston?" she asked.

"Yes, her favorite aunt died."

Thoughts tumbled through her mind. She remembered the letter that Sadie had received with threats from a family member of her dead husband. And then there was the matter of her gold-digging cousin.

"Please don't think this is presumptuous but will Sadie be inheriting any money?"

"Quite a bit, in fact. Not that she needs it. I plan to take very good care of her and the boys."

Louisa decided to withhold her suspicions for the moment. She didn't want to alarm Forrest, but she would be hanged before she let anything happen to his future wife.

Chapter 38
Ellen

Ellen steeled herself as she opened the door to the offices of *Mother Earth Magazine.* The anarchist publication had moved from a location in the Village to a spot in Harlem not far from Louisa's townhouse. A bell on the door announced her arrival.

Lulu looked up from a typewriter. Her black hair was twisted in a knot at the back of her neck. She had the same hypnotic gaze she'd had the last Ellen had seen her, the same full lips and pointed chin. Ellen's heart raced.

"Well, well, what light in yonder window breaks. It is my own sweet Juliet," Lulu said, leaning back in her swivel chair.

"Quoting Shakespeare now, are you? I thought we only quoted Karl Marx here." Ellen adopted a nonchalant tone.

"Didn't you drown when the *Lusy* went down?" Lulu brought a cup to her lips and drank.

"You know that I managed to survive," Ellen said. "I'm publishing a magazine, and I've brought you a letter from Emma. I saw her in the jail."

She held out the letter that Emma had dictated to her in the jail, but Lulu didn't take it. Instead, she stared at Ellen with mocking eyes.

"You're looking mighty spiffy there in your new duds. I haven't forgotten how you left me after the explosion. Not a word from you in what? Two years now?"

"That was a dangerous business. Making bombs in your apartment. No wonder those fools blew themselves up." Ellen had come too close to joining those fools in their quest for recognition.

"Do not malign our martyrs, Miss Malloy. But what about me? I thought we had something." Lulu stood up and moved close to her, hands planted on her hips. "I loved you."

Ellen stood dumbfounded. She had found Lulu intoxicating, sure, but she could not say that she loved her.

"I loved someone else, and I couldn't go on betraying her," she finally admitted.

"So, you betrayed me instead." Lulu stepped closer to her, a lioness about to go for the jugular.

"I suppose I did." Ellen had wrestled with the guilt, thought she was over it, but guilt had a way leaping out of dark corners. She dropped the letter on the desk.

"It was that wealthy woman, wasn't it? You couldn't resist the luxury, could you? It was she who took you on the *Lusitania* wasn't it? Saloon class, eh? The finest of everything. Satin sheets. Down pillows. Lamb and jelly for dinner. You must have thought you died and gone to heaven. Imagine a poor girl, born in the stink of fish, suddenly ensconced in the sweet smell of money. Yeah, I heard she left you a fortune."

"And what of it?" Ellen asked, restraining the anger that welled up inside her. "I'm putting that money to good use."

"Are you?"

Ellen pulled a copy of *The Ladies' Lantern* from her bag and tossed it onto the desk next to the letter from Emma. Lulu picked it up and opened it.

"Oh, I've seen this. Very slick. Naturally, you've got Louisa Delafield writing for you. That simpering society hack." She threw the magazine down.

"There's nothing simpering about Louisa," Ellen said. "And she's no hack."

"Maybe not." Then she smirked. "You know, Ellen, I don't think you really loved your rich lady friend. Oh, you loved the life she gave you all right, but you were only using her."

Ellen's hand flew of its own accord and struck Lulu across the cheek. After a stunned moment, Lulu burst out laughing. Then she grabbed Ellen by the arms and pulled her close. She smashed her mouth against Ellen's face in a violent kiss and grabbed her breast, squeezing until the milk leaked out. She jerked back in surprise.

"Look what I've done," she said, staring down at her dampened hand.

Ellen looked at the wet spot on her bodice and burned with humiliation.

"I have a baby," she said.

"A baby?" Lulu's smirk disappeared, replaced by an expression of utter astonishment.

Ellen turned her back to Lulu and walked toward the door. As she opened it, she heard Lulu say, "I'll be right here, Ellen. When you're ready. Bring the baby."

Ellen shut the door behind her.

That afternoon, she made sure no one followed her to the Lower Eastside to see her brother.

After a lunch of stew and slaw, Ellen and Martin took the boys to the park so Paula could get some rest.

While the boys did somersaults in the grass, they talked.

"I'll be leaving tomorrow for Boston," he said. "And then it's onto home."

"Just in time to get yourself killed."

"You know, Sister, it's too bad you're not a man. You'd be fighting at my side."

"Perhaps you're right," she replied.

"Sean Fear has made the Germans promise not to land any of their men until we've achieved our goal. And we pay for every gun we get. We take no handouts from them."

"I see. You poor, idealistic fools. That's why Devoy is always after giving money to von Igel, isn't it? He sends it straight to Franz von Papen in Germany."

"Ah, don't be that way."

He took her hand and she brushed a tear away with the other.

Chapter 39
Louisa

If Sadie was in Boston without Forrest, that meant she was unprotected. But unprotected from whom and what? Louisa wondered whether she was being foolish. And yet the nagging worry wouldn't leave her. The first thing to do was to read the Boston papers and learn something about this aunt who had died.

She went to the public library. There she perused the *Boston Globe* and found the obituary she was looking for. The funeral was the next day. There was no time to lose. She hurried home to pack.

"Ellen, I need to go to Boston," Louisa said, pulling off her gloves as she entered the parlor.

"Boston? Whatever for?"

"I want to do a story on the rampant censorship. 'Banned in Boston.' It's practically a cliché. But what makes it so? And who are these banners? I think we should publish an article about them."

"Not a bad idea," Thorn said.

Ellen looked over the story budget.

"I'm not sure we have room for it or the time to wait. But I can always save it for the next issue," Ellen said. "By the way, Martin is heading there, as well. The Boston Irish are as fanatical as our own New Yorkers."

"Then it's settled. I'll take a train today. We can travel with Martin. He was quite helpful when we exposed Mrs. Halle." Louisa didn't mention that Mrs. Halle did a fine job of exposing herself.

"And I'll come with you."

Louisa wheeled around. Anna had come into the parlor.

"I beg your pardon, Mother?" Louisa said.

"I'm coming with you. I used to love to visit Boston," Anna said. "In fact, I had a good friend from Beacon Hill."

"But, Mother, you haven't been out of the neighborhood, much less the city in fifteen years," Louisa said.

"Then it's high time, wouldn't you say?"

Louisa turned to look at Ellen, who was grinning.

"What a fine mother-daughter trip it will be. Let's make sure Mrs. Delafield has a few new dresses," Ellen said.

"Oh, yes!" Anna said. "And hats! I need new hats, too. With plumes."

Louisa rolled her eyes. How could she possibly investigate Sadie Treadwell's situation with her mother in tow?

"We don't have time to shop."

"We'll shop in Boston!" Anna said.

"Excellent idea," Ellen smirked.

"Ellen, I have an ulterior motive," Louisa confessed. "In addition to censorship, I'm concerned about Sadie Treadwell."

"Who?"

"Forrest Calloway's intended. I think someone might want to kill her. But they shot Mr. Kimura instead."

"Kill her? Why would someone kill her?" Ellen looked skeptical.

"Money, of course," Louisa said. "While I was visiting her in Brooklyn, she got a disturbing letter. Her cousin told me that her late husband's relatives have been threatening to sue her."

Ellen rose and came around the desk.

"Louisa, are you sure you're not on another wild goose chase?"

Louisa shook her head.

"I was there when Mr. Kimura was shot. At first, I thought the assassin meant to harm Forrest, but that doesn't make sense when you think about it. Mr. Kimura stepped in front of Sadie to help her out of the motorcar. She's in danger. She's in Boston for a funeral and I'd like to keep an eye on her."

Ellen sighed in resignation.

"A funeral? I haven't been to one of those since your father's," Anna said.

Martin sat in the seat across from Louisa and Anna, who couldn't stop staring at the young man. Like most members of her class, Anna harbored a deep prejudice against the Irish, but an Irish woman was paying her bills, and there was no denying Martin was an amiable young man with a pleasing aspect. Louisa thought the Irish Brotherhood had done well in recruiting him. He had a youthful zest that seemed to even put Anna at ease. But Louisa worried about his "cause" for so many reasons, not the least of which was that he would break his sister's heart if he should come to a bad end.

"I believe many Irish live in Boston," Anna observed.

"Indeed, there are, ma'am. They came over in droves after the Great Hunger. And once they got here, they couldn't afford to leave. It's a hard lot for them. But as Karl Marx says, the working man has nothing to lose but his chains."

"Who?" Anna asked.

"Karl Marx. Have you not heard of him, Mrs. Delafield?" he tilted his head in curiosity.

"No. Sounds German."

"He wrote *The Communist Manifesto*, Mother," Louisa said.

"Let me put it simply. Your Brahmins are much like the English. They keep a stranglehold on wealth and power," he said. "The men are paid so poorly their wives and children must work for the wealthy as well. The Brahmins have grown dependent on us and our labor."

Louisa sometimes thought that losing their family fortune had ultimately been good for her. She needn't have a house full of servants in order to carry on with her day. And there was something gratifying about being able to feed and clothe oneself. Since Suzie's marriage, Louisa felt an enormous sense of pride when she pulled off a decent meal.

"Martin, do you suppose there's some way to get a message to the servants who will be looking after Mrs. Treadwell? I'm afraid her life is in danger," Louisa said.

"Who is this Mrs. Treadwell?" he asked.

"She's the fiancée of my former publisher, Forrest Calloway," she said. "And she's from a Brahmin family in Beacon Hill. She's staying at the house of her aunt, the one who died. Here's the address." She handed him a slip of paper with the address.

"If the family is Brahmin, surely the servants will be Irish." He tucked the address into his jacket pocket. "I'll look into it and see what I can do."

The train pulled to the station in Boston. Anna was like a five-year-old child in her excitement. She gave the porter a penny tip, a symbol of largesse to her mind. Louisa followed it up with a quarter.

They said their good-byes to Martin and took a taxi to the Parker House Hotel where they got a room. It was a lovely hotel with marble floors, electric chandeliers and elaborate gilt-decorated elevators. The room was comfortable with an attached bathroom.

"When are you going to write about the censors?" her mother asked.

"On Monday. First, we're going to that funeral."

The funeral took place at the Central Congregational Church, a magnificent Gothic structure made of puddingstone in downtown Boston. Louisa and Anna entered the sanctuary and stood stunned for a solid minute.

"All the windows are Tiffany," Anna gasped.

"Mother, look at the chandelier," Louisa whispered. "It's magnificent. I believe that's Tiffany, as well."

A woman wearing a lovely deep purple dress overheard them and explained, "You're right. About 20 years ago, the church was going under, what with all the competition in the Back Bay. So, a new pastor was hired and insisted on hiring Tiffany's finest designers. It worked, our congregation has grown, but then he was fired. He broke the budget."

Louisa and Anna found seats in a wooden pew and continued to gaze around. It was like being inside a work of art. Everything from the mosaics behind the altar to the trusses and traceries combined to create a unified feel of perfection.

"I am not happy that Sadie Treadwell's Aunt Gladys died," Anna whispered. "but I would never have gotten to see this if she hadn't."

Louisa agreed. She had always felt there was something sacred about art, and though she generally did not ponder the great mysteries, her blood seemed to sing with a spiritual awareness in this church that was also such a thing of beauty.

She was here to protect Sadie if she could, but she could not stop thinking of Forrest, and she found herself praying, "Lord, if you hear me, let me think not of myself, but of the happiness of others. Give me the insight to know how to protect her from evil even as we walk through shadowy valleys."

She opened her eyes and gazed up at the window next to her. It was a depiction of the Madonna and child. She thought of Ellen and her darling baby. She hoped Ellen could overcome her grief and let herself love her baby as deeply as she had once loved the first Hester. The service ended, and Louisa had managed not to hear a word of it so lost was she in her own thoughts.

As she went through the receiving line outside the church, she mentally practiced her story. She reached Sadie, whose eyes widened when she recognized her.

"Miss Delafield, what a surprise. Are you covering Boston society now? Or did you know my Aunt Gladys?"

Louisa smiled as their gloved hands clasped.

"Neither, I'm afraid. My mother needed to come to Boston on some business and Mr. Calloway asked me check on you. He's worried since that ghastly incident."

"Poor Mr. Kimura. Is he out of the hospital?" Sadie asked.

"He is. It was apparently a flesh wound."

Sadie leaned in close. She smelled of rose water.

"Miss Delafield, I hope you and your mother will come to the house for the reception. Funerals can be such gloomy affairs, but Aunt Gladys lived a long and fulfilling life. So this will be as much a celebration as time of mourning."

Aunt Gladys' house, a big brick mansion with arched windows and a yard full of flowers, stood on a corner in

Beacon Hill. The house with its gold filigreed wallpaper and plush red carpet rivaled Alva Belmont's Marble House in ostentation. The butler directed them upstairs to the music room. All the servants were Irish as Martin had predicted. A Victrola in the corner played "Somewhere a Voice is Calling," which was fitting for a funeral.

Dusk, and the shadows falling,
O'er land and sea;
Somewhere a voice is calling,
Calling for me!
Night and the stars are gleaming,
Tender and true;
Dearest! my heart is dreaming,
Dreaming of you!

The *crème de la crème* of Boston society gathered in the large music room to commemorate the life of Sadie's Aunt Gladys. Even Anna, for once in her life, seemed awed in this pond of American aristocracy. Fortunately, Sadie's mother took over their introductions.

"These are Sadie's dear friends from New York," she told the mildly curious faces around them. The words "New York" were tinged with pity.

"How do you do," various mourners muttered. It was not a question.

"How do you do," Louisa and Anna replied.

"Ladies, may I introduce Mr. Godfrey Lowell Cabot," Sadie's mother said.

A serious looking man in his fifties with gray wings of hair on the side of his head descended upon them like a hawk on a couple of unlucky mice.

"You are a writer, are you not?" he said to Louisa.

She nodded, at a loss for words in the face of his intensity.

"What do you write? Not novels, I hope." His eyes narrowed.

She shook her head this time and managed to utter, "Journalism."

"A renowned chronicler of society," Anna interjected in Louisa's defense.

Louisa gathered her wits as she realized this was just the man she needed to interview for her article on Boston's excessive censorship.

She cleared her throat. "I understand you are the treasurer of the Watch and Ward society," she said, forcing her lips into a pleasant smile.

"I am indeed." His eyes shone with a mixture of passion and pride.

"And you ban books, is that correct? You decide what is acceptable reading material for the Boston public?"

"I do."

A middle-aged woman, attired in an elegant dark gray Worth gown, stepped in beside Mr. Cabot and said, "My husband enjoys reading very much, but the Watch and Ward Society does so much more than censoring inappropriate books. They stop evil in its tracks. They have shut down many gambling houses and ...other places." She would not utter the word "brothel."

"I understand that," Louisa said. "Quite admirable. But I do wonder what could possibly be offensive about Walt Whitman's *Leaves of Grass*?"

"You are much too innocent to understand," Mr. Cabot said in a particularly patrician tone.

Louisa managed to keep her eyes from rolling in their sockets.

"I'm writing an article for a magazine, Mr. Cabot, about the Watch and Ward Society. May I speak to you again?"

Mrs. Cabot once again interjected herself into the conversation.

"I suggest you speak to the Reverend Chase, dear. He knows more about the day-to-day operations. My husband is more of a ... benefactor." By which she meant, he spent a good deal of money to determine which books and magazines Boston citizens were allowed to read.

At that moment, Sadie's cousin, Edgar Morton, appeared at her elbow.

"Miss Delafield, how nice to see you again, even in these unfortunate circumstances."

Mr. and Mrs. Cabot wandered off to find more salubrious conversation, and Louisa turned her attention to the fortune hunter. She decided in that moment to forgive his past boorishness in order to learn what she could about the threat to Sadie.

"Mr. Morton, what a pleasure. I was hoping we would see you here."

"And here I am. You are as lovely as ever, and this is your mother." He turned to Anna with the warmth of the sun. "*Your* family, I believe, is even more distinguished than your late husband's, is it not?"

Anna's Old New York blue blood practically gleamed through her skin.

"Knickerbockers," she said with false modestly.

"Such deep history." He turned to Louisa. "Louisa, do you enjoy rowing?"

She stammered. "I was in a rowboat recently."

"I mean, to watch. There's a race tomorrow afternoon, and I'd love for you to join me as my guest. You, too, Mrs. Delafield, if you would like to come."

"Mother needs her rest in the afternoon," Louisa said and gave Anna a look.

Anna must have assumed that Louisa wanted to be alone with Mr. Morton for romantic reasons, for she meekly acquiesced.

Edgar gave her direction to tomorrow's date, and she agreed she would see him then.

After a few more superficial conversations, Louisa found Sadie and offered her condolences once more while a maid retrieved their wraps for them.

"Thank you so much for coming," Sadie said. She seemed genuinely touched.

In the taxi on the way back to the hotel, Anna asked, "Did you learn anything useful?"

"No," Louisa said. "But I'm glad I got a chance to see Edgar Morton again."

"Well, I learned a thing or two about him," Anna said. She clutched the handle of her cane.

"How so?"

"I insinuated myself into a conversation with Gladys' sister, who happens to be Edgar's mother. She let it slip she was worried about him. Seems he's got himself into debt. This is a much greater difficulty for men like him, you see. He absolutely must keep up appearances. Being born into wealth can be as much a curse as a blessing. I don't think he's a suitable match for you, dear."

"I am not interested in him as a possible husband, Mother. I'm interested in him as a possible murder suspect."

"Well, that's better," Anna said and brushed a bit of dust from her skirt.

Chapter 40
Ellen

The telephone in the hallway jangled. Carlotta picked it up and said in her most official tone of voice, "Delafield residence and office of *The Ladies' Lantern.*"

Ellen came down the stairs, took the receiver, and heard Hattie's gleeful voice.

"She's mine! Brigid is mine," she said, pealing the news like a church bell.

Ellen suppressed a groan. The wealthy would never understand that they didn't get to "own" a servant, even if she was indentured. On the other hand, she was relieved that Hugh Garrett had been thwarted. Brigid would not be subjected to his unwanted attentions as long as Hattie was around.

"That's wonderful news, Hattie," Ellen said. "Be sure to pay her a good wage. I don't care if she is 'indentured' to you."

"Oh, my husband takes care of paying the servants." Ellen huffed.

"Hattie, my girl, it's your household. Your job is to see to your staff. Are you truly allowing your husband to do your job? Are you going to be a little girl all your life?"

The line was quiet for a moment. No one ever spoke harshly to Hattie.

"No," she said. "I'll see that she's paid and paid well."

"At least your brother won't get his hands on her."

"I will not let him near her. I promise," Hattie said.

After the phone call, Ellen went back into the parlor. Thorn handed her a large packet.

"She's ready to go," he said with a self-satisfied smile.

"Our second issue," Ellen said, looking down at the package. "I'll take it to the printer right now."

She took the 9th Avenue El through Manhattan downtown to West Houston Street. From there it was a short walk past a church and a few businesses including an undertaker and a bakery to the Printing House on Hudson, one of the busiest printers in Manhattan.

She entered the building and laid the package on the counter.

"Help you, Miss?" the clerk asked.

"I've brought my magazine pages to print. Is Mr. Johnston here?" Johnston was the man who had assisted her with the printing of the first issue.

"I'll get him," the clerk said and pushed a piece of paper toward her. "In the meantime, please fill out this form here."

As Ellen finished filling out the form, she looked up to see Mr. Johnston approaching her in an ink-stained apron, his mouth set in a tight-lipped grimace.

"I'm sorry, Miss Malloy. We won't be printing your second issue. Your order's been canceled."

"Canceled? Says who?"

"It's been canceled," he repeated.

"I didn't cancel it. Mr. Thorn certainly didn't do it." Ellen was too confused to be angry. There must be some sort of misunderstanding, she thought.

"We won't be printing your magazine. Now kindly leave the premises." The man fidgeted as he stood there. He was nervous, Ellen realized, unaccustomed to turning away customers.

"I will not," Ellen said. "Not until you explain yourself."

"We will not be printing illegal information about babies and so forth, putting ideas in women's heads."

"But you haven't even seen the pages. There's no instruction manual inside here — just an interview with a woman who believes in the cause of birth control."

"Miss," he said in a resigned tone. "Please leave. We won't be printing your magazine no matter what is inside."

Ellen stood there in stunned silence before finally picking up her package. She walked out of the office, too baffled to be angry.

She stood outside the office. The sun shone above, and a breeze skipped off the river. Looking around, she noticed a red Rolls Royce parked across the street. The driver leaned against the hood and stared at her with his arms crossed. She stood with her feet stuck to the sidewalk. The driver spit, then cranked the engine, got in the motorcar, and drove off. There was her answer. Hugh Garrett had sent his thug of a chauffeur to threaten the printer. He must have known she had convinced Hattie to get Brigid away from him. And now he'd gotten his revenge.

Chapter 41

Louisa

Louisa and Anna had a breakfast of buttermilk griddlecakes in the hotel restaurant as Louisa plotted out her day.

"I need to go to the Boston Bookseller's Committee to learn what I can about their campaign of censorship in Boston. What will you do, Mother?"

"I will go shopping." Anna touched the brim of her oversize hat. It had been a while since she'd purchased a new hat.

"Not by yourself?" Louisa took a bite of her breakfast and licked maple syrup from her fork.

"Oh no, one of the ladies I met after the funeral has offered to go with me. She'll bring an extra maid."

"Thank heavens you'll have maids," Louisa said.

"You've never had a ladies' maid so you don't know what you're missing," Anna said.

"And I do believe I am better off for it."

"Let's not have that discussion again," Anna said with an exaggerated sigh. "I am looking forward to this."

Before leaving the hotel, Louisa called Martin at the phone number he had given her. He told her to meet him at a pub in the North End. She took a taxi and found herself in a shabby neighborhood that had once been rather grand but was now crowded with an immigrant population. In spite of its rather downtrodden appearance, there was a certain charm to the place. Every apartment house, it seemed, had bay windows. The wooden frames were painted green or brown. The taxi driver let her out, and as she walked through the swarms of children playing games in the street, she wondered what these streets would be like once all women had access to birth control. They would have a higher standard of living, certainly. These tribes of little savages would be no more. It might be a safer and more hygienic world, but a lonelier one as well. As an only child, she had always felt she was missing something by not growing up in a house full of other children.

"Miss Delafield," Martin said. He stood in the doorway of the pub. "Come in and have a plate of fish and chips."

He ushered her inside and found her a seat at a table while he went to order from the bar. A few minutes later he came back with two platters of fried cod and potatoes.

"I've found a couple young fellows to keep an eye on your lady friend. For a fee, of course."

"Of course," she said.

She handed him an envelope with some cash.

He looked inside the envelope and nodded with approval.

"Enough for the job and a bit leftover to support the cause."

"That's up to you," she said.

"Should I have someone keep an eye on yourself as well?" he asked.

"That won't be necessary. I do appreciate your concern."

"You mean a lot to my sister, Miss Delafield. For all your high class airs, she loves you. And my sister means the whole world to me, so I'll not have anything bad happen to you."

Louisa was taken aback. Ellen was not one to express affection. And neither was Louisa, but Ellen had opened up her world. It was as if she'd lived in a clam shell until Ellen pried it open. She vowed in that moment to do better to help Ellen make a success of her magazine.

Feeling assured that the servants were watching over Sadie, she decided to work on her story on the Boston censors. She started at a bookshop tucked into an alley just a block from the hotel. It turned out that they carried no books by Upton Sinclair or Theodore Dreiser—two favorite targets of the Watch and Ward Society.

After that she spent the entire day chasing down the Reverend Chase, the secretary of the Watch and Ward Society. He, along with his benefactor Godfrey Lowell Cabot, formed a cabal along with the proprietors of the Old Corner Bookstore to form the Boston Bookseller's Committee. It should have been called the Book Banner's Committee. They chose their titles in secret, but Louisa understood that for some publishers, getting "banned in Boston" meant increased sales elsewhere.

When she finally found the Reverend, he explained, "When sin endeavors to extend its sway and is aggressive, when money has been invested in special forms of temptation, especially against the young, our Society, supported by the better sense of the community, must make a vigorous fight against these sources of temptation."

Good heavens, he was verbose, Louisa thought. She wasn't going to include that quote. It would positively put readers into a coma.

"Did you find enough material for your story?" Anna asked when she got back to the hotel room.

"I believe I did. Did you go shopping?"

"We're going this afternoon. You do know that these censors do have the best of intentions," Anna said.

"Really, and what makes you say that?"

"Well, they come from the very best families," she said. "And from what I understand they had a social mission in their early days. They took care of the city's poor and under-privileged. It was what we always called, *noblesse oblige.* If you are born with great wealth or manage to earn it, then you are under certain obligations to society."

"I think the whole thing is rather sinister," Louisa said. "There is no public list. The books they decide are obscene are not even reviewed in the papers. They can't be sold. It's as if they never even existed."

"Perhaps they shouldn't exist," Anna said.

"Oh, Mother," Louisa said. "You love Walt Whitman as much as anyone."

Louisa took a taxi to meet Edgar at the stands beside the Charles River.

"You made it!" he said, a smile of delight on his face.

Though she was an avid tennis and polo fan, Louisa had never watched rowing before.

"Were you a rower in your day?" she asked as they climbed the bleachers to the top.

"Yes, I was the coxswain," he said as they found seats. The sun shone, the sky was dotted with fluffy bits of cloud, and a breeze tugged at her hat.

"Who's racing today?" she asked.

"The sophomores and the juniors though there is quite the 'row,' so to speak, over who should be in control of the teams. All started by the *Harvard Crimson*."

"I'm glad the future newsmen are learning how to stir things up at a young age," she said. "Who's in control now?"

"Each team elects a captain, but some of the men believe the coach should have full control over the teams as they do in football."

Louisa settled back on the bench to watch. For the most part, the crowd sat quietly as the teams churned down the river and back. The peaks of green water glimmered with sunlight, troughs of gray and blue. She noticed a handsome man, who could have passed for a film idol with his chiseled jaw, on a lower bench shift his eyes toward them and frown.

"Why does that young man keep looking at us?" she asked.

Edgar snorted. "He's angry because I gave him a D on one of his assignments. I can't help it. They earn what they earn."

When it came time for the finish, the spectators rose, throats clamoring for one team or another. The young men on the water pulled with all their might. Ultimately, the sophomores won by a half a length.

After the race, Edgar showed her around Harvard Square. The shade trees and brick buildings created a charming tableau. She was especially impressed by the new Widener Library, which had opened last year as a memorial to Harry Elkins Widener, a Harvard man who had died on the Titanic.

"I suppose you know the Widener family," Edgar said when they stopped to gaze up the steps at the immense pillars that formed a colonnade along the front of the building.

"I do. In fact, I knew Harry when I was a child. He was a few years older than I. Even then he always had his head in a book. What a spectacular memorial to him."

They continued along the sidewalk.

"Edgar, there's a reason I came here today and it's not simply to admire the campus or watch the rowing, though I am enjoying myself. I am worried about Sadie. You see, she is marrying someone quite dear to me, and I'm afraid someone may be intending to harm, or even kill, her."

She had expected him to be surprised, but instead she was the one who was surprised.

"I am worried as well, Louisa. And I believe I know who may be behind the attempt that resulted in injury to the chauffeur."

"Really?"

"When Sadie's husband died, he left everything to her. There was a great deal of resentment from his family, who are a lower-class sort. He was a self-made man who pulled himself up by his bootstraps. Of course, our family was scandalized by the marriage. Sadie was expected to marry a Brahmin, or barring that, at least some titled European. She might have been a baroness. Instead, she married for love."

Louisa nodded.

"Do you have any thought in particular as to who in Mr. Treadwell's family might want her dead?"

"There are a brother and a sister. It could be either one of them — or both. They most likely hired someone else to do the shooting."

"So you suspected that the shot that injured Mr. Kimura was meant for your cousin?" she asked.

"Yes. Miss Delafield, I love my cousin." He took her hand in his. "I hope you can find the culprits."

"I will do my best."

Louisa pondered his theory. He might be right, but he might also be deflecting suspicion from himself. If Sadie was dead, would he inherit Aunt Gladys' fortune?

Louisa looked across the green and saw the same young man who had been glaring at them from the bleachers watching them. He turned and quickly strode away.

Chapter 42
Ellen

Ellen walked to the office of Emma Goldman's *Mother Earth Magazine* and entered the cluttered room. Sasha Berkman was there, smoking his cigarette, in deep conversation with Lulu. He took off his spectacles and looked up at Ellen. She was struck by his keen eyes.

"Hello," Ellen said.

Lulu turned around, saw her, and smirked.

"Can't keep away, can you?"

"Seems I can't," Ellen said. "I'm here to ask for some help."

"And why would we give you any help?" Lulu turned back to the article in her hand.

"Because we're on the same side, Lulu. The side of justice. Our magazines are not in competition." She paused. "Hello, Sasha. It's good to see you again."

Sasha stubbed out his cigarette and looked up at her. Then his face broke into a smile.

"How can we be of assistance?"

Lulu rolled her eyes but didn't object.

"It seems someone is threatening the printer I was using to get my magazine done. I was wondering if you might direct me to your own printer. Someone who won't cave to the rich and powerful."

"As long as you're a paying customer, our man will print your publication, Miss Malloy. Have you got the pages?"

"I do."

"Then I'll see to it myself."

"Thank you."

She handed the package over to him.

"All the instructions are there."

Sasha Berkman had spent 14 years in prison for attempting to murder one of the robber barons, a poor attempt with a knife. Since his release he'd foresworn violence, but he still cared deeply about fighting injustice.

Ellen and Lulu shared a look. Funny, how difficult it is to translate the language of the eyes, but much was said in that moment between those two sets of eyes. Perhaps a bit of forgiveness transpired.

"Leave your number. The printer will call you when it's ready."

"Thank you both." Ellen said.

On the way back to Louisa's brownstone, Ellen cut through Morningside Park. Spring had sprung. Tulips bloomed like colorful chalices. The furious wind of March had changed into a docile breeze. Children's laughter danced in the air. She kept seeing Lulu's dark eyes in her mind's eye. Was there some chance she could still feel something for her? For so long, she had been dead inside.

Something caused her to look up. She gasped as a white bird faltered in the air and then tumbled in a flurry of feathers to the walkway below with a soft thump not five feet from her. Blood spilled from a wound just below its throat. The boy who had hit the bird with his sling shot yelled in triumph.

"Ah, what've you done, you little devil?" Ellen cried. The boy and his friends ran away, laughing.

She lifted the dying pigeon and held it close to her chest as the life seeped out of its body. Once it was dead, it's round black eye staring at the sky, she took it over to some bushes and buried it beneath a pile of old leaves and dirt.

Suddenly, she had a terrible premonition. Was this some sort of sign? Had something happened to her baby? She stood up quickly and ran along the walkway out of the park. She kept running, ignoring the stitch in her side. She had to get to little Hester.

She leapt up the steps and burst through the door and took the stairs two at a time, huffing, her skirt hiked up above her knees. She burst into the bedroom and saw Carlotta lifting the baby off the changing table.

"Oh, my Lord in Heaven," Ellen cried.

"What's got into you?" Carlotta asked.

Ellen couldn't answer, only reached for the baby. She needed to feel the life thrumming beneath her hands. She needed the reassurance of the wiggling legs and the solid weight of the child's body. Ellen held Hester close, felt the damp mouth against her cheek the fingers clasping a stray strand of hair. She worried her knees would buckle beneath her. It was as if her heart had never been freed from the box where she'd been imprisoned. Until this moment. She imagined this was how Jesus felt when the stone rolled away from his tomb.

"My darling babe," she whispered in the midst of her tears. "My own love. My girl."

Carlotta stared at her as if she'd gone balmy.

"Carlotta, have I told you how much I adore this wee girl?" Ellen asked, laughing and crying all at the same time. She looked at little Hester, looked into the depths of her eyes, and the child looked back at her, staring as if she could see into the reaches of Ellen's soul.

Chapter 43
Louisa

The Irish butler admitted Louisa to the parlor of the dead woman's house. Sunlight poured through tall windows onto an oriental rug. Sadie sat on the plush sofa, waiting for her, cookies and a silver service set on the table. She wore a black dress, which she'd adorned with a white orchid.

"Good morning, Louisa," she said with a welcoming smile. "I was surprised to get your call this morning. It sounded urgent. Sugar?"

"Yes, please. One lump."

Sadie poured coffee into a Noritake cup with a lump of sugar and handed it on a saucer to Louisa. Louisa decided not to sugarcoat her concerns.

"Sadie, I'm concerned that the bullet which hit Mr. Kimura was not intended for Mr. Calloway."

"It was probably some random attempt at robbery," Sadie said and took a sip of her coffee.

Louisa set down the saucer and folded her hands in her lap.

"I don't think it was that either. I have no evidence, but what if...what if the bullet was meant for you?"

"Me?" Sadie's eyebrows rose and her eyes widened. "Why would anyone want to kill me?"

"I know it sounds absurd. But you've inherited quite a bit of money. First from your husband and then from your aunt. It's possible that someone would want to get at that money."

Sadie's expression grew sober.

"My late husband's relatives have made quite a fuss over not getting anything when he died. But he'd had nothing to do with that lot for years. They even threatened to sue me."

Louisa measured her words carefully.

"If anything were to happen to you, it would break Forr...Mr. Calloway's heart. He loves you so much."

"As I love him. You are very fond of him, too, aren't you?"

"He was my publisher, and he did get me out of a scrape or two over the years." And we had a love affair, she thought.

"I understand. He's like a big brother to you, isn't he?"

Louisa gazed down at the intricate patterns in the rug and nodded. "Yes, he is like an older brother."

"Well, I don't think there's any reason to worry about me," Sadie said. She reached over and patted Louisa's hand. "Louisa, I know a bit of your history. I know you have uncovered sordid doings and various crimes. In fact, Forrest has spoken with admiration of your investigative powers, but do you think it's possible that these experiences have clouded your perspective? Perhaps you see plots where there are none."

Louisa couldn't argue with Sadie's logic.

"It is possible. In fact, I hope that's the case here, but would you humor me? I have an idea, and if I'm wrong about this, then at least I can put my mind at ease."

Louisa boarded the train, wearing Sadie's elegant black dress, her face covered by a heavy veil. Sadie's maid carried her valise for her. They found their seats and made themselves comfortable. Sadie's maid put on a show of helping "Mrs. Treadwell."

Anna boarded the train and sat a few rows away as if they were strangers. Louisa wasn't sure when or how or if the killer would strike, but she'd had an uneasy feeling ever since the funeral.

The train lapped the miles, as the poetess put it, and trees that had been bare were covered in small bright green leaves.

Louisa had a copy of Booth Tarkington's *The Turmoil* that she'd been waiting to read and this seemed a perfect time — except that the maid kept talking about one thing or another.

"I've been with the missus since she was a girl of eighteen," Jenny said. "What a lovely person. And so generous. Last Christmas she gave me my own silver watch. 'Course, that may be to keep me more punctual, but it's a pretty piece. And when my poor ma was ill, she gave me leave and the train fare to go see to her. It about broke my heart when my ma died."

"Jenny," Louisa whispered. "I'm supposed to be the missus. Perhaps you shouldn't talk about me to me."

Jenny opened a paper bag and loudly proceeded to eat a roll covered with seeds that spilled all over the place.

Since she could no longer talk about Sadie, she embarked on the story of her childhood.

"We had a small family. Only seven kids," she said. "And we was always fighting over every scrap of bread. My ma was a religious woman all the way up till little Johnny died of the rheumatic fever at the age of two. She stopped believing when he took his last breath."

Looking out the window, Louisa thought of those women in Greenwich Village, all fighting to help women limit their families. How could poor families possibly feed and take care of all those children?

She put away her book, and eventually Jenny stopped talking. Louisa laid her head against the window and against her will, fell asleep.

The train made it all the way to Stamford, Connecticut, without incident and Louisa began to think that the assassin wouldn't make his move. He, or she, would likely wait till they got to New York to try to take another shot at "Sadie." If they did, they could easily disappear into the crowds at Penn Station. And what if this time his aim was better?

She needed some fresh air.

Jenny had fallen fast asleep. Louisa stood, edged around the snoring maid, and lurched toward the back of the train. She passed her mother, who had also dozed off and made her way to the caboose. She pulled open the heavy door and stepped onto the platform on the back.

No one else was on the platform so she took off her hat and veil and looked at the scenery rushing behind them—trees, a field, gray boulders left over from continental upheaval, a red barn. Clouds gathered in the north, but the train would outrun any brewing storm.

The door opened and she glanced around. A woman wearing a dark dress, a boxy hat with a half veil and sturdy black shoes came out onto the platform. Louisa wasn't worried about maintaining her disguise in front of a stranger.

Louisa smiled and said, "Good afternoon."

The woman nodded but said nothing as she rested her hands on the railing. They passed a pond filled with ducks and then rode on in silence for several minutes. Louisa glanced down at the woman's hands. They were quite large. Fine black hairs covered the backs of the fingers. Those were not the hands of a woman. She took another look at the face and gasped.

"You!"

The young man moved quickly. Within seconds a knife appeared in his hand. He gripped her by the arm with his other hand.

"You should have minded your own business," he said in a low growl.

Louisa twisted free of his grasp, pulled away, and screamed, a scream which was swallowed by the train's plaintive whistle.

He lunged toward her. Dodging the slender blade of the knife, she grabbed his wrist with both hands. But he was too strong for her. He pulled away and clutched her neck with his free hand, pushing her against the rail.

"After I'm done with you, I'll find that bitch and kill her too, and Edgar will be mine."

Louisa struggled, beating against him with her fists, but he squeezed her throat and grinned. The point of his blade pierced her skin. She was quickly losing consciousness.

Out of the corner of her eye, she saw something dark coming toward them. Suddenly he released her neck and yelled in surprise. Louisa gasped for air, coughing, and heard a steady thwacking. Her mother stood on the platform hitting the man over and over with her cane. The knife clattered to the metal platform and then with a final jab of her cane, Anna Delafield, daughter of New York bluebloods, shoved her cane into the man's solar plexus and he tumbled backwards over the edge of the platform.

Louisa caught her breath and looked at the receding body of the man on the train tracks.

"Mother, what have you done?" she whispered.

"Exactly what needed to be done."

"Is he dead?" Louisa wondered.

"I don't know and I don't care," Anna said. "As long as you're safe."

Her mother had never been affectionate, but she reached over and patted Louisa's trembling hand.

"There, there," she said. "I told you I loved you. I always have."

Chapter 44
Ellen

Ellen hurried to get to Suzie's brownstone before Mr. Sweet left for work. Suzie had sent a message that Mr. Sweet had some important news for her.

When she arrived, Mr. Sweet, dressed in his butler's uniform was already coming out the door.

"Ellen," he said, "walk with me."

Ellen fell into step next to the elderly but vigorous man.

"You remember that fuss about the Welland Canal in Canada a couple years ago?"

"One of the Germans' foiled plots, wasn't it? They wanted to blow up the locks to prevent the transport of men and guns from Canada. Something like that, am I right?"

"Exactly. Only the spy they sent there was some drunken fool who got arrested and spilled the beans."

"Just one of the reasons they finally expelled von Papen," Ellen said. "But why are you telling me this now."

Mr. Sweet put his hand on her arm and faced her with a triumphant look in his dark eyes.

"I heard them talking about it the last few nights. Seems Wolf von Igel's still got the plans in his office. They're going to try again."

Ellen's breath caught. "No."

"Yes." He grinned. "Them fools are going to try to blow up the Welland Canal. Unless somehow the secret service was to find out."

They resumed walking. They passed a fruit vendor, and Mr. Sweet purchased a banana which he peeled and ate as they talked.

"The problem is that von Igel works for Count Bernstorff. He probably has diplomatic immunity," Ellen said.

Mr. Sweet pondered that for about a half a block as he finished the banana.

"Was he on the staff in 1914?"

"I don't know."

"The plans are from 1914, so maybe the immunity wouldn't apply."

"It's worth a look, Mr. Sweet," Ellen said. "Worth a look."

But how would she get that look, she wondered. It was time to contact Reggie Grant.

"Did you deliver it?" Ellen asked when Carlotta came in and removed the feathered hat she had borrowed from Louisa's closet.

"Sure did. Dropped it in a hankie right by his table," Carlotta said. "Had to cough a few times to get the big lug's attention, but I got it. He'll be there."

"Thank you. Hester's been fed and she's napping. I'm not sure when I'll be back but there's a bottle in the ice box."

Ellen put on a modest hat and checked her purse. The cash was there right where she'd put it.

"Wish me luck," she said as she left the house.

Von Igel's office was on the 25th floor of a building on Wall Street. She got off the elevator and went to the office. The giant bodyguard sat with his feet propped upon a desk. As soon as she entered, he stood up, towering over her.

"I'd like to see Herr von Igel," Ellen said.

Without a word the bodyguard went into the inner office. She heard voices and then the big man came back and signaled for her to enter.

The desk in von Igel's office was strewn with papers, and she saw something that looked like architectural plans. A safe stood in the corner, its door wide open.

"What brings you here, *Frau* Malloy?" von Igel said. His little mustache quivered over his lip.

"I have a donation for the cause."

"Do you? From Devoy?"

"No, it is a personal donation. If my brother is going to fight the English, I want him and his comrades to be well supplied. And if Devoy can purchase rifles from the German army, so can I. Whatever assistance we get from the Germans, we will pay for."

"A point of Irish pride?" von Igel asked.

Ellen answered his question with a question of her own. "Is it true you are an attaché of the German Embassy?"

"Why do you ask?"

"I want to know this investment is safe, that you won't get arrested for some foolishness," she said, pointing to the plans on his desk.

"The American secret service are so stupid, they do nothing but run around chasing their own tails," he sneered. "Yes, the Count appointed me to his staff last year so I have immunity."

So, Ellen thought, if those really are the Welland Canal plans from 1914, then he won't have immunity.

"As long as your men do their part to help Ireland, then we Irish will do ours to keep the English occupied," she said. "Here is the money. Please see that Franz von Papen gets it. As we both know, the uprising is imminent."

He snorted. "Just in time for the resurrection—of the Irish people."

She nodded.

"Thank you, Herr von Igel," she said.

He clicked his heels and bowed his head in a perfunctory gesture. She left the office.

When the elevator doors opened, she was greeted by Reggie Grant with four of New York's finest.

"The plans are on the desk," she told him.

The men barreled toward von Igel's office while she got on the elevator.

"First floor," she told the elevator operator. He pushed the brass door closed. She took a deep breath as the elevator went down.

Chapter 45

Louisa

"They captured him," Sadie said as she stood in the library of her Brooklyn mansion, gazing out the window. "He was critically injured but not dead."

"What did he have to say for himself?" Louisa asked.

Sadie turned and faced her. She looked older, sadder.

"It turns out he was in love with Edgar and thought he was helping him by getting rid of me."

"I take it Edgar inherits your aunt's fortune if you're not around."

"Yes. I feel terrible that Mr. Kimura was shot because of this."

"Did Edgar give this man cause to believe the love was reciprocated?" Louisa asked.

"Edgar has had affairs with men and women over the years, so it's possible but, of course, Edgar won't admit it. What he did admit to me, finally, is that he is deeply in debt. I don't know why he didn't just tell me to begin with. I gave him the money to pay off his debts, and he has promised to stop gambling."

"That was generous of you," Louisa said.

"I don't need it, after all." Sadie took Louisa's hands in her own. "I do apologize for my efforts at matchmaking. I had no idea that Edgar had no money and was only looking to marry someone who did. I hope you can forgive me for that."

"There's nothing to forgive. I actually enjoyed his company."

"And then you risked your life to save me. How can I ever repay you?" Sadie asked.

Louisa pulled her lips in tight and inhaled sharply.

"Just be happy," she said. "Both of you."

Tears sprang to her traitorous eyes.

"Oh, dear," Sadie said.

In that moment as the two women looked into each other's eyes, Louisa's secret spilled wordlessly out into the open: Louisa was in love with the man Sadie was going to marry. Instead of being angry, Sadie nodded in sympathy.

"I'm so sorry," Sadie said.

"Please don't be," Louisa said. "I'll be at the wedding with bells on. Now, I should be going."

"Of course," Sadie said.

Louisa held her shoulders back and her head high as she emerged from Sadie's mansion into the warm spring day. Sadie was a kind and generous woman. She would make a lovely wife for Forrest. As for Louisa, she had her friends and her work. And her mother, who apparently did love her after all.

"Wolf von Igel is Seized by Federal Agents After a Struggle," Ellen read the headline out loud to the other women at breakfast.

"A struggle?" Anna said with a touch of glee. "I wonder what sort of ruckus he caused."

Ellen read the article: "Wolf von Igel, intimate of Captain Franz von Papen, and according to his own and the German Embassy's claim — notice how they say it was a claim, not a fact — an under Secretary of the embassy, was arrested yesterday morning charged with having been concerned with Captain von Papen, the recalled German Military Attaché and others in the alleged conspiracy to dynamite the Welland Canal in Canada."

"What about the struggle?" Carlotta asked.

"It says here he 'fought like a tiger' and shouted that the seizure of his person and papers will mean war between the United States and Germany."

"Which is exactly what Reggie hopes will happen," Louisa said. "With every mistake the Germans make, I'm afraid the drumbeat for war grows louder."

"And the government says he has no immunity." Ellen smiled in satisfaction.

Chapter 46
Ellen

Ellen used a spade to dig into the soil in the tiny backyard in order to plant the bulb.

"What are you doing?" Carlotta asked, jiggling little Hester on her hip.

"I'm planting garlic. You must plant it on Good Friday so it will have the best medicinal properties. My gran taught me that." She placed the bulb into the ground and pushed dirt over it and then dug another hole.

"Are you religious?" Carlotta asked. "You never go to mass, but you also never eat meat on Fridays."

"If you're asking if I believe that Jesus Christ died for my sins, the answer is yes. It's just that the priests and I have differing views on what exactly is a sin," she said. "I think it's a sin to starve and abuse people. They think it's a sin to love others."

Ellen dropped in another bulb. The old tradition of planting garlic helped her not to think about what was going on in Ireland. The Brotherhood leaders had so little military experience. Dread settled in her belly. She'd not been able to eat a single thing since yesterday.

Ellen rose, took the baby from Carlotta's arms, and kissed her plump cheek. The baby patted her hands on Ellen's face.

The day passed slowly, but the night was even longer. She couldn't stop her mind from filling with images of destruction and always with something terrible happening to Martin, a gunshot to the chest, a building collapsing on top of him, his young body hanging from a rope.

The next morning Ellen lay on the bed with the baby. Carlotta sat at the foot of the bed.

"She's getting so big," Carlotta said.

Louisa entered the room.

"Ellen, have you seen the paper? Roger Casement has been caught on a German U-boat."

"What? When?"

"It says, 'on or about Good Friday morning.'" Louisa handed the paper over to her.

"Who's Roger Casement?" Carlotta asked.

"He's a fool is what he is," Ellen said, skimming over the article. "He thinks the Germans will make good allies for the Irish, ignoring what they did to Denmark. Christ on the cross! Now, he's been arrested. And who knows how his brethren will react?"

"What does this mean for the rebellion?" Louisa asked.

"Perhaps, they'll abandon their plans." Ellen sighed in relief. "Perhaps, Martin will be safe after all. Or maybe it won't make a difference and they'll go ahead on Easter."

Louisa tilted her head. "I thought the uprising was planned for June."

"I lied to you." Ellen couldn't meet her eyes.

"Why? So I would tell Reggie the wrong date?"

Ellen nodded. "But you didn't tell him. And I didn't either when I had the chance." She paused and then said, "I'm sorry. I thought I was protecting my brother."

"Oh, girleen," Louisa said in a poor attempt at an Irish brogue. "I'm afraid there's no protecting him now."

On Easter Sunday, Louisa and Anna went to church services at Saint Bart's. Carlotta went with them though she said that the Episcopal church wasn't a real church. Ellen stayed home with the baby.

"When I was a little girl," she whispered to Hester, "We used to go from house to house asking for eggs. It was grand fun. We always decorated our baskets with ribbons. Some day when you're just a wee bit older, perhaps you'll do the same."

The baby babbled. She was past two months old now and stared with wide eyes at the world, soaking it in.

Easter Sunday passed quietly. If the rifles had not reached the rebels, then she should stop worrying so much. Wolf von Igel was in jail, the Irish girl was safely ensconced in Hattie's household, and the magazine finally had a printer. Ellen might be able to catch her breath. She could start thinking about the next issue, and maybe this week, she would search out another space for the magazine.

The clock in the hallway struck nine when Ellen woke up on Easter Monday and saw the morning sunlight plastered on the window. She hadn't slept so late in months. She glanced around the room and saw that Hester's bassinette were empty. Carlotta must have taken her downstairs. Ellen rubbed her face. She'd been up in the thick of night with the colicky child, by turns nursing her and bouncing her in her arms. She didn't even remember when they'd both passed out, exhausted.

What a luxury it was to have a few moments to herself. But nature nudged her, so she got out of the bed, went to the bathroom, washed herself, and then put on a linen dress. Spring had finally landed in the city, and everything was a bit lighter.

Ellen spent the morning looking for office space. After a couple of hours of traversing Harlem, she found a set of two rooms on the first floor of a collection of shops and offices near 135th Street and Seventh Avenue. An ideal location. She would still be close to Louisa's house so she could go home to feed the baby or she could bring the baby to work with her. The rooms were large and clean. They needed painting but that would be easy to arrange. She imagined a sign "The Ladies' Lantern" over the door. She could even hang a lantern in the window. She asked the realtor to hold the rooms for her and promised to come back with a check. Then she hurried back to tell Louisa the news.

She opened the door and hung her bag on a hook by the credenza. She heard voices from the parlor, including a man's, which meant that Mr. Thorn was there. He would be pleased to have an office separate from their living space. She stepped into the parlor and stopped short. Reggie Grant sat on the divan with a cup and saucer in his hands. Louisa slumped in her chair by the fireplace.

"Ellen," Louisa said. "It's Reggie."

"What are you doing here?" Ellen asked, her heart skipping erratically in her chest.

He set down the cup and looked at her with a grim expression.

"Ellen, I've just gotten a cable. There's been an outbreak in Dublin."

"Outbreak? What do you mean?"

He stood and approached her. "Sinn Fein is in armed defiance of the crown."

"But how? They don't have the rifles?" She looked from Reggie to Louisa and back to Reggie. "And my brother?"

"I don't know. We don't have much information at this point."

She sank into the nearest chair, leaned over and placed her head in her hands. What had they done?

The week passed in a blur. Ellen tried to busy herself, finding stories for the next issue of the magazine, all while perusing every paper she could find for information about what they were calling the Easter Rising. No Irish newspapers reached America that week, and the only information she could find came from 'official sources' — the British. *"TROOPS CRUSH REVOLT IN*

DUBLIN; TAKE POST OFFICE SEIZED BY RIOTERS; MANY KILLED IN STREET FIGHTING" read one such headline.

The *New York Times* did publish the proclamation from the Provisional Government. She wept as she read it. "The Irish Republic is entitled to, and hereby claims, the allegiance of every Irishman and Irishwoman. The Republic guarantees religious and civil liberty, equal rights and equal opportunities to all its citizens, and declares its resolve to pursue the happiness and prosperity of the whole nation and of all its parts, cherishing all the children of the nation equally, and oblivious of the differences carefully fostered by an alien Government, which have divided a minority from the majority in the past." Such hopeful words. Such high ideals.

All for naught, for on April 29th, the rebels surrendered.

When Paula called and asked her to go to a rally put on by the Irish Americans that Saturday night at the George M. Cohan Theater near Times Square, Ellen agreed to join her. Paula met her outside the theater and gave her an Irish pin to fasten to her lapel.

Ellen thought it would be a somber affair because of the defeat, but it was quite the opposite. The place was filled to the rafters, including both balconies as her countrymen and women from the United Irish Societies of America gathered together in the name of Ireland. Paula and Ellen found seats amongst a group from the Irish Women's League. A band of musicians occupied a stall on the ground floor. They began with a rousing "Star Spangled Banner," which had the whole place on its feet. There followed "The Wearing of the Green," a nostalgic favorite. But Ellen was shocked when they played *Deutschland Uber Alles*," the Irish Americans all around her singing along. Then came the speakers. Local politicians and priests, and of course, John Devoy. The crowd erupted when he came on stage. All the speakers expressed unqualified support for the Rising and a belief that America would be on their side. "We are not defeated!" they declared.

Ellen couldn't help but be moved. She wanted freedom for Ireland as much as anyone else. Hadn't her own da been a constant thorn in the side of the invaders and a "guest of the crown" in an English jail more than once?

Her heart swelled with pride only to be pierced a few minutes later.

The speaker was a priest named Father O'Donnell. "This has been a week we have hoped and waited for," he intoned. "Our brothers at home are fighting for all that we have prayed for. Ever since the Germans torpedoed a munition ship, we have known they were on our side!"

Christ on the Cross, Ellen thought, he means the *Lusitania.*

The crowd roared its approval. Ellen overheard a man with a German accent shout that he hoped they would sink a lot more. She squeezed her eyes shut. And it all came back to her: the explosions, the fear, the life-boat tipping over, the screams, and then the swollen bodies of dead bodies in the sea, picked over by the seagulls.

She told Paula she wasn't feeling well and fled the building. More than a thousand Americans and Irish died that day in the Irish Sea, and her Irish-American brothers and sisters were cheering.

The next few days passed uneventfully. The rebellion had been broken. She had no word of Martin. On the morning of May 4, she descended the stairs and entered the dining room where Anna, Louisa, and Carlotta sat at the table. Ellen stopped at the sideboard and poured a cup of coffee. The three women were unnaturally quiet. Even little Hester slept in Carlotta's arms.

"I do enjoy silence," Ellen said, "but this has me worried."

She sat down and plucked a scone and took a bite, wiping crumbs from her mouth with a napkin.

Louisa passed her the front page of *The New York Times.*

Ellen stared in disbelief as she read, "Patrick Pearse, Thomas Clark, and Thomas MacDonagh executed for their role in the Easter Rising."

Immediately her mind conjured the scene: a barrage of bullets and then the bodies, crumpled on the ground, slaughtered.

"Did you know them?" Carlotta asked.

"I knew of them. Poets, playwrights, theatre directors. Patrick Pearse called the English education system forced on the Irish a 'Murder Machine.' He started schools in the Irish language," she said. "I always wished I was a better speaker of Irish myself."

Louisa looked on sympathetically. "I'm afraid America will be joining the war soon, sending off our young men to die. There's a 'Great Preparation Parade' starting at Bowling Green in just a few minutes," Louisa said, consulting her watch. "It's supposed to be 150,000 strong."

"They should stop preparing, and start doing," Anna said.

Ellen looked again at the newspaper article. A heavy silence descended on the table until Louisa said, gently, "Any word of your brother?"

Ellen shook her head, not trusting herself to speak.

"Will you keep Hester, Carlotta? There's somewhere I've got to go."

"What if she wakes up and is hungry?"

"Go to the milk bank and buy some more bottles, for crying out loud. I won't be a feeding trough today."

At Paula's house, Ellen found the leaders of the Irish Women's League gathered. The rage in the small parlor was a living thing, made of fire.

"They wouldn't even give 'em proper burials," one of the women complained. "Said it would make martyrs of 'em."

"I read that they're executing family members to-morrow," another said.

Ellen sat next to Paula. "Have you news of Martin?"

Paula nodded, tears in her eyes.

"I got a cable. He's been arrested," she said. "What if they execute him, too?"

Ellen took her into her arms and said, "I won't let it happen. I promise."

"What can you do?" Paula asked.

"Last year I helped expose the German saboteurs who were blowing up American ships at sea."

"You did what?" one of the women exclaimed. "Are you a traitor? The Germans are on our side."

"A traitor? For not wanting to turn my homeland over to the Huns? Only a fool would think that a better proposition."

"Are you calling Sir Roger Casement a fool?" an-other woman asked.

"I am," Ellen said. "He had good intentions. I knew him. But he made a fool of himself in Germany, thinking he might recruit Irish prisoners of war. They wanted nothing to do with him. And then for him to take a German U-boat into Irish waters..."

"With German guns for our fighters," the woman hissed.

"Leave her alone," Paula barked. "She was on the *Lusitania*."

There was a moment of silence before one of the woman said, "You mean the *munitions* ship?"

"There were Irish families on that ship. And Americans of every class. I saw them die." Ellen's voice rose despite her efforts to quell her anger.

Brigid Rafferty's Aunt Maeve stepped up.

"Ellen Malloy saved my niece from a terrible fate. If any of you speaks against her, I'll have your tongue!"

That did the trick. The women grumbled, but the conversation turned back toward the executions and how public sentiment was turning against the British for these outrages.

When Ellen got home, she wrapped Hester in a blanket and stuffed a valise full of baby clothes, diapers, and bottles.

"Where are you taking her?" Carlotta asked.

"To Katherine Murphy," Ellen said.

"But why are you packing all her things?"

"Because I'm going to Ireland, and I can't take her with me."

"You're doing what?" Louisa asked from the doorway.

"Martin's been arrested. You know what the English military is doing. Lining prisoners against a wall and shooting them as if they were nothing but animals. I can't let…" She was unable to finish the sentence.

"But what can you do?" Louisa asked.

Ellen met her gray eyes.

"You know full well the British owe me. And Reggie Grant will back me up if you ask him to."

"But the baby…"

"I must go. I have no choice," Ellen said.

"Why not leave Hester with me and Carlotta?"

Ellen shook her head.

"I know you love her, Louisa, and Carlotta's a good nursemaid, but I've arranged for Katherine and John Murphy to keep her should anything happen to me. You know as well as I do, heading into the Irish Sea means I might never return."

"Oh, Ellen. What a terrible choice for you to have to make."

On the way to the Murphy's apartment, Ellen held Hester close. Finally, she had felt maternal love, greater than anything she'd ever experienced. Even her love of Hester French had not been this powerful.

"Girleen," she whispered. "What am I to do now that you've conquered my heart? I canna give you what you need, the life you deserve. I love you like I love my life, little Hester Murphy. I'll always love you. But there are things I need to do, and I may not make it back."

She took the elevator up to the tenth floor where Katherine Murphy stood waiting with open arms. Ellen kissed Hester's soft cheek and inhaled deeply. The smell of her baby was a sweet perfume.

"Don't you worry, dear. We'll take good care of her," Katherine said.

Ellen walked out of the apartment and stepped onto the elevator. She saw a blurry vision of Katherine in the doorway, smiling at the baby in her arms. The doors closed.

Chapter 47
Louisa

Louisa took the Third Avenue El from Harlem downtown to Hanover Square in the financial district. She had told Reggie she needed to see him, and he had suggested she meet him at the India House, a gentlemen's club for men who were involved in foreign commerce. She crossed the street and climbed the steps of the whitewashed Italianate building with window boxes and ornamental lanterns. Of course, Reggie was a member, and while women were not generally admitted, members were allowed to show the art collection to female guests.

Reggie came to the foyer to retrieve her.

"Louisa, lovely as ever," he said, scooping her by the elbow.

"I'm honored to be admitted to such august environs." Sarcasm dripped from her tongue. She found the whole idea of these gentlemen enclaves offensive. Until recently she would have not even realized the harm done to women by these closed doors, but her work with the Heterodoxy women had opened her eyes.

The art collection housed in the main room was indeed stunning: a gilt eagle from a pilot ship, wooden models of merchant ships, a Chinese silk portrait of a warrior in an elaborate frame carved with serpents and gods.

"Why do they call it the India House?" Louisa asked.

"It has something to do with evoking the past when international trade was all about India. Spices from India, fabrics from India, tea from India."

"No actual Indian members?"

"Certainly not."

She stopped in front of a portrait of a sailing vessel with billowing white sails on a turquoise sea. The artist had painted the foreground in shadow, and she imagined her own ancestors crossing the Atlantic 200 years ago.

"Why did you want to meet me?" he asked quietly.

"Ellen's brother has been arrested. She's afraid he will be executed. She wants to know if there is anything she can do to save him?"

Reggie glanced around to make sure no one was nearby.

"There's always something she can do. Unless it's too late."

"Too late?"

"He may already be scheduled for hanging. Or for the firing squad."

"Oh, Reggie, you can't let that happen. Ellen will be devastated."

He guided her to an alcove sheltered by a large clock.

"There is something she can do," Reggie said in a low voice. "If she agrees, I'll send a cable immediately to halt any orders regarding her brother."

Louisa sat next to Ellen on the sofa in the parlor.

"You met with Reggie?" Ellen asked.

"He wants you to contact a man named Albert Sander," Louisa said. "He's the drama critic of a German newspaper here in New York. Apparently, Sander is recruiting journalists to go to England to report on conditions."

"Conditions? Such as?"

"How much food is available for the population, whether or not the people are experiencing distress, are the efforts of the German blockade working. They also want to know sailing dates for merchant ships."

"But I need to get to Ireland. How will that help me?"

"Reggie believes the Germans would send you there, to find out if the Rising is finished and what they might to cause further trouble. If you agree, he will cable Lord Wimborne in Dublin and forestall your brother's execution."

"Forestall? Why not cancel?" Ellen asked.

"I trust Reggie to make sure that happens."

"I don't trust anyone," Ellen said.

Louisa's chest felt hollow. She didn't want Ellen to leave, and she was stunned to realize how much she would miss the baby.

Chapter 48
Ellen

Ellen wore a large hat with a veil and sat in the lobby of the Ritz where she waited near an aquarium with colorful fish darting back and forth. She'd bribed the clerk to let her sit unmolested. It was almost midnight when Count Bernstorff stumbled in with a buxom young woman in a clingy dress attached to his arm. He was much too interested in the young woman at his side to notice Ellen get on the elevator with the two of them.

"Floor?" the operator asked.

"Nine." Bernstorff grinned at the young woman. He lowered his face to her neck and she squealed.

"Your whiskers tickle!"

"You just wait. I will tickle you in all the right places," he said and snorted.

He was quite drunk, oblivious to the elevator operator and to Ellen. When the elevator reached the ninth
floor, Ellen followed Bernstorff and the woman down
the hallway. They got to his room, and he dug in his
pocket, fumbling with the key.

"Count Bernstorff," Ellen said in a loud voice. "Does
your wife know about your activities?"

He whirled around and glared at her, his face was
purple from too much whiskey.

She lifted the veil.

"You! What do you want?" His nostrils flared in out-
rage. The young woman's crimson lips frowned.

"I want to speak to you. Alone." She adopted the im-
perious tone she had learned from Louisa's mother,
Anna Delafield.

"I'm busy now. Come back later." He waved her off.

"I want to speak *now*." She turned her eyes toward
the woman. "You can wait in the lobby, dear. This won't
take long."

Bernstorff's companion glanced in confusion from
Ellen to Bernstorff. The count nodded, and she swayed
toward the elevator with a huff.

"Come in and be quick about it," he said.

Ellen entered the suite. It was the height of luxury
with gilt chairs, velvet curtains, antique side tables, and
a plush settee. Bernstorff shut the door and wheeled
around to face her, his mustache quivering.

"What is it?"

"I need to get go to Ireland," she said.

"So go. I am not stopping you."

"No, but you can help me. And I can help you. You can use someone there who can get inside the Brotherhood. You need eyes and ears on the ground. And who better than someone who can pose as a journalist?"

"You're not a journalist," he scoffed.

"No? I have an entire magazine at my disposal. I would like you to put in a word for me with Albert Sander."

"Albert? The drama critic?"

"I know he's one of your men, and he's recruiting journalists. Do it now, if you please. Or I'll be making myself at home here in your lovely accommodations."

Bernstorff stuck his hands in his pockets and rocked back on his heels. "What happened with von Igel? It seems you were the last one to visit before his arrest."

"You want to blame me for his stupidity?" Ellen gave him an incredulous look. "I gave him money to pay for guns. It was my own money actually. And now that's gone. And the rebellion has failed. I've a mind to write a letter to Captain Nicolai and tell him about the incompetence of his men here."

Bernstorff glared at her, his cultured facade gone. Then he lumbered over to a desk in the corner of the room and picked up the telephone receiver. The Ritz was a modern hotel and had all the conveniences for its customers. When the call was connected, Bernstorff spoke in rapid German. Then he hung up the phone and glared at her.

"He'll meet you at the restaurant downstairs."

"Now?"

"In the morning at eight. Go! And tell that woman I was with to come back up here."

Ellen bestowed a polite smile on him and left the room.

Albert Sander happily enlisted her in the cause.

"You will go as a correspondent to Ireland. With your connections, you will learn the state of the rebel lion. Has it truly been quelled? Are there pockets of resistance? What is the mood of the Irish people? Size up the English forces, as well. The more of them in Ireland, the fewer there will be on the continent. If we sent more arms, are there rebels to use them?"

He gave her instructions and materials for using invisible ink to send correspondence and then booked her passage on the *SS Frederick VIII*. Most of the transatlantic passenger ships had been converted to hospitals or troop ships due to the war. Few people wanted to travel from America to Europe while there was a possibility of getting sunk by a German *untersee* boat. The *Frederick VIII* was one of the few.

Ellen stood on the stoop, waiting for the taxi to pick her up. Palen green leaves sprouted from the trees, flowers bloomed in window flower boxes and birds madly went about their bird business.

"Aren't you afraid of the U-boats?" Louisa asked.

"Not really. I believe the Germans learned their lesson with the *Lucy*," Ellen said. "They want America to remain neutral and sinking boats with civilians has proven bad for public relations."

"But being a double agent is so dangerous. I never should have gone to Reggie with this." Louisa frowned.

"Louisa, I must do whatever I can to save my brother," Ellen said.

"And then you'll come home," Louisa said. "And you'll live here with us. You and the baby. And Carlotta. You are always welcome here."

In an unprecedented display of affection, Ellen took Louisa in her arms and held her for a good long moment.

Then the taxi arrived. Carlotta stood in the doorway, looking morose.

"Arrivederci, Ellen!" she cried.

"Send a cable when you get there, please!" Louisa called out as Ellen got in the taxi. She looked back just once and then turned to face forward. She must have no second thoughts.

The SS *Frederick VIII* was nothing like the luxurious *Lusitania* had been, but it was comfortable enough for her. She had a cabin in second class. With Hester's fortune she could easily have afforded first class, but she would have been uncomfortable in that sumptuous environment especially without Hester. Second class was perfectly nice. The cabins were quite comfortable with mahogany furniture, wash basins and a sitting area. The water closets were just down the hall.

On the *Lusitania* she had befriended an entire gaggle of Irish women in third class, but on this voyage she kept to herself — except for an old man with whom she sometimes played backgammon. If they were all to die, she preferred not to know the names of her fellow victims.

Her arms felt empty without a baby in them, but then she thought of the sheer joy beaming from Katherine Murphy's eyes when she looked at Hester. The childless woman had been so grateful just to have her for a few hours at a time, and now, who knew how long it would be until Ellen returned. Already Ellen's milk had dried up and her breast size had returned to normal.

Ship travel was an odd sort of limbo, as if she were wandering around purgatory. All the worldly concerns were gone. She didn't think about suffrage for women, birth control, the rights of workers. The only thing that mattered right now was saving Martin. Ma had already lost one son.

Ellen had never been close to her older brother, Michael. But she had him to thank for her quick reflexes and her skill in self-defense. When they were young, he liked to hide behind the boat shed to ambush her or Martin. Sometimes he'd tie her up and leave her in the marsh until she'd figure out how to get free. He had a streak of cruelty, but it had been good training. That training had saved her more than once, but now she was a rich woman and a magazine publisher. She was beyond the need for the instincts he'd instilled. Rich people didn't need to worry about self-preservation. Only, she wasn't a rich person, she reminded herself. She was a poor person who had inherited a fortune after losing the person she loved.

Chapter 49

Louisa

"It's a letter for you," Carlotta said, coming into the dining room where Louisa and Anna were having breakfast.

Louisa opened the letter and read aloud:

Signorina Delafield,

Please to come to my office at the stable. I have information that you will want to know.

Yours truly,

Nicolo Morello

"What sort of name is Morello?" Anna asked.

"Italian," Carlotta said with a hint of indignation. Anna sniffed and resumed eating her breakfast.

"It seems we're out of coffee," she noted, blandly.

How could Nicolo Morello have information I would want, Louisa wondered.

"You want I should come with you again?" Carlotta asked.

Louisa shook her head.

"Oddly enough, I trust the man."

"I have heard he has honor," Carlotta said.

So Louisa found herself once again in Nicolo Morello's office in the murder stable on East 108th Street. He offered her a cup of coffee in a demitasse cup. It was delicious and strong enough to power a train.

"You said you had information that would interest me?" she said.

He leaned back in his chair, lit a cigarette, and blew a plume of smoke into the air.

"Would you care for a smoke?"

"No, thank you. You were saying you had information....?"

He lowered his elbows to his desk.

"I heard something that made me curious. A wealthy man sent his chauffeur to the stable. They wanted to hire someone to commit murder. That article in the newspaper about the 'murder stable' has the whole city believing we're a nest of assassins."

"This wealthy man wanted one of your people to murder someone?"

"Yes. On a boat. A woman."

Louisa was confused. What on Earth did this have to do with her?

"I remember you said you wrote stories for a magazine, something about a lantern."

"Yes, *The Ladies' Lantern.*"

"That's it. They want to kill the woman who makes that magazine."

Louisa suddenly felt sick. Someone hired an assassin to kill Ellen? But why?

He nodded.

"We turned him down. So they went to Brooklyn and found someone else. That's what I hear anyway. I thought to tell you." He tapped his cigarette ash into a glass bowl.

"Oh, dear," Louisa whispered. "Ellen is already on the boat headed for England."

Nicolo Morello studied her reaction with dark, deep-set eyes. It could have been sympathy he was trying to convey. "I would have told you sooner but only just found out about the Brooklyn hire. That territory belongs to the Camorra. No friends of mine."

Carlotta's family, Louisa realized.

"Do you remember what kind of car the chauffeur drove?" Louisa asked.

"Of course. It was a red Rolls Royce."

Louisa closed her eyes and blew out a breath. She knew who had done this.

Louisa hadn't seen Hugh Garrett since his wedding day. They had been friends as children — before her father died and their fortune was lost. Even after that, Hugh had remained friendly. Then, of course, she had found out about his treatment of the poor girl he'd gotten pregnant and worse things. A man as rich and powerful as Hugh was impossible to bring down, but she had hoped that after he married, some semblance of the kind-hearted boy she'd once known would take over.

She took a taxi to his five-story granite house just off Fifth Avenue. It was the same street on which she had lived as a child, but it may as well have been on another planet. She didn't even write about society any more.

It was evening. The family would be dressing for dinner. She assumed his mother still lived with him, probably making his poor wife miserable.

The butler, Mr. Strauss, answered. His hair had gone white, but he still had a kindly face.

"Miss Delafield," he said in surprise.

"Hello, Mr. Strauss. You look well," she said.

"Thank you, Miss."

"Would you please tell Hugh I need to speak to him. It's quite urgent."

"Of course, please come in. You may wait in the library."

The old man showed her into the library. It was a stuffy room filled with books that no one read and marble statues in the corners like prisoners. Unable to sit still, Louisa paced across the Persian rug until the door opened and there stood Hugh, her childhood friend, with his blue eyes and the cowlick in his hair that made him look like a perpetual boy.

"Louisa," he said. "I hope nothing's wrong. It's been ages. Why haven't you come to see Millicent? I know she's invited you to several soirées. You always send your regrets."

"It's not really my world anymore, Hugh."

"This will always be your world," he said, reaching his arms out expansively as if this stuffy, gauche room with its ugly landscapes on the wall represented the pinnacle of human achievement. "You're a Delafield."

"I'm not here to discuss my bloodline," she said. "I understand that you hired someone to murder my friend Ellen Malloy."

He stared at her. His cold blue eyes told her that she had guessed correctly.

"Oh, Hugh, have you become a monster?"

"I don't know what you're talking about. Why would I do anything to hurt your friend?"

"Would it have anything to do with the young woman Hattie recently hired as ladies' maid? Ellen had something to do with that. You wanted that girl for yourself."

Again, she saw guilt on his face.

"Hugh, if anything should happen to Ellen while she's on this voyage, I will hold you personally responsible."

"What can you do? You have no money, no power. You aren't even a society columnist anymore. You associate with rabble rousers and lowlifes. You are nobody."

"Really? You just said I was a Delafield. I'm not just a Delafield. I'm *Louisa* Delafield. I still have the power of the pen, and I have friends. In fact, I've already had a conversation with Captain Tunney. So, if anything happens to me, they'll come to you first."

Hugh shook his head and looked embarrassed.

"Louisa, I'd never hurt you. Never."

She almost believed him.

"Hugh, if there's any way you can stop this, do so."

He shook his head again.

"I have no way..."

"We used to be friends. How...?" she couldn't finish.

At that moment the door opened.

"Hugh? We're going to be late... Oh!" Hugh's pretty young wife, Millicent, stood in the doorway, a look of confusion on her face. Confusion that turned to concern and possibly disappointment, the heartbroken look of a woman who knew her husband sometimes strayed.

"Hello, Millicent," Louisa said, approaching with an outstretched hand. "I'm Louisa Delafield, an old friend of Hugh's. I wrote about your wedding for *The Ledger*."

"Oh, yes, I remember you." Millicent smiled in relief. She had pale, luminescent skin, but already two furrows were developing between her eyebrows. Marriage sometimes brought strange sorrows.

"I won't keep you any longer. I just stopped by to ask Hugh's advice on some investments. Do enjoy your evening. And Hugh, thank you for your help. I know you'll do whatever you can to make sure my investment is safe."

Louisa left the house. She did not believe that there was nothing Hugh could do. He was in the shipping business, after all. There must be some way to communicate with a ship at sea.

Fear for Ellen gripped her, and she bit her finger to keep from crying out.

Chapter 50

Ellen

The first inkling she had that something was amiss was when she came into her cabin after lunch and saw that her bags had been riffled. Sander had instructed her in using invisible ink, which is something she had not learned from her previous spymaster. In her bag she had several ballpoint pens and a brown wool scarf, the ends of which had been smeared with the invisible ink. She was to soak the end of the scarf in water to release the ink and use a ballpoint pen and rough paper to write her messages. But whoever had gone through her things must not have known what the pens were for.

Who would be snooping in her room and why, she wondered. Surely not the Germans. They believed she was in their employ. No reason for the Irish to be interested in her. Perhaps it was just a thief looking for something to steal and finding nothing. Aside from the cheap wedding band, she owned not a single piece of jewelry, and her money was in a safe.

She went to the library in the second-class section and settled in to read a book, but the book didn't hold her attention. She thought of that moment when she had finally looked deeply into her child's eyes and felt that indissoluble bond. That moment would stay with her the rest of her life.

Dinner was served in the second-class dining room. She was seated at a long table with several other single travelers as well as a young couple. The conversation was pleasant. No one wanted to think about the war, much less talk about it. The baked haddock and boiled rice tasted good. She followed it with a plum pudding.

When she went back to her cabin, she saw that no one had been in during her absence, and began to think it may have simply been a steward who had been in the room. After a quick trip down the hall to the water closet, she came back to the room and put on her nightclothes. She fell asleep quickly, but woke up in the night with her heart racing. She'd been dreaming of the dark shape of the torpedo heading toward the *Lusitania.*

Restless, she rose from her bed and got dressed. Before the war, the first-class passengers would still be drinking and dancing, but now the ship moved in darkness. She left her cabin and made her way to the promenade deck. Through a window, she saw a couple of old men in the smoking room next to the deck, but on the deck itself she was alone. She leaned against the rail. Light from the sliver of moon stippled the surface of the water. Above her the splatter of stars shone like so many winking angels. She inhaled the scent of the ocean. This was not the *Lusitania*, she told herself. This ship would not go down. The ocean had already taken the woman she loved. What more could it want?

She heard footsteps and turned to see one of the stewards approaching her.

"Nice night, isn't it?" he said.

"'Tis." She turned her gaze to the sparkling firmament above.

"So many stars." He stood next to her at the rail.

At that moment, she thought of her brother, Michael. How he would sidle up next to her before shoving her into the water trough. She wheeled around to see a champagne bottle coming for her head. She ducked, turned, and ran.

"Help!" she screamed before he grabbed her and clamped his hand over her mouth.

She bit the hand as hard as she could. He released her mouth, then grabbed her hair and shoved her up against the rail. He was wiry and strong. Thrusting her head toward his face as hard and fast as she could, she nailed his nose. The bone crunched, and he grunted in pain. She slipped out of his grip and dropped low.

"No, you don't," he said.

He leaned over her, slipping his hands under her arms. She twisted and jammed her elbow into his throat. He gasped, and staggered backwards. She started to run again, but then stopped. She must use the element of surprise.

She turned toward him and dove toward his feet, knocking him off balance. Then she leapt up and went for the throat again, this time with the heel of her boot. She stomped just above his collarbones. Blood gushed from his mouth. He thrashed but she pushed harder until her boot touched his backbone. Death showed more mercy than she did and came quickly.

Should she leave his body there? *No.* There would be too many questions. He was not a particularly large man, but he would be the very definition of dead weight. However, she was strong and her blood sang with that power that comes from a heady dose of fear. She would use the strength of her legs and back to push him up over the rail. All she had to do was lift him onto her shoulders, using the same principle she'd learned as a girl when helping her father bring in a net full of herring. She squatted next to the body and took his arms. The coppery smell of blood swarmed around her. She wormed her back underneath him, and awkwardly staggered upright. She shoved his torso over the rail, and then it was a matter of tipping his lower half upward. She noticed his shoes as they brushed past her. They were new with rubber soles, and she wondered if he'd purchased them just to sneak up on her. As she leaned over the rail, she saw his body break the surface. Then he was sucked under the ship.

She stood there with a dead man's blood soaking through her dress. She had killed him. She should feel something, but she didn't. She didn't feel a thing. Except relief.

A strange sensation, first cold and then warm, passed through her and the smell of lavender tickled her nose.

"Did I do a terrible thing?" she said aloud.

A gentle voice in her head said, "No, my love. You are bravery itself."

Below her the white crests of the waves twinkled in the moonlight.

Chapter 51
Louisa

The taxi pulled up to the curb a block away from the church. A morning in May. A perfect day for a wedding. Virgil Thorn walked by Louisa's side.

"Lucky for me, crying at weddings is allowed," Louisa said in a low voice as they approached the church among a sea of other guests — Boston Brahmins, Broadway stars, publishers of every major newspaper.

"Allowed? It's positively *de rigeur*," Thorn said. "I might join you."

As former employees of Forrest Calloway, it was perfectly appropriate for them to attend the wedding together. She was glad she didn't have to come alone.

They found seats in a pew towards the back of the church. Louisa sat on the aisle. To distract herself from the fact she was witnessing the marriage of the man she loved to another woman, she imagined she was once again a society writer and that she was covering the wedding for her column, as she had covered so many weddings in the past.

She took mental notes: As Sadie was a widow and this was *en second noces*, she wore a satin gown of pale violet and a delicate toque adorned with white lace instead of a white dress. She carried no orange blossoms as women did for their first wedding, but instead held a bouquet of purple orchids, tied with a satin ribbon. According to Louisa's mother, in the last century, widows wore their first wedding ring on their finger and the new husband had to slide the new band next to the old one, a little reminder that he was not entering "virgin" territory. Fortunately, that tradition was dead and buried along with husband number one.

As soon as the Episcopal priest said, "Dearly Beloved," Louisa imagined it was she standing there in Sadie's place.

After the vows were said, Sadie's youngest child, a boy of about three, carried her bouquet back down the aisle and the other boy, who was about five, walked at his side. The music was "Ode to Joy," which was more appropriate for a second wedding than "The Wedding March."

As she came down the aisle, Sadie smiled at Louisa. Louisa returned the smile and wiped away a tear.

Louisa declined to go to the wedding breakfast, and Thorn had no interest in it either.

"What shall you do now that the publisher of *The Ladies' Lantern* has absconded across the water?" he asked in the taxi on the way back to Harlem.

"I'll wait for her to return," Louisa said. "I suppose I'll catch up on a few stories in the meantime. I never did find Djuna Barnes. And I still need to write the story about the Boston censors for the next issue."

"Louisa, I'm not sure writing about poets and censorship and so forth is really your bailiwick," he said.

"What do you mean? When I was writing for *The Ledger* I wrote several topical articles under the name Beatrice Milton, if you recall. You edited and published some of those stories. I wrote about abortion, contraception, and the trafficking of women."

"I remember. And they were good stories. But those stories gave you the chance to do real investigations. I got the sense that it was the adventure that drew you in. You do realize you solved three murders in the past month."

"I suppose I did," she said, surprised as she realized the truth of what he was saying. Was she on the wrong path in her life, she wondered.

He cleared his throat.

"I have some news to tell you," he said.

"Yes?"

"I'm going back to England. What with this damnable war going on, I feel I can't stay here any longer. I've gotten a job with the war office."

Louisa felt her world falling out from under her feet. Ellen was off in Ireland. Forrest was married. And now Thorn was leaving.

Louisa went home, and worked on completing her story about the Boston conspiracy of censorship, but it felt rather like wasted effort. Who knew when Ellen would come back and now Thorn wouldn't even be around.

She realized she had forgotten all about dinner when she noticed a strange odor. A good one. She went downstairs, following the lure of the aroma. It was... garlic. In the kitchen she found Carlotta standing over the large pan, red sauce bubbling inside.

"I thought you couldn't cook." She stared at Carlotta in shock.

"Of course, I can cook. I'm Italian. It's in my blood." Carlotta stirred the sauce. "It's almost ready."

Louisa, Anna, and Carlotta sat down to eat. Anna had insisted on bringing out the Wedgwood china with the bramble pink pattern that had been her wedding gift.

"Food that smells this good should be eaten on the best plates," she said.

Carlotta's spaghetti was as good as any Louisa had tried in a restaurant. Her Italian childhood must have been more influential than she ever admitted.

"I have to go out tonight," Louisa said after she finished the last bite of her dinner.

"Go out? Have you an invitation somewhere?" Anna's voice was petulant and hopeful.

"No, Mother. I have received no invitations to a ball or a *soirée* or anything of that nature. I simply want to go out."

"By yourself?"

"I'm 28 years old. I do not require a chaperone."

She took the subway to Greenwich Village, which was teeming with revelry. She wanted to be around the poets and playwrights and artists who made up Bohemia.

The myriad gift shops were closed. She sat in a basement cafe, surrounded by long-haired men in flowy ties and short-haired women smoking cigarettes, wearing makeup. Louisa enjoyed the crackling energy. She would never be a Bohemian herself, but she could appreciate their *joie de vivre*. She had just finished her coffee when she felt a presence at her side.

"Hello, you."

Louisa looked up into the face of a woman with full red lips, a pointy chin and dark eyes filled with curiosity. She wore a pork-pie hat pulled over one eyebrow and looked as though she might burst out laughing at any moment.

"I hear you've been looking for me," the woman said in a voice as warm as molten gold. The scent of sandalwood wafted about her.

Louisa knew her without a single doubt.

"Djuna Barnes, I presume?"

"The one and only. Shall we go to the Cafe Lafayette for a New Orleans fizz?" Djuna asked, though it was more of a command than a question. She was tall and angular and had a magnetic force that pulled Louisa up out of her seat and onto the streets.

They went to the cafe on Ninth street. Twin awnings jutted out to the street. It was an odd-looking place, three townhouses patched together. Inside was warm and cozy. Every single waiter they passed, nodded to "Miss Barnes." It seemed all of Bohemia was inside. They got a table by the window.

Louisa rarely drank liquor; she preferred wine or beer. She took a sip of the gin fizz.

"This is delicious," she said. "We don't have clubs like this in Harlem."

Djuna lit a cigarette.

"It is not where one washes one's neck but where one moistens one's throat that matters," Djuna said.

And so Louisa Delafield's night of debauchery ensued. They "painted the town" or at least Greenwich Village, flitting from cafe to cafe to rooftop garden to private studio. They drank New Orleans fizzes and did the one-step and the two-step and the tango with whatever fellow was willing to cut the rug. Djuna dispensed nuggets of gossip along the way as they encountered the denizens of the Village. She seemed to know everyone.

"That one's a dancer who thought herself in love with a Cossack. And there's George who is planning to erect a Toy Theatre on Washington Square. And this is Christine," Djuna said, greeting a gaudy woman who might have actually been a man. "She would have been a great goddess in another century."

Christine laughed gaily, and they moved on to the next spot, Romano's, for a midnight dinner. Oddly enough, in spite of her spaghetti dinner earlier, Louisa was ravenous. And she was astounded at the pronouncements that flowed from the lips of Djuna Barnes. She had an opinion on everything.

"Greenwich Village is the only place in the world where the waiters feel free to cultivate their innermost longings and acquire a soul. It's a place where everyone is as good as everyone else."

Djuna told Louisa a bit of her history, growing up with both her mother and her father's mistress in the home. She'd been married unhappily and briefly. Now she supported her mother and brothers with her writing. Louisa told of her own struggles to support her mother and how she had only succeeded by defying her boss and writing yellow journalism.

The more they drank the more erudite Djuna became.

"I once knew a girl who was born laughing," she said. "She had a laugh that sprang up from the gutter like a flower. Her eyes were set in her face like a child's peering over a wall."

Eventually, they came to a park beside the Hudson where they sat drinking champagne from the bottle, watching the river slide past.

"The waves are like soldiers slouching toward oblivion," Djuna said.

"Or wild horses stampeding shoulder to shoulder," Louisa countered.

"They are ghosts in empty coats."

Louisa giggled. She was quite drunk and yet her mind operated with crystal clarity.

"It's all so ephemeral," she said. "None of this was here except for the river and the sky a hundred years ago. And who knows what it will look like in another hundred."

"You and I will be forgotten, my dear," Djuna said.

"I will be. But 'they' will remember your work."

The night dissolved into a blur until finally they found themselves drinking coffee in a cafe that claimed to be closed but was open to Djuna Barnes.

"I hear so much about free love," Louisa said, "But I'm afraid it's not for me."

"How many men, or women for that matter, have you made love to, Louisa?" Djuna asked.

"Not many. There's the man I'm in love with, whose wedding I just attended, and then there was an unpleasant experience with a Frenchman who turned out to be a murderer, and then a spy who was engaged to another woman. At least sex with him was not unpleasant. In fact, it was fun."

"No women?" Djuna asked.

"No. My friend Ellen was in love with a woman, but I am not made that way."

"I love who I want to love. It doesn't matter if they are a man or a woman." Djuna leaned back and spread her arms.

"I suppose that widens the field," Louisa said.

"Yes, it also means there are twice as many fools who can break your heart." Djuna spoke as one who had also had her heart broken.

They wound up watching the sun rise from the balcony of the cafe, a sliver of orange sliding like a thumb nail through a crack in the clouds.

"Marcus Aurelius said that each day should be treated as the last. Do you agree?" Djuna leaned on the railing as beams of light pierced the sky.

"I think I may not have many days left if I treated them all as the last," Louisa said, laughing.

Djuna took off her hat and turned it like a wheel in her hands. "Will you write about this night for your friend's magazine?"

"No," Louisa said. "I think I'll keep this one for myself."

For a moment she thought Djuna might kiss her. But the moment passed.

Louisa found a taxi to take her back to Harlem. For someone who hadn't slept in 24 hours, she felt oddly refreshed. She dug into her purse for her compact and opened it to see what damage the night had wrought. The woman in the small round mirror was someone she was only beginning to know.

Chapter 52

Ellen

When she arrived in Dublin, Ellen was astounded at the destruction. The streets smelled of dead horses and charred ruins. Hordes of children ran among the bombed-out buildings, screaming and playing at war. The window of a candy shop was nothing but jagged shards of glass, where a boy sliced his leg going after the chocolate. He hobbled past her, blood dribbling down his leg, his mouth bulging with candy.

She stared at Liberty Hall with its crumbling walls. She wandered down Sackville Street and found abandoned trucks and more buildings turned into rubble by British gunboats. Houses were missing their doors and windows. Others had caught fire and were now a heap of smoldering ash. She walked past the trenches in St. Stephen's Park where the rebels had been slaughtered like lambs from snipers in the surrounding buildings. The walls of the Union Workhouse had been breached. But the General Post Office on O'Connell Street where the rebels had headquartered was the most shocking of all. All that was left of the imposing granite building with its Roman pillars was a tangle of stone and metal rafters.

The rebels had not been savvy enough to bring the people with them on their crusade. The ordinary Irish citizens, many of whom had not supported the uprising to begin with, stared with sullen faces from windows and doorways at what was left of their city.

Ellen felt a slow rage burning in her belly, but she couldn't tell if she was angrier at the English or the foolish poets who had no business picking up a gun. And under the anger was a simmering grief. Joseph Plunkett, who had befriended her in Germany the previous year, had been shot on May 4, the day after marrying his sweetheart. He had been the kindest, most idealistic man she'd ever known.

No of the trolleys in the center city were working, so she made her way down the main thoroughfare and found one on a side street to take her to Kilmainham Gaol.

She entered the arched doorway of the stone building, gray as a mausoleum. There milled women — old and young — with crying babies.

"I need to know if you have a Martin Malloy," she said to a man behind a barred window.

"We have 1400 prisoners. It may take days to find him." He didn't even look at her as he spoke.

"Can you tell me then where I might find Captain Hanks? I've been referred to him by British Naval Attaché Sir Reggie Grant in New York."

"Is that right?"

"It is. I have important information for him from Mr. Grant."

The man heaved a sigh and stood up. He went into a back room and after a bit returned, followed by a stout man in an olive drab Captain's uniform.

"Can I help you, Miss...?" he asked.

"Malloy. Ellen Malloy. Mr. Grant, the British Naval Attaché, said he would send word that I was coming. Can you tell me if my brother, Martin Malloy, is here?" she asked.

"If he was one of the fighters, then he's in here," the captain said.

"Is there any way to see him or talk to him?"

"Why don't you come outside with me? To the courtyard." He shoved his hands into his pockets.

Confused, Ellen followed him down a hall.

"I do recall hearing about your brother. Seems he was a courier?" The man turned and looked at her.

She shrugged.

"Pretty important fellow in the Brotherhood," he said, opening a heavy iron door and showing her into a courtyard.

"No, he's just a boy, really," she said.

She stepped out into the sunlit courtyard. Her stomach lurched when she saw the blood-spattered wall. The smell of gunpowder lingered in the air, and she could hear the echo of rifles in her head. This was where the heroes of the Easter Rising had been shot, where Joseph Plunkett had died.

"And what of their bodies?" she asked. "Did they not even get a decent funeral?"

"No need to create more martyrs," the captain said, puffing out his chest. "General Maxwell has promised there'll be no more treason whispered here for a hundred years."

She jerked her head toward him, clenching her fists, willing her legs to stand firm. He had a pock-marked face and a pouting, self-satisfied expression.

"They call it treason when people fight for the right to rule themselves?" Her voice shook with rage.

He shrugged. "The Irish can't rule themselves. The leaders are nothing but a collection of half-mad poets."

She turned her eyes away and stared up at the looming prison walls. Her brother was in there somewhere among the other hundreds of men and women. He would be scared, but he would not show it. Her gaze traveled back down to the wall before her with its dark stains. As someone who colluded with John Devoy and the Germans, Martin was sure to face the firing squad.

"You have a choice to make, Miss Malloy," the man said in a jovial voice, as if he found the situation somehow amusing.

"Do I?" she asked.

"I suspect General Maxwell will want to talk to you. He's up at the castle."

When she left the jail, she went straight to Dublin Castle. After speaking to first one lackey and then another and then waiting on a hard wooden chair for hours, she finally was called into the office of the General. She'd bitten the nails down to the quick.

"The Naval Attaché gave us quite a bit of information about you." He sat across the table from her in an office on the second floor of the castle. The man continued in his droning voice. "He praised your work in helping to expose the German saboteurs, working under von Papen."

"I had my reasons," she said.

"Yes, I understand you were on the *Lusitania* when she went down. That must have been terribly frightening."

Frightening didn't begin to cover it, she thought, but said nothing. She hated this man, hated everything he represented, and hated most of all that the rebels had failed in driving these arrogant bastards out of Ireland.

"Grant also mentioned that you are well versed in the craft, thanks to the Germans."

"Craft?"

"Spy craft."

"I'm a magazine publisher these days, and I've other things on my mind than saving the bloody British empire, and when I say bloody, I'm being literal."

"You aren't wrong, Miss Malloy. The events of the month have been especially unfortunate, but you must understand we are fighting a war, a war we *cannot* lose. You know as well as anyone that if the Germans invade Ireland, they will make British rule look like nursery school."

She crossed her arms and gazed out the window, thinking of Martin right now in a cell, probably starved and terrified for his life. The lump in her throat threatened to strangle her.

As if reading her mind, the General said, "Your brother will be shot tomorrow."

Ellen's mouth gaped open.

"Of course, you can stop it. In fact, you can set him free."

His lumpy face was the color of a boiled potato. When he spoke his lower teeth glinted like yellow tombstones.

"How so?" she asked, though she knew the answer.

"We want you to work for our military intelligence division."

"I've already got a job."

"Not anymore. We've offered your Mr. Thorn a lucrative position in our propaganda office and he's accepted. Mr. Grant made sure your magazine's banned not just in Boston but in other cities as well. Besides, would you really choose a magazine over your brother?"

He knew the answer to that question.

"Why did the Germans send you here?" he asked.

"To monitor the state of the rebellion, search for pockets of resistance, and to relay information about English forces in the country. The number of troops, that sort of thing."

"That's fine. We can give you false information to send them, but at some point, we'll threaten to arrest you. You will escape and somehow make your way back to Germany. We'll even give you some 'secrets' to share so you can ingratiate yourself with the *Abteilung III b*. We have several agents in Berlin, and we may need you to help them escape if they are found out."

Ellen took a deep breath.

"And what about my baby? You expect me to abandon my child?"

The General gazed at her thoughtfully. "You already have, haven't you?"

Ellen remembered Katherine Murphy holding little Hester, gazing at her with adoring eyes. The child would have every material advantage. She would also have something Ellen couldn't give her. A love undiluted by grief.

"Your choice, of course," he said as if he were offering her either pudding or cake.

She said nothing. At least, now she knew what mother love felt like. That love that would give her the strength to let the child go.

He leaned closer, his voice deepened. "Remember what the Germans did. Can you forgive those who sent a torpedo into the side of a civilian ship, killing upwards of 1,200 souls?"

She closed her eyes and shook her head. She would never be able to swallow that bitter pill.

The man continued, "Not to mention, a man disappeared from the SS *Frederick VIII* on the trip from New York. I don't suppose you know anything about that."

Still, she said nothing. She opened her eyes again and stared into his cold gaze. Her silence told him everything he needed to know.

"Right. Then I'll give the order to cancel your brother's execution. After a brief investigation, it will be determined he did nothing wrong, and he can go back to his mother's bosom."

"I won't go to Germany until he's free," Ellen said. "I want you to send him to New York. My mother, too."

He considered her request.

"We can do that. We've scheduled some additional training for you. Though at this point, it seems you're quite capable of taking care of yourself."

"I am, indeed," she said.

She walked out of Dublin Castle into a misty rain. As she strolled down the street, she removed the wedding band from her finger and tossed into the gutter. A band of children rushed past her, waving broken rifles and screaming like blood-thirsty savages.

Chapter 53
Louisa

For months, Louisa had longed for her home to be returned to a semblance of orderliness, and yet now with both Ellen and the baby gone, it felt a bit like a tomb. Carlotta cleaned the house in a desultory fashion, and then sprawled on the sofa reading *Motion Picture News*. Anna fretted like a petulant child, constantly needing this thing or that, and even the ginger cat yowled in displeasure at odd hours of the morning.

It was one such morning that Louisa woke up and saw it was still dark outside. She looked around her room and felt an irresistible urge to get out. She dressed, having no idea where she was going until she was outside on the quiet streets. She walked toward the platform of the El, and climbed the steps. No one except for a tired looking man in workman's clothes waited for the train.

She got on the train and decided to stay on until the end of the line, which is how she found herself standing on the beach at Coney Island, fixated on the horizon where an orange crescent bulged in a purple sky. The ocean inhaled and then exhaled in a rush toward her feet.

Arctic terns kipped as they made lassos in the sky. Once upon a time she had heard or thought she heard the sound of women whispering in her ears — a susurration like the waves spreading their foamy hands along the shoreline. Then she remembered the first time she had lain eyes on Ellen. Had it only been three years earlier? It felt as though they'd lived a lifetime together. Ellen had saved Louisa's life, and Louisa had saved Ellen's. They had done the sort of work women weren't supposed to do. Especially unarmed and untrained women. They had trapped a man who trafficked in girls. They had solved murders and foiled plots. They had connived and spied and stolen secrets. If not for Ellen, Louisa would still believe that civilization's social order had been decreed by divine right and not by the forces of greed and hunger. Ellen had revealed the world to her in all its hideous glory — monstrous and yet also precious.

She was beginning to understand something about herself. Being a society writer had cured her of the need she'd so desperately felt to belong to that staid old crowd. She could mingle in society if necessary, but now she saw through the façade to the emptiness within. She had changed. She also realized she would never be the writer that Djuna Barnes was. She simply didn't have her sharp wit and the urge to live her life on a precipice that seemed to be part and parcel of the whole enterprise. The thing that thrilled her was exactly what she had been doing these past months as she sought to protect Forrest: digging, discovering, exposing the truth. She supposed she could join the police force, but she didn't want a bunch of officious men telling her what to investigate or how. Whatever she did from now on would be on her terms.

The sun had risen, round as a gold coin. The sky lost its purple mystique and donned its daytime dress of blue. As Louisa stood there, warming in the light, she heard the whispering once again. But this time it was not the voices of many women. Instead, one woman whispered a message from across the sea, and the message, which dropped her to her knees, was this: "I'm sorry, my friend. I shall miss you."

Epilogue

Louisa stood before the altar of the church next to Katherine and John Murphy. In a pew at the back of the church, Martin and Paula Malloy sat with Paula's two boys, one on each lap. Carlotta and Anna watched from a pew near the middle of the church. Suzie and Mr. Sweet occupied the space next to them.

The baby wore a white gown; a white ribbon circled her head. Louisa had expected the baptism to be in a Catholic church, but Katherine was Episcopalian and that was how they would raise Hester. Katherine had not found a suitable godfather, so Louisa would be the child's sole godparent. The Episcopal priest asked Louisa as godmother if she would promise to help the child grow into the full stature of Christ. She said she would. He then asked the family and the congregation to renounce a variety of evils and sins. The parents, Louisa, and the congregation promised to support the child in her life in Christ. Then he took little Hester in his arms in front of a marble font and poured holy water and oil on her head, saying "I baptize you now in the Name of the Father, and of the Son, and of the Holy Spirit." Then he marked the child on her forehead with the sign of the cross. "You are sealed by the Holy Spirit in Baptism and marked as Christ's own for ever." Louisa found the ceremony oddly touching. She may not ever be a mother, but to be a godmother was a great honor indeed.

At the end of the service, the priest raised his arms and said, "The peace of the Lord be always with you."

"And with thy Spirit," the congregation responded.

A half a world away, Ellen Malloy strode into an ornate white building on the *Nieuwe Maas* river in Rotterdam.

"I would like to speak to the Imperial Consulate General," Ellen said in perfect German to an officious soldier behind a desk in the lobby.

He looked her up and down and asked, "Who are you? And why should he want to meet with you?"

"Tell him that I work for Walter Nicolai," she said, gazing down her nose at him.

The man's pale face turned even paler.

"Right away, *Fraulein*." He rose from his desk and hurried away.

Ellen thought back to Wolf von Igel and how she had once wondered how he managed to squelch any human feeling. Now, she understood that certain times called for such a gift, and if you were in possession of it, you had a duty, a calling.

"He will see you now," the soldier said, his eyes cast down.

"*Danke schön.*" She followed him down the marble hallway.

Banned in Boston
by Louisa Delafield
Unpublished article

To be "banned in Boston" is a badge of distinction in some circles. Publishers find that readers in other cities hurry to acquire books that Boston has banned. However, for the residents of Boston, this patently unfair system robs them of their choices of reading material and infantilizes people who are intelligent enough to decide what they want to read on their own.

In the past decade it has been common practice for members of the Boston Watch and Ward Committee to raid bookstores and arrest the booksellers for selling such scandalous titles as *Leaves of Grass.*

Eventually, for the sake of self-preservation, the booksellers joined forces with the censors to create the Boston Booksellers Committee to determine which books and magazines may be offered to the public. Now, the Old Corner Bookstore has become one of the staunchest censors in the city. A small group of men gets to be judge and jury for every book that comes into the city to be sold.

This secret committee is composed of six people, three of them chosen by the booksellers. They are voracious readers, and they peruse as many books as they can. If they deem it acceptable, then Boston booksellers can sell it without any fear of reprisal. However, if they determine that a particular book is immoral or obscene, then woe to the bookseller who puts that book on his shelves.

Boston's newspapers know better than to advertise or review a condemned title and the police have stayed out of the matter entirely, rarely prosecuting a book on their own. If a book seller won't sell and a reviewer won't review the book, it might as well never have been written.

Rev. Chase, the Watch and Ward secretary, is in charge of the organization's day to day, but he is guided in his decisions by some of the most prominent members of society, including Lowell Cabot who, according to all accounts, reads voraciously. One wonders why certain books are permissible for him to read, but not for others.

The only way to deal with these self-appointed guardians of morality may be through ridicule for their mandate is indeed a ridiculous one. Someday they will go too far and when the public pushes back, it will do so laughing.

Author's Note

I love to immerse my fictional characters in real world events, and there are plenty of them in *The Ladies Lantern*. Notably, a plethora of magazines were constantly popping up – especially among the Bohemians of Greenwich Village. It was a time of great change and great foment for change. The Heterodoxy Club existed as both a counterpoint to the myriad clubs for men and as a vehicle for progressive women to effect change. I found a great deal of information about them in the excellent book *Hotbed: Bohemian Greenwich Village and the Secret Club that Sparked Modern Feminism* by Joanna Scutts. As that book pointed out, both Emma Goldman and Margaret Sanger were jailed for their activism in the cause of birth control.

The German spies in this book are all based on actual German spies. Count Bernstorff (whom you may remember from Secrets and Spies, Book 4) was still active in the United States. Franz von Papen was expelled but his assistant Wolf von Igel, who had an enormous bodyguard, was arrested with plans to blow up a canal in Canada on his desk. A *New York Times* article "VON PAPEN'S AID ARRESTED. WOLF VON IGEL SEIZED BY FEDERAL AGENTS" from 1916 describes the event in delicious detail.

In a fascinating article by Louise E. Wright in the *Journal of Lawrence Studies (1992-93)*, I learned that Sir Guy Gaunt (the basis for Reggie Grant) "intercepted a spy bound for England." That spy became an informant and told the British that Albert Sanders, a drama critic in New York, had instructed his agents to visit Ireland to determine "the possibilities of further trouble there." *The Scientific American* (April 5, 2014) has an article about the use of invisible ink.

The goal of the Germans and the Irish-Americans who were in favor of the Uprising were closely aligned. Neither group wanted America to enter the war on the side of the British. It was fascinating to read the memoirs of John Devoy and to see his viewpoint on British "aggression." Many other sources clarified the reasons for Irish desperation to get out from under the yoke of the British. An article by Michael Quinlan in *The Irish America Magazine* (Feb/Mar 2016) explains:

Ireland's Home Rule movement was put on hold as the British fought a bloody war with the Germans. Irish men and boys were being recruited to fight and die in trenches on the continent. War taxes were being levied amidst high unemployment and poverty. Draconian laws such as the Defense of the Realm Act allowed authorities to deport or imprison Irish men and women on unproven charges and to suppress newspapers from criticizing the English government.

As someone who is one half English and one quarter Irish, I'll admit the Irish voice inside me dominated as I wrote about the Easter Uprising. The English subjugation of the Irish -- stealing their resources and attempting to quash their culture -- for eight centuries was an unconscionable act of barbarism. I have enormous admiration for the "mad poets" who tried to end it, and whose sacrifice ultimately led to at least partial freedom.

The 1936 film *The Plough and the Stars* based on the play by Sean O'Casey and starring Barbara Stanwyck provides a riveting depiction of what actually happened in Dublin during the Easter Uprising.

For the story of Brigid Rafferty, I was inspired by the stories of the Irish girls in *Bad Bridget: Crime, Mayhem and the Lives of Irish Emigrant Women* by Elaine Farrell and Leanne McCormick (Penguin, 2024). A fabulous piece by Dorothy Day in *The New York Call* (11) from November, 1916 describes going to the women's night court and introduced me to the word "slooping."

While much of Louisa's investigation in this book is fictional, certain elements are inspired by true events, including the fact that a lawyer in deep debt really did shoot himself in the Woolworth Building, Al Jolson (in black face! Ugh) did star in a play about Robinson Crusoe on Broadway in 1916, and a mathematics professor of Boston Brahmin origins at Harvard was accused of murdering someone for money. In addition, Nicolo Morello, the boss of the Sicilian Mafia in Italian Harlem at the time, was murdered shortly after the events in this book. If you want to learn more about the New York Mafia at the time and the "Murder Stable," check out my blog at trishmacenulty.com/2025/07/02/a-murder-stable-yikes/.

Louisa's article about censorship, led by the Reverend Chase and his benefactor, is informed by the book, *Banned in Boston: The Watch and Ward Society's Crusade Against Books, Burlesque, and the Social Evil* by Neil Miller.

I was fortunate in my research trip to Boston to meet Simone DeVito at the Church of the Covenant, who explained the history of the church to me along with the origins of the stunning Tiffany windows and other decorations.

Finally, I attempted to pay homage to one of the most original journalists of the early 20th century – Djuna Barnes, who was also a poet, playwright, illustrator and novelist. Her quotes in her conversations with Louisa come directly from *Djuna Barnes's New York*, a collection of her journalism, edited by Alyce Barry (Virago, 1990).

As always, I have relied on *The New York Times* archives, The Bowery Boys Tours, *The Irish Times*, and the Hathi Trust as well as the Internet Archives for accurate information.

I am so grateful to my fellow "histfic gals," Gina Hogan Edwards and Melody Harris, for their insightful feedback along the way; Susannah Reed for editing; P.V. LeForge and my brother, John, for proofreading, and my husband, Joe Straub for reading, supporting, and making the magic.

My grandparents, whom I never got to meet, John and Katherine MacEnulty, are the ones who inspired me to begin this series and serve as the model for John and Katherine Murphy.

There is at least one more Delafield & Malloy mystery in the pipeline. After all, Louisa and Ellen both deserve a happy ending. Louisa will continue her discrete investigations in future stories or novellas. For an example, check out the Louisa Delafield novella, *The Envious Vamp*. Most importantly, if you're curious about what happens to Ellen's child, Hester Murphy, stay tuned. Her story in *The Spymaster's Daughter* is coming soon!

If you haven't already done so, you can sign up for my newsletter at <u>trishmacenulty.com</u> for updates and links to my blog where I write about historical fiction, recommend books, and share fun things I discover during the research process as well as the occasional personal story. And please be sure to review and rate this book!

The Delafield & Malloy Investigations

If you liked *The Ladies' Lantern*, enjoy the other
DELAFIELD & MALLOY INVESTIGATIONS

Book 1, The Whispering Women: A pair of female sleuths dig into 1913 New York's elite, and its dark underbelly!

Book 2, The Butterfly Cage: Buffalo Bill, the Prince of Monaco, panic attacks, and a mysterious string of abductions to Panama!

Book 3, The Burning Bride: Dynamite-wielding anarchists, hungry alligators, a raging fire, and Louisa and Ellen's wayward hearts!

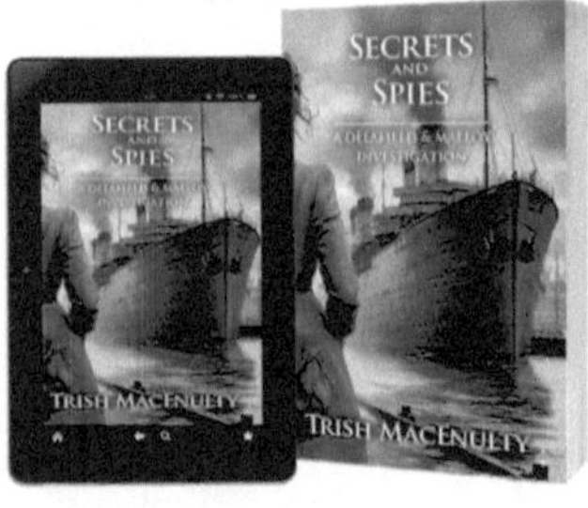

Book 4, Secrets and Spies: Subterfuge, deception, German saboteurs, and the sinking of the Lusitania!

Book 6, The Furies in Winter: *1917:* Two women. Two cities on the edge of chaos. One bond that defies distance!

The Furies of Winter
Chapter 1
Louisa

Snowflakes swirled outside the window of the silk shop. Louisa checked her watch. Almost closing time. She'd been working every afternoon for two weeks now and still no sign of the thieves. She closed the *Delineator* fashion magazine she'd been reading, stood, and meandered among the bolts of silk stacked on tables in the center of the cavernous room, losing herself in the piles of cloth — the bright jewel tones, the brocades, the gold-threaded flower patterns. With travel to Paris canceled due to the war in Europe, America's silk trade was at a peak. Some of the bolts were worth upwards of ten thousand dollars. She unrolled a bolt of turquoise silk and held the cloth up in the pale light, eking through the windows. She envisioned a dress, swirling around her calves as she danced in Francis' arms at the Paradise Club.

The bell above the door tinkled, and a blast of cold air barged in, raising goosebumps on the back of her neck. The silk slid from her fingers. Louisa turned to see a stout, middle-aged woman bundled in a dark wool coat and a black rolled-brim hat, snow dusting her shoulders, with a boy about seven years old at her side. The woman smiled as she approached. She was missing a front tooth.

"May I help you?" Louisa asked.

"I believe youse have a package of ribbons for me."

"Your name?" Louisa walked over to the counter where the packages were kept.

"Mrs. Smith," she said.

Louisa looked through the small packages under the counter. "Ah, yes, here it is." She brought the package to the counter.

"Coldest winter I ever remember," the woman commented.

"At least the snow seems to be letting up," Louisa said, glancing at the window. "That will be one dollar and forty-five cents."

The woman handed her an envelope. "Keep the change, dearie," she said.

Louisa peered inside the envelope, swallowed when she saw the sum, and then looked up at the woman. This kind-looking lady and child were the thieves? Her heart rate accelerated. "Th-thank you."

"And would you mind looking after the boy for me? Just for a while?" The woman nodded at the child, a sullen-faced boy in knickers and a jacket with a tweed cap on his head.

"The boy? You want to leave him here?" Louisa asked, dumbfounded.

Even though there was no one else in the shop, the woman leaned forward and said in a tight whisper, "That's the way it works, sweetie."

"I see." Louisa eyed the child once more.

The boy came around the counter, and sat down on an overturned crate.

The woman leaned over the counter and pointed her finger at the boy. "You be good for the nice lady."

"Wait," Louisa said as the woman turned to leave. "What do I do?"

"Close up shop like always. The kid'll be fine." She strode out of the store, clutching her package of ribbons.

Louisa looked at the boy hunkered down on the crate.

"Do try not to touch the silk," Louisa whispered, then realized that was a stupid thing to say as he was part of a gang planning to haul as much of the valuable fabric out of the shop as they could.

The boy ignored her. He propped his elbow on his knee and put his chin on his fist, posed like the statue of *The Thinker*. He was awfully young to be a criminal. She wondered what would happen to him.

Of course, the silk thieves had to be stopped, Louisa thought. Recently, they had killed a night watchman. Then after months of robbing shops, train cars, and designers' lofts, the gang finally made a mistake and approached an honest clerk to see if she'd be willing to take a bribe. She said she would be, then promptly told the owner what had happened, and quit her job. The police had been no help as a crime had not yet been committed. Hence, the owner turned to Louisa Delafield's "Discreet Investigations."

At five o'clock, Louisa looked outside. The snow had stopped falling. She donned her coat, her fleece cloche, and wool scarf and locked up the shop. The boy hadn't moved from the crate where he sat. It was an ingenious plan. Train a child to hide in the store and then unlock the door when the thieves arrived later that night. He would probably have to wait for hours. She wished she'd had some food to leave him.

Louisa walked briskly along Park Avenue, checking her reflection in the store windows to see if anyone was following. Three inches of snow had settled onto the sidewalk, but her boots were sturdy and warm. At the Belmont Hotel on 42nd Street, she entered the massive lobby and glanced around. No one had followed her inside. She found the concierge and asked to use the telephone. He showed her to a desk in an alcove.

"Operator, please connect me with police Captain Tom Tunney. He's at the Centre Street location in the fifth precinct."

When Captain Tunney's gruff voice came on the line, she informed him of the bribe and the forthcoming burglary. "Do be careful," she said. "There's a child involved."

Fifteen minutes later she dashed up a flight of steps inside a building on Broadway and opened the door to the offices of Francis Holland, Esquire & Associates. Over the past few months, Francis had steered several investigations her way. Working together, consulting on cases, dining in restaurants to discuss the details—they'd grown close. The dinners had turned into dancing, and dancing had turned into kissing and touching. Which is where their relationship lingered for the moment.

The secretary was gone for the day, and since Louisa was the only "associate," she hung up her coat in the reception area and walked directly into Francis' office, where she found him bent over a contract. He looked up at her and smiled, broad smile that reached all the way up to his warm hazel eyes. He had perfect teeth and an adorable cleft chin.

"The discreet investigator returns," he said.

"The owner of the store was right. An older woman came in with a bribe just before closing time." Louisa dropped the envelope with the money on his desk.

He straightened up—tall, lanky, and boyish in his gabardine suit—and came around the desk. "So how do they do the heist?"

She pulled her gloves off finger by finger as she spoke. "You'll never guess. They leave a child hidden in the store to let the thieves in later."

"Starting them young, I suppose." He picked up the envelope, looked inside and whistled.

"We can paint the town with this."

"No, we can't. You're taking it straight to your uncle at the precinct. He's expecting you."

"Too bad. I was going to let you buy me a steak at Delmonico's," he teased, pulling her close to him. The warmth of his body made her tingle.

"Delmonico's is too stuffy." She gazed up at him. This close she could see the end-of-day stubble. She rubbed her index finger across his sandpapery jawline.

"How about I take you to Cafe Montmartre instead. Friday night?" he asked. "I want to celebrate."

"Solving this crime?" she asked.

"Maybe," he said. "Maybe something else."

She looked into his eyes and saw a yearning that surprised her. Her breath caught. Did he intend to propose? She lowered her gaze. "I'm not sure I'm available Friday night."

"Is that right? Just how many suitors do you have, Miss Delafield?"

"Only a dozen or so."

His lips landed warm and soft on hers. She kissed him back and felt a fire at the back of her throat. What if he did plan to propose? What was she so afraid of?

"Of course, I'm available Friday night," she said.

He smiled. "Then it's a date. In the meantime, I'll run this bribe to the precinct station and make sure the police do their job."

"Who would have imagined silk houses would lose so much money to thieves?" she wondered. "The stuff is worth as much as gold."

"And now it will stop thanks to you."

The next day, when Louisa returned home from the Silk House with several yards of the turquoise fabric the owner had given her in return for her services in addition to her fee, she found Martin Malloy sitting on the sofa in the parlor with Carlotta. Martin usually came by about once a month to find out if she'd heard anything about his sister, Ellen. This time he'd brought Paula O'Neil's older boy, Sean, with him. At least something good had come out of it all, Louisa thought. Paula had been left a widow much too young. How surprised Ellen would be that one of the first things Martin did when he got to New York was to join the police force and second, to marry Detective Paddy O'Neil's widow. The Irish lawbreaker was now a law enforcer.

"There she is," Carlotta said as Louisa set down her package. "Martin's been telling me all about his latest arrest. Plenty of excitement. They nabbed that gang of silk thieves."

"Bang. Bang!" Sean said, startling the cat from her perch on the windowsill.

"A whole family of crime stoppers, aren't you?" She tousled Sean's dark hair, black like his dead father's.

"Thanks to you," Martin said. "We caught the thieves red-handed – or silk-handed."

Sean piped up. "Pops is still a rookie, but they let him arrest the old lady!"

"And she seemed like such a sweet old thing," Louisa said. "What will happen to the little boy?"

"Reformatory, I s'pose. Thievin' is no life for a wee lad."

"Louisa didn't even take me on the job," Carlotta said, piqued. Since Ellen had left them to go to Ireland last April, Carlotta had been Louisa's right hand on her "discreet" investigations, but the silk house had been a one-woman job.

"You would have been bored," Louisa said to mollify her.

Carlotta scoffed and turned to Sean. "Say, Sean, let's go down to the park and chase some pigeons so's your Papa and Miss Louisa can talk."

After Carlotta left with the boy, Louisa poured herself a cup of tea from the silver service on the coffee table, sat down in the overstuffed armchair, and gazed at Martin. Gingin the cat jumped on her lap and settled down.

"Are you enjoying married life?" she asked.

"Aye, Paula's the best. And I love the two boys as if they were my own. They were mighty young when Paddy was killed, so they don't remember him well. You knew Paddy, didn't ya?" Martin's lilting Irish cadence reminded Louisa so much of Ellen.

"I did," she said. "He was a good detective. His death was horrid." Paddy had died when a pallet "accidentally" fell on him at the docks where he'd been investigating German saboteurs. "Marrying you is a decidedly better outcome for Paddy's widow and his two boys than if you..."

"Than if I'd been shot by a firing squad in Dublin. I know what you're thinking," he said. "You're thinking of the sacrifice my sister made to save me."

Louisa sipped her tea, set down the cup, and ran her fingers over Gingin's soft fur. "Ellen made that choice of her own free will."

"Did she? What sort of choice is that? Her brother's life in exchange for losing all she'd managed to accomplish, even giving up her baby to go back to Germany and be a spy?"

Louisa understood the guilt he felt. If he had not been a member of the Irish Brotherhood, if he had not been hellbent on casting off the British yoke during a time of war and gotten arrested in the Easter uprising last year, Ellen would still be in New York, publishing *The Ladies' Lantern* and raising her child. But Ellen had given it all up so the British would commute her brother's sentence and send him and their mother and her youngest brother to America.

Louisa was loath to admit how bereft she'd been since Ellen's departure. Not to mention the baby. Even with three women living in the small Harlem townhouse, the rooms felt empty without Ellen, publishing a magazine in the parlor, the baby sleeping in her little swing. At the time it had seemed a nuisance, and she'd told Ellen in no uncertain terms she should find another office space. Was that part of the reason Ellen gave up the baby and left? Louisa understood Martin's guilt because she had so much of her own.

"Something occurred to me," she said. "Ultimately, Ellen would never have been satisfied simply publishing a magazine. She's the sort of person who has to do things. Publishing stories about women's rights, the plight of children, and the troubles of workers — that would never have been enough for her. Ellen has a drive to change the world. And the magazine, for all the good it did, was simply not enough. That's why she left to go to Ireland as soon as she knew about the uprising.

And that's why she went to Germany to be a double agent when the British told her to go." Louisa wasn't sure if she was trying to make Martin or herself feel better.

Martin rubbed his cheek and frowned. With his trim blond mustache, his face had acquired a distinguished, handsome look. "And what about the baby?"

"Ellen loves Hester, but..." Louisa hesitated. Ellen *had* loved the child, but there was an enormous wall of grief in the way of her expression of that love. Not to mention the circumstances behind Hester's very existence. "Did you ever meet the man who...fathered the child?"

"No, he was someone she met in Germany. I wasn't there." He pounded his knee with his fist. "I never shoulda let her go there. I encouraged her. I thought she could help the Brotherhood get weapons from the Germans for the uprising. Dammit to hell."

"Young man!" Anna Delafield stood in the doorway of the parlor, leaning on her cane.

"Pardon me, Mrs. Delafield," Martin said, rising.

"Oh, sit down. I assume you two are discussing the whereabouts of Ellen Malloy." Anna headed over to her favorite armchair by the window. "Well, don't let me interfere."

Martin stayed standing. "Thank you, but I must be off at any rate. Miss Delafield, if you run into your British friend, that Grant fella, you might ask him the whereabouts of my sister. At least, let us know she's alive. For poor Ma's sake."

"I will." Louisa walked him to the door. "You'll find Carlotta and Sean down the street at Morningside Park."

After she shut the door, she turned and leaned against it. She felt it again, that yawning chasm in her chest whenever she thought of Ellen. Europe was in the throes of a war that seemed it would never end, and her friend was somewhere in the thick of it. She imagined mustard gas seeping across a continent, the slaughter in its wake. A roaring sound filled her head.

Stop, she told herself. Do not think of it. She strode into the parlor and put a record on the phonograph. Beethoven's Fifth Symphony. She lay down on the sofa and let the music drown out the clamor in her head.

About the Author

Trish MacEnulty is the author of the historical fiction series, *Delafield & Malloy Investigations*, as well as the YA historical novel, *Cinnamon Girl*, two memoirs — including *The Hummingbird Kiss*, and *My Mother's Requiem* (2024) — a short story collection, and children's plays. She currently lives in Florida with her husband and teaches for the School of Journalism at Florida A & M University. She writes features and book reviews for the *Historical Novel Review*.